A Sly and Sinister Tail

A Sassy Sarcastic Cat Cozy Mystery

Rachel Woods

BONZAI
MOON

BonzaiMoon Books LLC
Houston, Texas
www.bonzaimoonbooks.com

Prologue

Before the unfortunate incident—which I don't want to get into right now, but will explain later—Callie, the Calico cat who helps me solve mysteries *did not* talk. At least, she didn't talk to me. And maybe she didn't talk at all.

Then, out of the blue, or all of a sudden, or for no apparent reason, the cat spoke to me. Nevertheless, I want to be clear that, at first, the cat *didn't* speak. Eventually, she started talking, but only after—

Wait.

I'm probably getting ahead of myself.

I should probably tell this story from the beginning, so you understand. So it all makes sense. However, I must warn you that the tale (or, would that be tail? Too early for a cat pun?) of Callie the talking Calico will never make sense.

Because talking cats don't make sense.

Chapter 1

At seven o'clock on a sunny Tuesday in August, I'm not doing what I would normally be doing at seven in the morning, which is enjoying a cup of hibiscus tea with lemon and berries and eating donut holes drizzled with mango icing, while listening to the online police scanner for the St. Mateo Police Department, keeping my ears attuned for crime story ideas to pitch to Martin "Marty" Edwards, my boss, the Managing Editor of the *Palmchat Gazette* St. Mateo satellite office, where I currently work as a Junior Reporter.

Instead, at this moment, I'm being chewed up and spit out by Marty, who paces back and forth behind his desk, squeezing a stress ball between his palms. "I have to tell you, Sophia, that I have become increasingly disappointed with and infuriated by your performance."

Sophia, I think, concerned by his use of my given name.

Though my byline reads, Sophie Carter, technically, my name is Sophia.

However, no one has ever called me Sophia. And I suppose I don't see myself as a Sophia, which I imagine to be a sultry, raven-haired vixen, very glamorous and proficient in the art of cunning seduction. Now, don't get me wrong. I can look rather fetching when I'm all dolled up, but normally, people consider me "pretty cute," with my springy, corkscrew curls, heart-shaped face, ski-jump nose, and youthful appearance, which makes sense because I'm only twenty-two. Anyway.

The fact that Marty called me *Sophia* worries me. Makes me think this performance review meeting is going to be more confrontational than constructive. His use of the words *disappointed* and *infuriated* is also quite distressing. Nevertheless, I am determined not to be alarmed. Unless, of course, I should be.

"It appears you don't understand the requirements of your job," begins Marty, who is short and very muscular with spiky blonde hair that looks like blades of brittle hay sprouting from his head. His skin is blotchy and red, possibly from rosacea, a bad sunburn, or the results of one of those trendy vampire facials.

"I understand the requirements of my job," I insist, though, admittedly, Marty's dubious stare makes me wonder if I actually don't.

"You can't possibly understand," says Marty. "Because if you did, you would have written the stories I assigned to you last week—"

"I did write those stories," I tell him.

"Yes, you did," he says. "And you did a wonderful job."

"Thank you," I say, though I'm not sure he's giving me a compliment.

"I don't think you understand your job requirements because you were supposed to write the stories I assigned to you ... and *only* those stories."

"Oh ..." I say, suddenly realizing why he's miffed.

"You also wrote three additional stories," says Marty. "Three stories that focused on crime."

When I worked at the *Palmchat Gazette* main office in St. Killian, I was given many chances to show off my investigative and crime reporting skills.

Since I started the job at the St. Mateo office, Marty has assigned me lifestyle features. In other words, soft news. Profiles of political candidates, fledgling cricket athletes, and wanna-be Caribbean socialites. Sometimes, I'll cover the opening of a new restaurant or club, which is cool, I suppose, because I'd get a free meal or instant entrance into the latest celebrity hotspot.

Nodding, I say, "True, but only because I was in the right place at the wrong time. Or rather, the wrong place at the right time. I was in the bank cashing my paycheck when the attempted robbery occurred. And I had just gotten on the jitney bus when those guys got on and tried to hijack it. And I was shopping at the grocery store when the deranged customer tried to kidnap the cashier."

"The point is, Sophia," says Marty, "that you *do not* cover the crime beat."

"Right," I agree. "But—"

"You should have called the paper and informed the assignments desk about what was happening at the time," Marty says. "Then the assignments editor would have informed me and I would have assigned the story to the reporter who covers crime—Ruth Rice."

"Right," I say, biting my lower lip and averting my eyes—so I won't roll them.

And, honestly, I shouldn't roll them, because doing so is pointless and juvenile, considering that Ruth Rice is my coworker.

She joined the *Palmchat Gazette* a year ago, and in that time, somehow, she's managed to convince Marty that she's Lois Lane, Brenda Starr, and Nellie Bly all rolled into one. This, in my opinion, is not the case, although maybe she is a superstar reporter, but I doubt it, and no, I have no evidence to support my skepticism, but still …

I'd like to say Ruth and I are friendly, polite coworkers but I can't, because it's not true. Our relationship is not friendly or polite. And our mutual animosity is not my fault. It's not even mutual. I have nothing at all against Ruth. But she seems determined not to like me, even though I have made every effort to be cordial to her.

Okay, well, maybe not *every* effort, but I've tried my best.

I greet Ruth each morning with a smile and pleasant hello. I offer to get her coffee from the breakroom when I step away to make more tea. And I've invited her to lunch countless times, my treat.

Nevertheless, Ruth has resisted and rebuffed each and every one of my attempts to develop and cultivate a friendship, or even a friendly working relationship.

"You know what your problem is, Sophia?"

"My problem?" I ask, wary of what he's about to tell me.

"You think you can be insubordinate because you're the boss's pet."

"The boss's pet?"

"I am well aware that you're good friends with the publisher, Leo Bronson, and his wife, Vivian," says Marty.

Vivian Thomas-Bronson, the Managing Editor of the *Palmchat Gazette*'s main office in St. Killian, isn't just a friend. She's also my idol, a beautiful former foreign war correspondent, and someone I look up to and aspire to be like. Vivian's journalistic accomplishments are legendary. Her husband, Leo, recommended me for the position in St. Mateo, and was one of my biggest supporters.

"I suppose that's true," I agree. "However I wouldn't say I'm their ... *pet* ... I don't even think they like animals."

"Is that supposed to be funny?" Marty growls.

"Well, um ... not really, but ..."

"You know I don't mean that you're an actual pet," says Marty. "But you do have the privilege of their friendship, which you believe gives you preferential treatment and exempts you from following my instructions."

Shaking my head, I say, "I don't think—"

"You think you can write whatever you want to write because Vivian likes you!"

"That's not true," I insist, even though I suppose it is. Well, the part about Vivian liking me is true. I'm fond of my former boss, as well.

"Let me tell you something, Sophia," says Marty. "Vivian doesn't run the St. Mateo office. I do! And that means what I say goes, and I say you cover lifestyle, not crime. Do you understand me?"

"Yes," I tell him, then add, "... and no."

"What?"

"I understand that you want me to cover lifestyle stories," I say.

"But why can't I cover crime stories, too? I wrote articles about crime in St. Killian."

"Well, in case you haven't noticed, Sophia, you're not in St. Killian anymore," he says.

He's certainly right about that.

I was born in St. Killian, the largest island in the Palmchat Island chain, but I'm currently living in St. Mateo. Even though I'm St. Killian through and true, I moved when I was offered a reporting job at the *Palmchat Gazette* satellite office in St. Mateo.

"And if you want to know the truth," says Marty. "I don't want you covering crime because you're not good at it."

"Not good at it?" Staring at him, I swallow the lump growing in my throat.

"That story about the attempted bank robbery was just the facts. Staid and uninspiring."

"Staid and uninspiring?"

"The jitney bus hijacking was boring and apathetic."

"Boring and apathetic?"

Marty stops pacing and glares at me. "Are you a parrot?"

I blink. "A parrot?"

"Are you going to repeat everything I say?"

"Well, not everything you say but ..." I trail off as Marty's eyes narrow into razor-thin slits. "Sorry."

"Your problem is you don't have enough experience," says Marty, stroking his chin as he stares at me. "Remind me: How long have you been working for the *Palmchat Gazette*?"

"Since I graduated from university," I say, feeling woefully inadequate, as though my journalism degree isn't worth the paper it's printed on.

"When was that? Three years ago?"

"Two," I say.

Shaking his head, Marty scoffs. "Only two years of sinperience and you think that's enough to cover the crime beat. Sophia, crime is brutal. Criminals are ruthless. Crooks are heartless. Covering crime will eat you alive. Rip you to shreds. Leave you gasping for your last breath. Bleeding out in a ditch. It's chaos. Madness. You want to write crime? You need to suffer. And you haven't suffered!"

Concerned by Marty's flushed skin, I say, "Maybe not."

"Sophia, I'm going to give you the cold hard facts," says Marty. "Straight with no chaser. You can't cover crime because you don't have 'it' …"

"I don't have … it …" Confused, I stare at Marty. "What's … it …?"

"Why am I not surprised that you don't know?"

"Is that a rhetorical question?" I ask.

Marty smiles, but there's no mirth or warmth in the curve of his lips. "Sophia, 'it,' which you don't have … is experience."

"You mentioned my lack of experience," I remind him. "And I know I've only been a reporter for two years, but I wrote a fair amount of crime stories when I was at the St. Killian office."

"A fair amount is not enough," says Marty.

"But—"

"No buts," says Marty, dropping down in the chair behind his desk. "The point is, and the fact remains, that you were hired to cover lifestyle, arts and entertainment, travel and leisure."

"Yes, I know," I say, trying to sound confident, though I hear a slight tremor in my voice. "However, I really believe that I'm a good crime reporter. And I believe that I would be an asset and a benefit to the paper if I covered lifestyle *and* crime. After all, Ruth can't cover all the crime stories. I could—"

"Sophia, you seem to be having a comprehension problem," says Marty. "So, let me put it plainly. You were hired to cover lifestyle stories. You do not cover the crime beat. I do not want you covering crime stories. Do you understand?"

Trying not to feel discouraged, I nod. "Yes, I understand."

Marty takes a deep breath. "Now, I have an assignment for you."

"Great!" I say, as enthusiastically as I can, even though I don't feel great at all. I feel as though Marty is punishing me for my lack of experience while at the same time preventing me from getting more experience.

It's an unfair Catch-22.

How can I get more experience writing crime stories if I'm not allowed to write about crime?

"A new tour company has opened up in Guavatown," says Marty. "You need to do a review of the walking tour they're offering."

"A review of the walking tour," I repeat, determined to stay positive, even though the assignment sounds less than riveting.

"I've spoken with the owner," Marty says. "He's open to signing a contract for print and online advertisements with the paper, so a good review would help us accomplish that goal."

"Got it," I say, understanding the point of the assignment. Advertising dollars. Which are important, of course. That's how the paper brings in revenue so the employees can receive a salary. Still, I'm more than a little bummed that Marty gave me another lifestyle feature and won't give me a chance to prove I'm a good crime reporter.

"Before you head out," says Marty. "I want to make something clear …"

"Okay …" I say.

Marty's gaze is shrewd. "I run the show at the St. Mateo office. Not Vivian. I assign the stories to the reporter I feel is best capable of covering them."

"Right, I understand that," I say, feeling a tad desperate to plead my case. "But I can cover crime. Let me show you."

"Okay, Sophia, I'm putting all my cards on the table. Face up," says Marty. "It's not just your lack of experience that bothers me."

"It's not?" I ask.

"You got this job because of cronyism."

"Cronyism?" I stare at Marty, flummoxed. "You mean, you think Leo only hired me because—"

"Because you're friends," says Marty. "You're chummy with the boss and something about that isn't right, in my opinion."

Shaking my head, I say, "But, you have it all wrong. Leo is friendly to me, but we're not *friends* friends. We don't hang out together, or anything. However, I have gone to lunch several times with Vivian.

And once, we went out to this club, and a girl I knew named Phoebe ended up—"

"Sophia, I could care less, okay?"

"You do know that actually means that you do care, right?"

Marty scowls. "What I know is that I don't want you writing any more crime stories. I mean it, Sophia. You write the stories I assign to you. If you can't do that, then maybe you shouldn't work here."

"No, of course I can write the stories you assign me," I say, worried by the idea of losing my job. "And I will write only the stories you want me to write."

"You better," says Marty. "Because if you don't shape up, I will ship you out!"

Chapter 2

At nine in the morning, the sun is warm and bright, a stark contrast to my gloomy thoughts.

Marty has strictly forbidden me from writing crime stories, which is to say that he has effectively dashed my hopes and crushed my dreams. My goal has always been to build a career as an award-winning, top-notch investigative reporter, writing exciting and informative articles about murder and mayhem.

How am I supposed to do that if I can't cover the crime beat?

Of course, Marty's point about my lack of experience is valid, and I agree with him. I do need more experience covering crime stories. That's one of the reasons I was so excited to accept the position in St. Mateo.

At the St. Killian office, I competed with three other coworkers for assignments, and often lost out to the more thrilling stories. When I arrived at the St. Mateo office, and realized the only other crime reporter was Ruth Rice, I thought the distribution of assignments would be more equitable. I'd get opportunities to tackle stories about crime and corruption and build my resume. But that hasn't been the case. And now, after the conversation with Marty, it feels like it'll never be the case.

Marty won't give me a chance because he doesn't think I deserve the job, but he won't let me prove that I wasn't hired because of cronyism.

He also doesn't think I've suffered.

Well, he'll be happy to know that I'm suffering now, knowing that my investigative journalism career might be over before I got the chance to really get it started.

Despite my predicament, it's a gorgeous day in St. Mateo, one of the main islands in the Palmchat Islands, an archipelago comprised of dozens of sister islands, atolls, and sandbars.

A few days out of the year, it's rainy and overcast. But, mainly, the weather is sublime, as are the islands. Nothing but white sand, turquoise waters, palm trees, and sunshine. Each year, millions of people converge on the islands to enjoy the lush, natural beauty.

A salty sea breeze, carrying the faint smell of bananas and fresh fish, lifts my springy curls from my neck and across my cheek.

After a deep breath, I survey my surroundings.

Guavatown is a lovely, lively fishing village named for the abundance of guava trees throughout the area, most of them planted by Europeans settlers in the 18th century. Though scenic and quaint, it bustles with robust activity. Local fishermen catch fresh seafood from Guava Bay. Visitors meander and loiter, traversing the wooden jetties, and bargaining with vendors hawking wares at stands, stalls, and kiosks.

Colorful boats, skiffs, dinghies, canoes, kayaks, and an assortment of personal watercraft bob in the brilliant turquoise water. The main weather-beaten wooden plank boardwalk is lined with a variety of souvenir shops, restaurants, and tour companies offering any and all types of excursions, from culinary tours to ziplining to deep sea fishing.

A few minutes ago, I disembarked from a jitney bus crowded with tourists eager for a day of sun, surf, and sightseeing. Besides myself, a few local Palmchatters—which is what folks born in the Palmchat Islands are called although, since I'm in St. Mateo, I could refer to the residents as St. Mateans—were wedged into the cramped, twenty-passenger bus.

Now I'm in the thick of the throngs of people strolling the boardwalk, headed to meet the director of the walking tour. According to the text he sent me when I reached out to him, he should be waiting for me at an abandoned fruit stand on the far northern end of the boardwalk, where a one-lane side road leads to a neighborhood of brightly colored shanty homes behind the waterfront.

As seagulls fly overhead, laughing their distinctive screech, I continue on, slipping between industrious locals and lackadaisical tourists. When the boardwalk ends, I step onto the road leading into the neighborhood. As the road curves to the left, I come abreast of a large guava tree.

And immediately stop in my tracks.

As clusters of tourists maneuver around me, some giving me eye rolls and scowls, confusion and excitement race through my veins.

Through the leaves of low-hanging branches, I spot nearly a half dozen St. Mateo cops, plus two men in suits and a guy wearing a white jumpsuit, disposable mask, and shoe coverings. The contingent of law enforcement surrounds the boarded-up fruit stand, a crumbling structure of weather-stripped wood, the colors faded, the paint cracked and flaking.

I wrinkle my nose at the salty, fishy, guava-scented air, which holds the faint stench of something rotten and putrid.

Thirty feet away, beneath the shade of more guava trees, a cluster of twenty or so tourists talk and whisper among themselves, gesturing toward the fruit stand, craning their necks as they stare at the police. Their faces register a mix of horrified shock, fascinated excitement, and perturbed confusion. There's a lot of head shaking, hand wringing, and cell phone camera videoing. Two girls, one dressed in hot pink and the other neon orange—which reminds me of Starburst fruit chews—take selfies, seemingly using the fruit stand as a background.

Two guides in T-shirts advertising the excursion company—St.

Mateo Top Tours—stand apart from the group, cell phones pressed against their ears. They look frustrated and impatient.

I bite my bottom lip, wondering what's happening. Why are the police here? Why do they seem to be questioning the tourists? Why does the air smell like something is decomposing? And why do I get the feeling that I've stumbled into yet another crime story?

Shaking my head, I tell myself not to panic, or jump to conclusions, as I remember Marty's warning. After all, just because the area is swarming with cops and shell-shocked tourists doesn't mean something bad happened? Right?

But, what if something bad has happened? What if a crime has been committed? A terrible travesty of justice that needs to be covered and then published in the *Palmchat Gazette?*

Well, if that's the case, I can't report the story.

Marty made it painfully clear that he'll fire me if I do.

My assignment is to review a Guavatown walking tour. So, that's what I'm going to do. Despite my rabid curiosity, I'm not going to test Marty's patience or give him a valid reason to get rid of me. Without further ado, I head over to one of the tour guides.

With a gentle tap on his shoulder, I say, "Excuse me—"

"Look, I don't know anything, okay?" says the tour guide, a young Palmchatter with a slender build, a mop of curly hair, and large eyes that dart frantically back and forth. "The police haven't told us anything. We're trying to contact the owner to figure out what to do."

"Well ..." I start, gearing up to introduce myself and inform him that I was supposed to take the walking tour. Instead, for some reason, I find myself asking, "What happened? What are the police doing here?"

Dragging a hand down his face, his expression desolate, the tour guide says, "The tour group I was going to lead found a dead body behind that abandoned fruit stand."

"Are you serious?" I say, trying to ignore the jolt of adrenaline racing through my veins, telling myself it's the tea I had this morning. But I didn't get to have my tea. So I know I'm excited about the prospect of covering a crime story.

"I wish I wasn't," says the tour guide. "The fruit stand is our meeting spot and we were waiting for the rest of the group when someone started screaming about a dead body."

"Oh my gosh …" I say, biting my bottom lip, wondering if I should ask—

The tour guide's phone rings, and he answers it, launching into a conversation as he turns and heads away from me.

I glance toward the fruit stand. The two men in suits, who I assume are the detectives assigned to the case, are walking away from the crime scene, heading down the strip of road that leads back to the boardwalk.

Feeling conflicted, I wonder what to do. Marty's warning floats into my head, just as foul as the smell wafting from the back of the fruit stand.

On one hand, I know I need to let Marty know about the dead body and let him assign the story. But on the other, if the only reporter he could assign the story to is unavailable, and I'm right here at the scene of the crime, then shouldn't I at least get some details? The quick facts. Just the who, what, when, where, and why? Marty couldn't possibly be upset if I did that, could he? After all, I wouldn't be writing the story. I'd just be gathering information about it. Information I would pass along to Ruth, so she could write the story. Unfortunately.

Throwing caution to the wind, I hurry after the detectives, one of which is Detective Francois—a surly, hulking grump who has made it known, loud and clear, that he hates the press.

Chapter 3

Chasing the detectives is not something I'm super excited about. Detective Richland François is one of the five "François brothers" detectives.

In the Palmchat Islands, the François name is famous. The brothers are known for their superior ability to solve crimes. They inherited their investigative skills from their father and grandfather. Both elder lawmen were responsible for capturing The Fury—a heinous serial killer who stalked the islands for decades.

Detective Richland François is known for his impressive crime-solving, but not his compassionate bedside manner. Although, I suppose that's not a good analogy because Detective François is not a doctor, so he wouldn't have a bedside manner. So, let's just say that he's not very nice. Or patient. Or tolerant. Or accommodating.

Nevertheless, seconds later, I find myself running up behind him. "Detective François? Do you, um, have a second?"

The detective stops mid-stride. After a pause, during which I desperately pray that I'll be professional and intelligent, and not dull and dim-witted, François faces me.

Scowling, he barks, "A second for what?"

"Okay, yes, well, um …" I clear my throat. "First of all, my name is Sophie Carter, and—"

"I know who you are," says François, his tone curt, impatient. "What do you want?"

"Okay, yes, well, um …" I clear my throat again and glance at François' partner, a slightly older man with wary eyes and an expression of pity. "I'm covering the story of the dead body that was found behind the fruit stand by the tourists …"

"Is that right?" Francois asks, his gaze dubious, as though he knows I'm not being honest, as though he's well aware I've been given an official directive not to cover crime stories.

Clearing my throat, I say, "Well, I'm getting details about the story and I wanted to know—"

"Ms. Carter," interrupts the detective. "I have no comment at this time."

"Okay, yes, well, um …" I decide not to clear my throat. Instead, I take a deep breath. "Listen, I absolutely understand why you wouldn't want to comment, but I really think the *Palmchat Gazette* readers deserve to know—"

"Ms. Carter, here's what you and your readers need to know," says the detective, giving me a sly, predatory grin. "I will never have a comment for you."

Taken aback, I stare at him. "Never?"

"Ever," he confirms, crossing huge arms over a muscular chest.

Disappointed, I say, "But—"

"Ms. Carter, what part of 'no comment' did you not understand?" he demands, his grin now a grimace.

Shrinking beneath his withering scowl, I try to work up the nerve to tell him that I understood every part of 'no comment' but François turns his back on me. Forlorn and frustrated, I watch in bitter defeat as the detectives continue down the road, and then onto the boardwalk, and out of sight.

Exhaling, I try not to feel like a failure. And yet, I can't help thinking that Marty said I shouldn't cover crime because I don't have enough experience. Because I haven't suffered.

A long-suffering, more experienced reporter could have gotten François to talk, Marty will probably tell me. And then, he'll remind me that I don't have *it*.

Unfortunately, he might be right.

Chapter 4

"Excuse me, miss …?"

The voice behind me is deep and succinct, but with traces of curiosity and compassion.

With a deep breath, I turn.

And promptly lose my breath.

The police officer standing in front of me is breathtakingly handsome. Although, I suppose that shouldn't be surprising since I lost my breath when I turned around.

He's handsome but has a boyish charm. Dimples frame an engaging, enticing smile. He's tall and fills out his police uniform quite nicely. The nameplate on his white shirt says NOAH CUETEE. And he certainly is a cutie, but I don't have time to swoon, as my grandma would say, even though I wouldn't mind falling into Officer Cuetee's muscular arms.

"Are you with the tour group?" asks the cute cop. "If so, can you tell me if we've already taken your statement, or not? And if not, then I need to take your statement."

"Oh, no, I'm not with the tour group," I say, then fish around in my cross-body for my PRESS credentials. "I'm a reporter from the *Palmchat Gazette*. Sophie Carter."

The officer glances down at my *Palmchat Gazette* identification. Nodding, he smiles at me. "Are you covering the story?"

Clearing my throat, I stare into Officer Cuetee's light ocean-blue eyes and say, "Actually, I am … gathering information about the story. Unfortunately, François wasn't in the mood to give me any details."

"François doesn't trust the press," says the good-looking policeman. "He thinks you guys just impede his investigation while you obstruct justice and publish fake news."

Rolling my eyes, I say, "I'm not trying to impede investigations, obstruct justice, or publish fake news. I'm trying to get more experience. And maybe suffer a little."

"Suffer a little?"

"Oh, um …" I shake my head, mortified for mumbling my thoughts out loud. "It's complicated. Anyway …"

"Listen, I can probably give you a few basic details," says the cute cop. "But, I can't be quoted."

"You can be an anonymous source," I tell him, excitement coursing through me as I reach into my purse to get my smart phone. But it's not there. I push aside several items: my compact mirror, a tube of mascara, my wallet, a bottle of nail polish, a pocket dictionary, my brush, four fine point felt-tipped pens, some frizz-control serum, lip gloss, reading glasses, a mini calculator, my keys, and a 5 x 7 spiral notebook.

"What's the matter?"

"I don't have my phone," I say, upset that I won't be able to use my notetaking app. "I must have accidentally left it at work."

"That's too bad," says Officer Cuetee. "What are you going to do?"

Glancing down at the notebook, I say, "Guess I'll have to do things the old-fashioned way. I'll actually have to take notes."

Smiling, Officer Cuetee says, "I'll talk slow."

For the next ten minutes, or so, Officer Cuetee gives me the who, what, when, where, and why. And although he doesn't yet know who the victim is or why he was killed, the basics are as follows:

The group was on a walking tour, led by two guides, when they came upon the abandoned fruit stand. Immediately, they noticed a horrible smell. And then one of the tourists screamed. A quick investigation by several others in the group revealed the horror—a dead body in an advanced stage of decomposition. The guides called the cops. The woman who screamed fainted and had to be transported to the hospital by ambulance. Someone vomited. Another person lost control of their bladder. The rest of the group begin snapping photos and recording videos.

"So that's what happened," I say, furiously writing.

Officer Cuetee says, "More or less."

"Which is it?" I ask. "More? Or less?"

Giving me another heart-stopping smile, he says, "I'll let you know when I get more details."

As he walks back to the cluster of officers conversing around the fruit stand, I focus on the tourists huddled beneath the guava trees. Should I try to interview them? Will doing so make Marty think I'm trying to cover the story when he warned me, in no uncertain terms, not to? Or will Marty appreciate my efforts and view me as a team player, gathering information about the story to help out a coworker?

I'm not sure. And yet something tells me Marty will be less than pleased. He'll probably demand to know why I didn't call the paper to let him know about the dead body. And maybe that's what I should do. Forget about the information gathering and follow my bosses' orders. Resolved with my decision, I reach into my cross-body purse, and—

Shoot!

I don't have my phone. I forgot it at work. So, I can't call Marty, even though I want to. But, since I can't call him, I might as well get details and gather information, right?

Fortified by the justification of my actions, I march toward the tourists.

Chapter 5

The tourists are hesitant, wary, and slightly suspicious of me even though I give them bright smiles and properly introduce myself.

Still, there is a reluctance to answer my questions.

But, then an elderly man with a cane steps forward to "say his piece about this wicked business," which he does, though I'm not sure I follow his logic. But, that's okay because he's the catalyst for change. Or, maybe not change, exactly, but he's the reason why the other tourists eagerly jump in with their two cents about the horrid discovery.

The outlandish girls in pink and orange chime in with their opinion.

"He was probably in that gang," says the one in orange, preening as she takes another selfie. "You know, the AR-15?"

"It's not the AR-15," says the girl in pink, sucking in her cheeks and making duck lips as she takes a photo of herself. "It's the B-52. No, wait. The DC-10. No, wait. It's the—"

"PC-5," I supply, not that I want to bring up the dreaded island cartel.

Scowling at me, the girl in pink says, "No, that's not it, either."

I'm absolutely certain it is the PC-5, but something tells me proving my point would be pointless.

"Anyway, like I said, the guy probably got killed because he was in that gang," says the girl in orange, striking several more poses as she documents her existence. "You know what they say: snitches get stitches."

"That ain't why he died," announces another wizened old man, also with a cane, who gazes at me with intense, rheumy eyes.

"Why did he die?" I ask, flipping to a clean page in the notebook. "And may I have your name, please, sir?"

"Bob Pennyworth, spelled just like it sounds," he tells me. "And he died on account of what that lady down at the beach said yesterday."

"What did the lady down at the beach say?" I ask.

"A bunch of foolishness," says the woman next to him. "Nothing you need to put in your paper."

"And your name, ma'am?" I ask.

"Bobbie Pennyworth," she says. "He's my daddy and he's had too much sun. We need to get back to our hotel so he can take his medicine, but the cops haven't released us to leave, and the tour guides don't know anything."

"They know," says a guy with slicked back reddish-blonde hair wearing an I 🩶 the Palmchat Islands T-shirt and a matching baseball cap with the bill turned to the back. He takes a last drag on a cigarette, then flicks it to the ground, mashing the cherry out with the tip of his sneaker. "They just don't want to tell us."

"And your name?" I ask.

"Zeke Kelly," he says, then asks, "You said you're with the *Palmchat Gazette*?"

Glancing up at him, I nod. "Yes, I'm a reporter at the paper. Sophie Carter."

"I have a friend who works there," says Zeke Kelly.

"Really?" I ask, slightly intrigued. "Who?"

"Ruth Rice," says Zeke. "Do you know her?"

Forcing myself to smile, despite the sour taste in my mouth, I say, "Yes! I know Ruth. She's a ... great reporter."

"I'm surprised she's not here," says Zeke. "I know she covers crime."

"Oh, well … " I clear my throat. "She probably got assigned another story."

"Wait until Ruth finds out I'm going to be in the paper," says Zeke. "I'll tell her to look for my name in your article."

Panicked, I say, "Oh, no … you can't do that."

Zeke frowns. "Why not?"

Clearing my throat, I say, "Well, because … you might not be in the story."

"Why not?" asks Zeke, his gaze slightly suspicious.

"Because I might not write the story," I say. "I'm just gathering information … the editor will decide who writes the story … or if the story is even written at all."

Zeke scoffs. "Why wouldn't the story be written? A dead body behind a fruit stand is front page news."

"True," I acknowledge. "However—"

"I hope we get our money back," says a squat, heavyset woman who steps between me and Zeke Kelly.

Grateful for the interruption, I turn to her. "Did you ask the tour guides about that?"

"I've been trying to call the tour company, but I can't get an answer," she says. "I've left six messages. I want my money back. My name is Erica Harris. Erica with a 'k', not a 'c'."

"Got it," I say, making sure to write her name accurately.

"If I don't get my money back," says Erica with a 'k', "I'm going to sue."

Zeke scoffs. "You probably won't win. And can you imagine how long it would take for your case to get through the courts down here? This is a small island. Most you could do is hope the company will settle to avoid negative publicity."

"We're going to do a podcast," says the girl in the orange outfit. "Like, a murder in paradise true crime podcast. It's going to be Tammy and Sasha—I'm Tammy, she's Sasha—well … we gotta think of the name but it's going to have our names in the title."

"We sort of feel like we have to do the podcast, you know?" says Sasha. "I mean, this is like fate, right? Like instructions from the universe."

"Instructions from the universe?" I ask, not sure I follow her.

Snapping another selfie, Sasha says, "Like, that guy died so we could do a true crime podcast."

"That's not why he died," says Zeke, sneering at the girl.

"He died because he got shot, right?" asks Erica with a 'k'. "Somebody said they overheard one of the cops say he got shot."

"What Sasha meant was," says Tammy, "that if we don't do the podcast, then that guy's death will be in vain, you know? We have to let the world know what happened to him and that he mattered, you know?"

Actually, I don't know that. Or think that. But—

"I just want my money back," reiterates Erica with a 'k', pulling out her phone, and dialing a number with blood red stiletto shaped fake nails. "I didn't come to this island for murder in paradise."

"He died because that lady said so," says Bob. "That lady was right!"

"That lady claimed she could read seashells," says Bob's daughter, rolling her eyes.

"Oh, I see," I say, nodding. "Well …"

I've heard of women, usually with indigenous ancestry, claiming the ability to read seashells, jellyfish tentacles, or even sand. They set up stands and stalls on the beach and lure tourists with the promise of predicting future events. Of course, it's all a sham. A lucrative scam.

Fanning herself with a limp tri-fold brochure, Erica with a 'k' says, "And somebody needs to tell us how we're going to get back to our hotels. We came from all over the island. Most of us were picked up from the King Palm Hotel and Suites, but—"

"Not us," says Bob. "We're at the Hibiscus."

"Nice," I say, impressed by the fancy digs even though the luxurious, seven-star property always makes me think of its sister hotel, the equally posh but somewhat mysterious Heliconia Hotel, which some say is a hotel that allows women to indulge in secret fantasies.

"Those two silly twits," the old man pauses to point his cane at the wanna-be Instagram models taking more selfies near the abandoned fruit stand, "were at the Royal St. Mateo. Then we got Zeke from the Neptune Inn & Suites." Nodding, I quickly scribble the information Bob Pennyworth spouts. "And there's a family of five that was at the Ocean Bay Villas," Bob Pennyworth continues. "Nice place. The husband, he's a lawyer, I believe he said—" "Daddy, what are you doing?" demands Bobbie Pennyworth, turning away from the conversation she'd been having with the guy in the backward cap and toward her father. "You shouldn't be telling where people are staying. What if they don't want anybody to know?" "I'm just trying to be helpful," protests Bob. "And you were, Mr. Pennyworth," I hasten to assure him. "You were." "Come on, Daddy. I've called us a cab." Pursing her lips and scowling at me, Bobbie Pennyworth guides her father away. "We need to get back to the hotel so you can take your medicine." As father and daughter leave, the other tourists disperse, as well, leaving me alone under the guava tree. Glancing at my notes, I frown. Despite the fact that the tourists started talking to me, I realize they didn't say very much. No one really saw anything. No one had any viable suspicions. No one had any clues. So much for my information gathering. All I learned was that a group of people are upset that their tour ended in disaster before it started. They want their money back and worry about getting back to their hotels. I didn't get anything riveting, exciting, or … informative. It would be different if one of the tourists had seen a suspect fleeing the scene. Or had found the murder weapon. Or had overheard something suspicious. If so, I might have been able to convince Marty that my blatant insubordination was justified. But I have nothing to show for doing the very thing Marty warned me not to do. With a sigh, I shove my notebook back into my purse. As I walk toward the boardwalk, I can't help wondering if I'll lose my job. Marty was serious about his promise to ship me out if I don't shape up.

Chapter 6

An hour later, I'm back from Guavatown, traipsing across the small employee parking lot behind the *Palmchat Gazette* building.

With each step, my anxiety and apprehension increases.

Marty is going to ask me about the walking tour, and I'll have to tell him I wasn't able to do the tour so I can review it, and he'll demand to know why …

And then I'll be forced to tell him about the dead body the tourists found behind the abandoned fruit stand, where I was supposed to meet the tour director.

And because anytime a dead body is found, it's considered a crime story, Marty is sure to ask me if I tried to cover the story, even though he warned me not to. And then what will I tell him?

I'm still not sure.

As I sat on the jitney, headed back to downtown St. Mateo, I imagined dozens of ways to convince Marty I wasn't covering the crime beat, even though by questioning witnesses, I kinda, sorta was. I cycled through several scenarios, but in the end, I saw myself being fired. Saw Marty telling me he was shipping me out because I hadn't shaped up.

Walking along a line of Seagrape trees around the perimeter of the lot, I wish I had taken a detour to Tea 4 Too, my favorite teahouse before returning to work. A steaming cup of mango lemon chamomile tea and donut holes rolled in powdered sugar cane would have calmed my nerves and given me the courage to—

A strange, plaintive wailing wafts in the breeze.

Curious, wondering where the sound came from, and what it is, I glance around and—

A desperate, frantic, high-pitched screech mixed with a crazed rustling startles me. Arrested by the sound, I stop, curious about the increasing volume and frequency of what I can only describe as a hissing yowl of pain. What on earth?

With tentative steps, I follow the sound to the Seagrape bushes, peering at the wide, round hanging leaves. The high-pitched wailing hiss seizes my attention as I discern what sounds like ...

Meow ... meow ... *meeeeeoooooowwwww* ...

A cat, I think, not quite sure. But what else could it be except a cat? What other animal meows?

The Seagrape leaves rustle again, as though being disturbed by something. Walking to the tree, I push the leaves aside, searching for what I think might be a cat. The intensity of the yelping meow worries me. Poor thing, I think, wondering if the cat is hurt.

"Here, kitty, kitty ..."

Scanning the clusters of leaves, I spot the cat wedged between two intertwined branches. Looks like a Calico with distinctive orange and black patches on its back. But I could be wrong, as I'm not exactly a cat person.

Struggling valiantly, the Calico tries to free itself but doesn't seem to be able to ... and I can see why. The branches are bent, forming a small, tight opening, like a vise of thin bark around the cat's body.

"Oh no ..." I say. "Poor little thing. How did you get in there?"

After extracting the cat from the tree, I hold her up like the monkey held up Simba in The Lion King.

"There, there, little kitty. You're okay now. You're free. You—"

Hissing in my face, baring sharp, pointy teeth, the cat swats its right paw against my jaw, then its left paw against my chin before it head butts me in the nose.

Shocked and startled, I shriek, then drop the ungrateful Calico, which, not surprisingly, lands on its feet.

Looking back at me, its eyes narrow and it hisses again before shooting off like a bat out of hell. Or, rather, a cat out of hell.

I shake my head at the ungrateful feline, who probably would have died in that Seagrape bush if I hadn't rescued it. Removing my compact from my purse, I take a deep breath, and inspect my face for damage, thankful that psycho cat didn't claw my eyes out.

Chapter 7

Back in the building, I'm about to sit down at my desk in my cubicle when the phone next to my computer rings.

I glance at the caller ID and wince.

It's Marty.

My anxiety and apprehension rachet up several notches. Staring at the phone, listening to the ringing, I hesitate. I don't want to talk to Marty because I know he's going to ask me about the review of the walking tour and I'm still not sure what to tell him.

Of course, I have to tell him that I didn't have a chance to talk to the tour director or go on the tour, and when he asks why, I'll have to inform him about the dead body. Once he finds out I couldn't complete the tour because a crime was committed, he'll demand to know why I didn't call the office and tell him. And I'll admit that I accidentally left my phone at the office.

But the conversation won't end there.

Marty will question me about whether or not I tried to cover the story.

And what will I say? Do I tell the truth? Admit that I interviewed a few of the witnesses who were planning to go on the tour when the body was discovered? Or do I keep that bit of information to myself, considering that I didn't find out anything crucial anyway?

I don't want to lie to my boss, but what if the truth gets me fired? I don't want to be shipped out because Marty thinks I haven't shaped up. Marty thinks I need more experience to be a good crime reporter. I want him to give me a chance to get the experience I need, but that won't happen if I'm no longer working at the *Palmchat Gazette*.

The ringing continues.

Exhaling, fighting my reluctance, I press the button to answer. "Hi, Marty!"

"Sophia, come to my office. Now."

"Okay, yes, I'll be right—"

The line disconnects.

"There …" I mumble under my breath as I hang up, then stand to my feet. With shaky legs and much trepidation, I walk to Marty's office.

At the half-open door, my heart races as I knock, secretly hoping he won't be in his office, that in the few seconds, or so, it took me to walk down the hall, he was called away, possibly to some important symposium taking place in at the end of the world, in Patagonia, and he'll be gone for six months.

"Come in …" Marty calls out.

Sighing, I step inside. "You wanted to see me?"

Turning from his computer, Marty asks, "Have you finished the review of the walking tour?"

"Oh, um … well, you see, " I begin. "I actually didn't go on the walking tour."

"Why not?" demands Marty, scowling.

"Because … " I say, biting my lower lip as I take a seat in one of the chairs in front of his desk. I'm stalling. Wondering what to tell him. Trying to decide if I should come clean.

"Because?" demands Marty, his face deepening to a darker shade of crimson.

Clearing my throat, I say, "Because … it was, um … cancelled."

"The walking tour was cancelled?"

"Right," I say, feeling like a coward and a failure. Why didn't I tell Marty the truth? Why didn't I explain that the tour was cancelled because a dead body was found in Guavatown? Despite the fact that I learned about the tourists discovering the dead body, I didn't try to cover the story. I only tried to get some information from them, which I was going to give Ruth, but none of them had much to say, so technically, I didn't ignore his warning. Which means, he doesn't have to ship me out because I have shaped up.

"Well, these things happen, I suppose," says Marty, retrieving a file from the stacks of papers and documents on his desk.

Shocked at his nonchalance, I say, "I suppose they do …"

Opening the file, Marty says, "Sometimes they don't have enough people. Most of these tours need a certain number of bookings to make a decent profit."

"Right," I say, feeling both relieved and worried, like I got away with something I shouldn't have, something I didn't want to get away with.

"Tourists come to the islands to go to the beach," says Marty. "Walking tours aren't as popular as swimming, snorkeling, and laying out in the sun."

"I totally agree," I say, feeling slightly less apprehensive, but still somewhat upset about not coming clean.

"Nevertheless, we still need the ad dollars," says Marty.

"Of course," I say.

"So you need to write a story about the walking tour," says Marty, giving me a shrewd gaze. "Whether you're able to take it, or not."

"Right," I say. "I can call the owner and interview him."

"Good idea," says Marty.

Reignited with eagerness, I say, "He can give me an overview of the tour, including the points of interest and places a tourist would visit on the tour, and I could check them out on my own."

"Make that happen first thing tomorrow," says Marty. "We need a very detailed overview of the tour."

"Absolutely!" I say. "The article will be full of detailed details!"

Frowning, Marty says, "Detailed … details …"

Realizing I should probably bridle my unbridled enthusiasm, I give him a shaky smile. "It's just something I say sometimes ..."

Leaning back in his chair, Marty stares at me. "Sophia, I'm sure I don't have to remind you that walking tour article is very important. The lifestyle stories matter more than you think. They bring in significant revenue in the form of ad dollars."

Nodding, I say, "I understand."

"Here's something else you need to understand," says Marty. "Don't drop the ball. And don't take my warning lightly. I will ship you out if you don't shape up."

Chapter 8

"Oh, Sophie, I wouldn't worry about being shipped out," says Candace, the paper's receptionist, a sixty-something woman with a cute salt-and-pepper pixie cut and a bright smile, dressed in a crisp royal blue suit that matches her eyes.

At a quarter to six, fifteen minutes before the official end of my workday, I'm sitting in the *Palmchat Gazette* breakroom, a large airy space with glass walls that allow lots of natural light to brighten the area.

At the table with me are my coworkers, Candace and Clark, whose name is, believe it or not, Clark Kent. And I know, that's the name Superman adopted because he couldn't tell people he was really Kal-El, but believe it or not, there are really guys out there named Clark Kent. The local staff photographer is one of those guys.

And even though it would be totally ironic if Clark Kent didn't look like Superman, that's actually not the case. Because he does look like Superman. Clark Kent is a total Clark Kent. He's tall, handsome, and well-built. He even wears glasses, but they don't distract at all from his intense gray-green eyes. Over tea, for me, electrolyte water, for Candace, and black coffee, for Clark, I told them about Marty's warning this morning, and how I sort of ignored it when I questioned those witnesses about the dead body in Guavatown.

Once I finished, I solicited thoughts and opinions as to whether, or not, Marty will ship me out because I didn't shape up.

"So, you wouldn't worry?" I ask, a bit hopeful that Candace doesn't think my predicament is hopeless.

Shaking her head, Candace takes a sip of her healthy electrolyte water, then says, "Well, unless, of course, you're afraid of water."

Confused, I ask, "Afraid of water?"

"Or boats," says Candace.

Frowning, Clark says, "I don't think Marty meant that he would literally ship Sophie away on a boat."

"Oh," says Candace. "Well, then, in that case, Sophie, if I were you, I'd probably start updating my resume."

Hopes dashed, I feel my heart sinking.

Clark says, "I don't think Marty will actually fire Sophie because she didn't come clean and tell him she asked a few witnesses questions about the dead body."

"Who said anything about Sophie getting fired?" Candace asks.

I stare at her. "You said I should update my resume. Why would I do that if I didn't think I needed to look for another job?"

"You need to update your resume because it's good to do so every six months, or so," says Candace, chugging more water.

I sneak a glance at Clark, who's sneaking a glance at me, and I can tell we're thinking the same thing.

"Anyway," Clark says. "I don't think Marty will be too upset. Especially since you didn't even get any information."

"But doesn't that make it worse?" I ask. "I interviewed those witnesses for nothing. I didn't get any clues."

"Are you sure you didn't?" asks Candace.

Glancing at her, I say, "I don't think so. If I did, I didn't realize it. Which also makes it worse."

Nodding, Candace says, "Makes you look incompetent. Like you're not a good reporter. You don't know what you're doing."

"Thanks ..." I mumble, biting my lip, hoping I won't cry.

"Just because the tourists didn't have any information doesn't mean you're incompetent or not a good reporter," Clark disputes. "The tourists didn't tell you anything because they didn't know anything."

"Unless they did," says Candace. "But they didn't want to tell you because they didn't think you were a good reporter."

"What did the tourists tell you?" Clark asks.

"Well, as I said, not much," I tell them, recalling the scant details I wrote in my Steno pad. Details which were not, to my chagrin, very detailed. "They were mostly upset about not being able to go on the tour. They wanted their money back. They wondered how they would get back their hotels. Two girls wanted to start a podcast because they saw the murder as a sign from the universe about justice ... or something."

"Not much you can do with that information," says Candace.

"Which is why I don't think Marty will fire you if he finds out what you did," reiterates Clark.

Sighing, I take a sip of tea, then say, "But he specifically told me not to cover any crime stories. And I'm worried that interviewing the witnesses falls under covering the crime beat."

"I suppose he could see it that way," Clark allows.

"He also specifically told me that if I see a crime in progress or find myself in an area where a crime has been committed," I say, "then I need to call the paper and let the assignments editor know. But I didn't do that because I couldn't."

"Why not?" asks Clark.

Shaking my head, I say, "I forgot my phone at the office."

"And whose fault is that?" Candace asks.

I give her a look.

Shrugging, she says, "Listen, Sophie, I know you don't want to hear this, but I have to say it ..."

"Do you really?" I ask, preparing myself for a shady, snarky comment.

"I think Marty would have a legitimate case if he wanted to fire you," says Candace.

"I disagree," says Clark.

Candace says, "You didn't heed Marty's warning and you lied to his face when he asked you about the article. He told you not to cover crime and you interviewed witnesses about a dead body. He told you to call the paper if you saw a crime story unfolding in front of you, but you didn't."

"Because I left my phone," I insist. "I couldn't call the paper."

"But what if you hadn't left your phone?" Candace asks, her gaze shrewd.

"What do you mean?" I ask, even though I know exactly what she means. I'm just not sure how to answer her.

Candace asks, "Would you have called the paper to tell the assignments editor about the dead body? Or would you have interviewed those witnesses anyway?"

"I'd like to know the answer to that question as well …"

Chapter 9

Recognizing the voice, I wince, then turn in my seat to look at the person standing behind me.

Ruth Rice scowls, arms crossed.

Tall, svelte, and aloof, Ruth has alabaster skin, cupid's bow lips, and a pretty heart-shaped face framed by ink-black wavy hair cut in a classic French bob.

"Well, isn't that interesting," says Ruth, shaking her head.

Candace asks, "Isn't what interesting?"

I'm wondering the same thing, but I'm even more curious about the strange, Cheshire cat who swallowed the canary look on Ruth's face.

"Sophie, it seems that you're not just a bad reporter," Ruth begins.

"Excuse me?" I stare at her.

"But you're also a dishonest employee," Ruth says, sneering, "who doesn't know how to follow the boss's orders."

My heart drops into my stomach as the realization hits me like a kick in the gut.

Ruth overheard me talking to Candace and Clark about interviewing the witnesses in Guavatown when Marty told me not to cover the crime beat.

"I don't know what you mean," I say, glancing at Clark, who looks slightly worried, which increases my anxiety as I struggle to think of how I'm going to convince Ruth that she didn't hear what she thinks she heard.

Candace says, "Sophie, I think Ruth means that you weren't honest with Marty about the fact that your interviewed witnesses about the dead body found in Guavatown when Marty told you not to cover any crime stories."

I glare at Candace, though I'm not surprised she's not on my side.

"That's exactly what I mean," says Ruth. "Which I'm sure Sophie knows."

Exhaling, I jump up and turn to Ruth. "Listen, I know what you overheard but I can explain."

"I don't want your ridiculous explanations," snarls Ruth. "I just want you gone!"

Shocked, I gape at her. "You want me … gone?"

"You don't belong here," Ruth says. "You shouldn't even be a journalist. You're not a good reporter and your writing is horrible!"

"If I didn't belong here," I say, "then I wouldn't have been hired, but I was and it's because I'm a good reporter and a good writer."

Ruth scoffs. "What you are, Sophie, is a silly little twit who's good friends with the publisher and his wife. That's the only reason why you have this job."

"That is not true," I dispute, annoyed by her cronyism claims. "My relationship with Leo and Vivian had nothing to do with why I was hired!"

"That is the only reason why you were hired," says Ruth. "Leo and Vivian like you. They feel sorry for you. Because you're a bad reporter. You don't know what you're doing. That's why you can't cover crime stories."

"I don't cover crime because Marty assigned me to work the lifestyle beat," I tell her.

Rolling her eyes, Ruth says, "Fluffy nonsense that no one reads!"

"Actually, that isn't true," says Candace. "My choir members at church love reading about the society section, following the exciting and glamourous lives of the rich and famous."

"And the guys in my running club scour the travel section, looking for new trails," says Clark.

Shaking her head at Clark and Candace, Ruth says, "Of course you two enablers would encourage her incompetence."

"I'm not incompetent," I tell Ruth, growing sick of her insults.

"Oh, is that right?" Ruth smirks. "So, you interview witnesses about the dead body they found behind the abandoned fruit stand and find out … what? Nothing at all?"

"Only because they had nothing to say," I tell her.

"No, because you don't have the necessary interviewing skills to be a crime reporter," says Ruth. "Did you find out which one of the tourists actually found the body? Did you bother asking if any of the witnesses recognized the dead man? Did you ask the witnesses how it felt to be involved in such a violent act when all they wanted was a peaceful vacation?"

"Well, no, I didn't," I say, feeling as incompetent as Ruth believes I am. "But only because—"

"Because you didn't think to ask them those things," Ruth says. "And why would you? How could you? You're not a crime reporter and you never will be!"

"I've reported on crimes before, at the St. Killian office," I say. "And I'll convince Marty that I can work the crime beat here, in St. Mateo—"

"Not if I can help it," Ruth informs me.

"And how would you help it?" asks Candace. "And, exactly what do you mean by it?"

Ruth glares at Candace. "Did I invite you into this conversation?"

Candace says, "Well, pronouns, like 'it,' do require antecedents."

Nodding, Clark says, "As a reporter, you should know that."

Rolling her eyes again, Ruth exhales. "I'm going to make sure Marty fires you."

Frowning, I ask, "And just how do you think you're going to accomplish that?"

"I'm going to tell him the truth about your lies," Ruth says.

"The truth about my lies …" I repeat, confused for a moment … until I understand exactly what Ruth plans to do. "No, you can't tell Marty—"

"Can't I?" Ruth arches an eyebrow as she smirks. "Oh, I absolutely can and I absolutely will! Marty is going to know that you ignored his warning to stay away from the crime beat. You blatantly went behind his back and interviewed witnesses—albeit pathetically and poorly—when you were supposed to call the paper and tell the assignments editor about the dead body in Guavatown."

Panic and desperation threaten to overtake me. "No, Ruth, please don't. If you tell Marty, he'll—"

"Get rid of you?" Ruth lets out a mirthless cackle. "Yes, I know. That's why I'm going to tell him."

As Ruth saunters away, I resist the urge to pick up my empty mug and hurl it at the back of her head. But violence never solves problems. Instead, I sit down at the table, where Candace and Clark are giving me sympathetic looks.

Sadness and anger threaten to overtake me. Ruth is such a horrid troll, but I won't let her get to me.

"Don't let her scare tactics worry you," Clark tells me.

"How can I not be worried?" I ask. "Marty was serious about shipping me out if I don't shape up. When Ruth tells him what I did …"

"Even if she does," Clark says. "That's no guarantee that Marty will fire you."

Shaking my head, I say, "Marty said—"

"You have to explain your side to him," Clark says. "Plead your case. You didn't mean to ignore his warning. You interviewed the tourists because you were trying to help. You weren't going to write the story."

Candace says, "Look at the bright side. If Marty does fire you, maybe you can ask Leo or Vivian to rehire you."

Pinching the bridge of my nose, I shake my head. "I can't do that. It's bad enough that Marty already thinks I got hired because of cronyism. I need to prove that I deserve this job despite my friendship with Leo and Viv. And I need to find a way to stop Ruth from telling Marty the truth."

Candace says, "The good news is that Marty is gone for the day, but there's always tomorrow. Ruth will probably talk to him first thing in the morning."

"I can't let that happen," I say, struggling to fight the panic and desolation brewing within me. "I won't let Ruth destroy my journalism career ..."

Chapter 10

After leaving the breakroom, I head back to my cubicle.

Panic, rage, sadness, and confusion have my stomach twisted into nautical knots. I can't stop thinking about my confrontation with Ruth in the breakroom. Can't believe how much she dislikes me. How she wants me to be fired because she doesn't think I deserve my job.

No wonder she never wanted to go to lunch with me.

At my desk, I power down my computer, then grab my purse and keys. Apprehension and a dreadful sense of impending doom swirl within me. Whenever I get anxious, I crave cinnamon tea with apple streusel donut holes. A stop at my favorite tea shop might be just what I need to calm down and think rationally.

There has to be a way out of the mess I'm in.

Clark and Candace think I should intercept Ruth's plans and talk to Marty before she does. I need to come clean and explain to him that I wasn't trying to ignore his warning. I really wanted to help Ruth and I thought getting information from the tourists would help foster a collaborative spirit among us. I wasn't trying to work the crime beat. I really wanted to call the paper about the dead body found in Guavatown but I accidentally left my phone at the office.

Candace asked me if I would have called the office had I not left my phone and I'm sure I would have.

Leaving my office space, I walk through the maze of cubes, heading toward the back door that leads to the parking lot.

A few feet ahead on the right is a cube I plan to rush by.

It's Ruth's cubicle.

Earlier, when I passed Ruth's cube on my way from the breakroom, I quickly glanced over and determined she wasn't there, thank goodness.

Hopefully, she's gone for the day.

And, maybe, on her drive home, she's having second thoughts about trying to destroy my career. I doubt it, though. Something tells me I'll have to focus my efforts on Marty. I need to convince him that I took his warning seriously. That I plan to do whatever it takes for me to shape up, so he won't have to—

"I will do what you say," continues Ruth. "You won't have to kill me ..."

Stifling a gasp, I slow to a stop, frowning. *You won't have to kill me?* Wait. What? Did Ruth really just say that? My heart slams.

Is someone in the cube with her? Or—

"... we can meet at my place, okay?"

The hushed, worried tone floating out into the hallway definitely belongs to Ruth. I'm less than a foot from her cube now. As she continues to talk, her voice rises an octave. Inching closer to the opening of her cubicle, I listen.

"I will give you the jump drive ... yes, I know, but—"

What's going on? Who is Ruth talking to? What jump drive is she talking about? Who is she going to give it to? Obviously, I know I shouldn't eavesdrop, but—

"You don't have to threaten to hurt me ..."

Frowning, I bite my lip. Why would the person Ruth is talking to threaten to hurt and kill her? Who could she be talking to? A confidential source? A witness? A disgruntled reader who didn't appreciate her word choice or the structure of her sentences, which, in my opinion, can be somewhat complex and hard to understand and—

"And then you'll leave, right?" asks Ruth.

Silence ensues, and then Ruth curses. Rigid, I stand rooted to the spot, wondering what to do, if anything. Part of me wants to forget what I heard. Just turn and keep walking toward the door, out of the building, and across the parking lot to my car. After all, Ruth was having a private conversation. It's none of my business.

And yet, despite her firm, bossy tone, I heard hints of fear. And how could she not be terrified? *You won't have to kill me.* Whoever she's talking to threatened her life. Part of me also thinks that, despite our animosity—which, trust me, after the confrontation in the breakroom is now mutual—I need to make sure she's okay.

With determination and trepidation, and against my better judgment, I walk into Ruth's cube. "Is everything okay?"

Ruth spins around to face me.

For a few awkward seconds, she doesn't say anything, just stares at me in shock. I see several emotions playing across her face. Embarrassment. Chagrin. Apprehension.

But then Ruth scowls. "What do you want?"

Reminding myself not to cower, I clear my throat. "I was just wondering—"

"Wondering … *what*?" Ruth glares at me.

I take a cautious step toward Ruth and lower my voice. "Is someone trying to … hurt you, or—"

"Hurt me?" Ruth's glare morphs into an amused sneer. "What are you talking about? No one is trying to hurt me."

"Are you sure?" I ask. "Because you said—"

Ruth's eyes narrow. "Said *what*?"

"Well, I heard you saying that—"

"You were eavesdropping on my private conversation?" Ruth's glare makes a comeback.

"Well, technically, yes," I admit. "But I wasn't trying to—"

"How dare you …" Ruth steps closer to me, invading my space.

"I accidentally overheard you," I say, stepping back. "And you seemed to be having a heated discussion with whoever you were talking to on the phone. You told that person they wouldn't have to kill you, and—"

"I don't know what you think you heard," says Ruth. "But stay out of my life, okay?"

"You can tell me the truth," I tell her. "I would never betray your confidence, or—"

"The truth is that you need to mind your own business, you silly little twit," admonishes Ruth. "And start looking for another job because after I talk to Marty, he's going to get rid of you ..."

Chapter 11

Taking a small sip of lemon, mint, and chamomile tea, I recline on the chaise lounge on the veranda of my small apartment.

As I drove home, I ruminated on Ruth's last words to me.

Ruth promised to tell Marty that I was attempting to cover a crime story when he warned me not to. After Ruth left for the day, I spent a an hour in my cubicle worrying and fretting that Marty was going to call me into his office and fire me. When he didn't come, I glanced in his office and found him already gone. I tried to convince myself I wouldn't have to look for another job. That somehow, someway, I could keep my position at the *Palmchat Gazette*.

I was hoping Ruth would relent and realize she didn't want to ruin my career. If she was still focused on taking me down, I knew I'd misinterpreted the conversation I'd overheard between her and the unknown caller. Anyone worried about being killed wouldn't have time to plot my demise, yet Ruth seemed determined to do just that. My only hope was that if she did snitch to Marty, he would be angry but would find it in his heart to give me a second chance.

I take a deep breath, trying to think positively.

Despite Ruth's threat, I don't have to jump to the worse conclusions. And yet, I feel as though I should prepare myself for the worst. Just in case. The panic in my limbs turns to full-blown fear. I can't lose my job. All I've ever wanted to be was a journalist. And, specifically, I've longed to write stories about crime and corruption.

When I was in high school, I wrote for the paper, but my love for investigative journalism was born when I was in primary school. In my third year, I single handedly solved what I like to call, The Case of the Missing Library books.

When classic, beloved books began disappearing from the school library, it was believed that they had been misplaced or that students had forgotten to return them. Soon, it became apparent that the books were being stolen.

My classmates and I wondered who the thief might be, but I ventured to search for evidence. I eventually realized that there were always crumbs near the shelves where the books had been taken from. A rudimentary analysis of the crumbs led me to suspect they were flakes from the cranberry croissants sold in the cafeteria. Croissants that most of the students didn't like. But I knew there was someone who did like the croissants. Someone who was always eating them and asking the cafeteria manager to put a few back for him.

The school janitor, Mr. Bosenberry.

With a suspect in mind, I knew I would need proof. One afternoon, I stayed after school and snuck into the library. With the camera on my phone, I was able to record the janitor removing several books and shoving them into a large sack. I went home, showed my parents the video, and the next day, we went to school and had a meeting with the principal.

When confronted with the evidence, Mr. Bosenberry broke down and confessed.

As it turned out, he had a secret illegal side hustle selling the books to local bookstore.

After I exposed the culprit, I was lauded for my cunning ingenuity and intrepid observation. Most people thought I might make a good police detective. However, when I was interviewed for the local paper, I was a bit shy so the reporter asked me to write the story in my own words. Doing so gave me a rush of elation and euphoria. And the newspaper editor decided to publish my story. There's a framed copy of it on the living room wall at my parents' house in St. Killian. Not only was I immensely proud, but at that moment, I knew I wanted to be an investigative reporter.

Trying not to cry, I sit up and lean forward, dropping my face into my hands. What am I going to do? If I lose my job, what will happen then? I'll be forced to go back to St. Killian, where I'll look like a failure. Even my former coworkers in St. Killian will think I didn't have what it took to be a good crime reporter. They'll think I was forced to beg Vivian and Leo for another chance, and they rehired me because they felt sorry for me—not because they believed in my ability to be a good investigative journalist.

Taking another sip of tea, I try to relax. And not panic. I need to think. But I can't. Well, actually, no, that's not true. I can think.

About one thing.

Or, rather, one person.

Ruth Rice.

If I'm going to keep my job, and maintain my dignity, I need to convince Ruth not to tell Marty I interviewed witnesses about the dead body found in Guavatown. Someway, somehow, I have to get through to Ruth. I have to make her see that ruining my career would be the worst thing she could do.

Standing, I try to convince myself I'll be able to turn this horrible situation around. I need to talk to Ruth tonight. Walking back into my apartment, I glance at the clock on the microwave oven in the kitchen. 7:51 p.m. It's not too late to head to Ruth's place. Of course, she won't be expecting me, and proper etiquette states I should call her first, but if I do, she probably won't answer the phone.

Showing up at Ruth's door out of the blue is my best bet to talk to her, and hopefully convince her to hear me out.

And maybe, just maybe, she'll have a heart, show some grace, and give me a break.

I'm not ready to throw in the towel yet.

And I won't.

Chapter 12

The front door to Ruth's duplex home is slightly open.

Apprehensive, I shift my weight from one foot to the other, unsure of what to do.

A minute or so ago, after I exited the JEEP, I made my way up a broken concrete sidewalk. Brown grass and half-dead weeds grew between the cracks. The chain link fence creaked and groaned as I pushed it open and continued, approaching the porch. Carefully, I navigated five warped and splintered wooden steps. As I did, I was thinking Ruth probably wouldn't answer the door. Actually, I was hoping she wouldn't. Behind the fence, the bushes are dense and thick. The early twilight heat and humidity, and the incessant buzzing of insects, made the atmosphere feel like the jungle. It was just minutes after sunset, and the porch was dim and shadowy.

I was glancing around, hoping someone wouldn't pounce on me from out of nowhere, when I raised my hand to knock on the door and realized it was already open.

Now I'm confused and worried.

The door is not supposed to be open and I can't help but wonder why...

Maybe I should just turn around, go back out to my JEEP, and go home. What was I thinking? Ruth can't stand me. She thinks I'm a horrible reporter who doesn't deserve my job at the Palmchat Gazette because I got it through cronyism. She's never going to change her mind about snitching on me to Marty. Why did I ever think she would?

I bite my lip.

I should just leave.

And yet, I'm not leaving. I'm still standing on the porch, staring at the space between the doorframe and the door as though I'm contemplating pushing the door open and entering Ruth's home. But I'm not going to do that. Am I?

Exhaling, I raise my hand and place my palm against the door.

I think I am going to push it open.

And I do.

The door swings back, revealing a gloomy, dim foyer.

"Ruth …" I call out, anxious about stepping over the threshold since I can hardly see two feet in front of me. "Ruth … are you home?"

I hesitate. I don't want to enter the house. I may not be an investigative reporter, but I do know that a half-open door usually means bad business. People just don't accidentally leave their doors open. And in a neighborhood like this, if a door is partially open, it's probably because someone broke into the house.

So I shouldn't go inside.

And yet, for some ridiculous reason, I can't bring myself to leave without at least trying to plead with Ruth, even though my efforts will most likely be for nothing.

I take a deep breath and walk into the foyer.

Gloom dissipates around me as ambient light reveals an interior starkly different from the ramshackle exterior. The inside of the home is posh and pristine. Shockingly and unexpectedly, I find myself surrounded by expensive modern furnishings, pristine marble flooring, and brushed platinum fixtures. Above me are tray ceilings and a chandelier. There's crown molding and wainscoting. Serious art adorns walls painted slate gray. And when I say serious, I mean like I think I recognize Picasso. Chagall. Basquiat. And Quark, the quirky, trippy, otherworldly Palmchatter whose work always sets the world on fire.

Of course, I don't know for sure if the paintings are real, but I've been to enough museums—and I've been to the mega-mansion of my coworker Stevie's family—to know when I'm looking at something museum quality. Stopping in front of what appears to be the Basquiat, I try to wrap my mind around Ruth's house. On the one hand, I suppose maybe I shouldn't be surprised since Ruth is regularly decked out in haute couture. And yet, I guess I've always thought her Chanel was fake. But could those tweed suits be real? As real as this Basquiat seems to be?

I bite my lower lip. It's possible, but … one thing I wonder is—

Glass shatters.

Startled, I turn and look over my shoulder.

From a short hallway off the living area, Ruth Rice emerges.

"Help …" gasps Ruth, her voice barely above a whisper. "Please …"

Ruth's eyes are glassy, her hair is unkempt, she's pale, sweaty … and covered in blood.

Chapter 13

Horrified, I hurry toward Ruth.

"Oh my God! Ruth, what happened?" I ask. I know, I know, it's a ridiculous question. It's obvious what happened to Ruth. The handle of a large knife protrudes from the center of her chest. The sight of my co-worker, bloodied and shuffling toward me like a zombie has rendered rational and realistic thought useless. I don't know what to think, let alone what to say. But words don't matter now. Ruth needs help.

Hurrying to Ruth, I grab her shoulders as gently as possible, then grab the knife. I pull it from her body and fling it toward the couch. Quickly, I gather the hem of her bloody T-shirt and press it against the wound, hoping to staunch the flow until I can call the paramedics.

Ruth clutches me, her trembling fingers grasping and clawing as her eyes widen. Her mouth opens. I get the feeling she wants to say something, but the only sound that tumbles from her lips is a wheezing gasp.

"Don't talk," I tell her. "Save your strength."

As I struggle to guide Ruth to the couch, and keep pressure on her wound, we stumble around, doing a drunken dance.

"This way," I tell Ruth. "Come on … you need to lie down, and—"

Ruth stiffens, pushing me away. Then her body goes limp, and she falls, crashing down onto the coffee table, the weight of her body shattering the table, sending hunks and shards of glass flying and scattering all across the living room.

Stumbling, I cover my head and dive onto the couch.

Seconds later, I venture to take a look toward the shattered glass coffee table. Not surprisingly, Ruth is sprawled out, face up on her back, across the broken glass. I rise slowly to a sitting position, then stand. On shaky legs I walk to Ruth, then take a knee next to her.

Seconds later, pressing two fingers against her neck, I cry out in shock even though I'm not surprised that there's no pulse.

Ruth is dead …

Chapter 14

I never should have gone to Ruth's house.

Exhaling, I glance around at my surroundings, which happen to be, at this moment, an interrogation room at the St. Mateo police department. The space is small and austere. Sterile and scary. A cause for panic and alarm. My heart is slamming. It hasn't stopped since the police arrived at Ruth's house.

Two responding officers were the first to show up, and they were quickly joined by what seemed like every cop on the force. Plus a host of crime tech guys. And a few paramedics. The place was swarming with law enforcement. Immediately, I felt surrounded, as though they were all crowding me, staring at me with narrowed, skeptical, and suspicious eyes as I gave my statement.

The words tumbled from my mouth in fits and starts, and to my own ears, they sounded false and phony. Like a manufactured narrative. Something I'd come up with to hide my involvement in some malicious malfeasance.

Which was ridiculous because I wasn't involved in any malicious malfeasance.

The extent of my involvement was the following: I went to my coworker Ruth's house because I needed to talk with her about something, then I heard a noise, turned, and watched in horror as Ruth collapsed and died.

I told the cops that, but I don't know if they believed me. They insisted that I come with them to the police station to repeat my story to one of the St. Mateo detectives, who would probably have more questions for me, they said. It sounded like a warning.

Taking a deep breath, I rub my damp palms against my pants.

My nerves are shot. I shouldn't be worried about being questioned by Detective Francois, but I just can't help it.

After all, I'll be telling the truth. And it makes sense that the detective would want to hear the story from me directly.

Still, I can't help thinking that sitting in an interrogation room is something very bad.

I feel as though I've been here forever.

At least three hours, which I know is, technically, not forever but it's a very long time.

Enough time to make me wonder if maybe the cops didn't believe me. And they want the detective to get me to confess to something I didn't do …

If that's true, it has to mean they want me to confess to killing Ruth.

I take another deep breath.

I can't help thinking the detective is making me wait on purpose. Because he has the power to do so. He wants me to squirm. And he's using some passive-aggressive interrogation technique designed to make me spill my guts all over the stainless-steel table.

But, what would I spill my guts about? And why would François want me to spill my guts? Why would he think I had any guts to spill?

My mind shifts back to the first responders I spoke to.

Do those cops think I killed Ruth? If so, why? How could they? It doesn't make sense.

Well, okay, I suppose it's not out of the realm of possibility that the cops might perceive me to be guilty. After all, the police arrived at a ghastly scene. Ruth was dead on the floor with blood all over her. And I had Ruth's blood on me. Smeared across my peach-colored eyelet blazer. Staining my right palm and the fingertips of my left hand. Plus I was sort of forced to admit that I entered Ruth's house uninvited, but only because the door had been open. And, no, I didn't have any proof of that, but …

Panic flares within me as I bite my lower lip.

Okay, so maybe the cops do have reason to suspect me. But they shouldn't because I didn't kill Ruth. I wouldn't have done that. The detective is just going to have to believe me. I'm telling the truth. And, besides, there is no evidence against me, and—

The door to the interrogation room opens.

Startled, I jump.

Seconds later, Detective François enters and then slams the door behind him. Swallowing, I shrink back, apprehensive. As the detective strides toward me, much like a panther eyeing its prey, I can't read his cool expression.

"Ms. Sophia Carter …" says the detective.

His tone is as enigmatic as his gaze, but I'm not surprised. I read somewhere that François detectives have an uncanny ability to discern while remaining undiscernible themselves. They can be both deceptive and deductive. You never know what they're thinking but they always have you figured out.

Somehow, that gives me hope.

If Detective Richland François is as good at investigating crimes as he's purported to be then he should already know I'm innocent, right?

"You are Sophia Carter …" prompts the detective, stopping behind the chair on the opposite side of the small table.

"Huh? Oh. Right. Yes," I stumble over my words. "Absolutely. That's me. Sophia Carter. Sophie Carter. Well, Sophia is on my birth certificate, but no one calls me Sophia. Well, except for my boss, Marty, he calls me—"

"Why did you go to the home of Ruth Rice?"

"Why did I go there?" I echo.

The detective stares at me. Again, I can't read the look. I don't even try. I just say, "Um, you see, Ruth is my coworker and—"

"Why did you go to her house?"

Clearing my throat, I ask, "Didn't the responding officers tell you—"

"You need to tell me."

"Right. Yes. Well, okay." I clear my throat again. Wipe my damp palms on my jeans. "I went there to talk to Ruth."

"About what?"

I hesitate, struggling to remember what I told the first responders. The last thing I want to do is tell a conflicting story. But I don't recall telling them what I wanted to talk to Ruth about, just that I hoped to speak with her.

"Well, we'd had sort of a disagreement," I start.

"What did you disagree about?"

Terrified that I've made a mistake, that I've made myself look suspicious, as though I had a reason to kill Ruth, I say, "She thought I was eavesdropping on her personal conversation and I wanted to apologize."

"Did you eavesdrop on her conversation?"

"Accidentally," I say, recalling the disturbing things Ruth had said when she was on the phone in her cube. "Not on purpose."

The detective frowns. "And you decided to go to her house to apologize?"

"Right."

"Ms. Carter, did Ruth Rice know you were coming?"

Shaking my head, I say, "No, if I had called first, she wouldn't have answered, and if she had, she would have told me not to come."

"Why is that?"

"Ruth didn't like me," I say, remembering Ruth's threat to snitch and her rude words about my skills as a reporter.

"Why not?"

"She thought I got the job at the paper because of cronyism," I say, rolling my eyes. "Which is absolutely not true. Sure, I'm friends with the publisher and his wife, but they gave me the job because I'm a good reporter."

"Ruth didn't think so?"

"No, she wanted me gone," I say. "She wanted Marty to fire me."

"Marty?"

"My boss," I explain. "The editor of the *Palmchat Gazette*. Ruth was going to tell Marty that I ..."

I trail off as something in the detective's gaze seems to switch, and for the first time, I get the feeling he's amused. But not like he finds something funny. It's more like this smug satisfaction.

"That you ...?"

Clearing my throat, I say, "Ruth was going to tell Marty that I did something he told me not to do."

"What did he tell you not to do?"

Figuring that honesty is the best policy, I decide to come clean. "Marty doesn't want me covering the crime beat. He says I don't have enough experience and that I haven't suffered enough."

"Interesting," remarks the detective.

Shaking my head, I say, "Well, you remember I was in Guavatown when the tourists discovered the dead body behind the fruit stand, right? And I asked you for a comment? Well, I questioned a few of the witnesses, as well, but I wasn't supposed to do that, and ... she threatened to tell Marty."

"And you didn't want her to do that, right?"

"No," I say. "Marty explicitly told me that he would ship me out if I don't shape up. If Ruth told him I was covering a crime story, Marty would have fired me."

"So, you had to stop Ruth from talking to Marty, right?"

"I went to her house to beg her not to tell him," I say. "I was hoping she might feel sorry for me and decide not to ruin my career."

"I thought you went to Ms. Rice's house to apologize for eavesdropping on her private conversation," says the detective.

Sheepish, I attempt a smile. And fail. "Well, I was going to mention that, but my main reason for going to see her was to plead for mercy."

"But you didn't get a chance to beg for mercy, did you?"

"Unfortunately, no," I lament.

Tilting his head, the detective says, "Ms. Carter, I'm curious. What were you going to do if Ms. Rice had refused your plea for mercy?"

Confused by, and wary of, his question, I say, "Well, I'm not really sure what I would have done."

"But you wanted to stop her from talking to your boss, correct?"

Nodding, I say, "That's the last thing I wanted her to do."

"So, is that why you killed her?"

Chapter 15

"Wait a minute," I say, stuttering slightly, my heart slamming. "What? No ... I didn't kill Ruth."

"But you had to prevent her from talking to your boss," says the detective. "And you said she didn't like you, so she probably would have refused to show you any mercy."

"Maybe not," I tell him, feeling as though I'm wilting beneath his withering glare. "But still, I didn't kill her. I wouldn't have done that. You have to believe me."

Detective François crosses his arms. "I only believe the evidence. And I believe the evidence proves that you killed your coworker, Ruth Rice."

"What evidence?" My heart races. "There's no proof that I killed Ruth!"

"You have blood all over your clothes," says the detective.

"I only have her blood on me because I was trying to help her," I explain. "I told the responding officers this. Ruth came into the living room. She had blood all over her. So, I ran to her and tried to help her to the couch, but she grabbed me and that's how her blood got on me. I didn't stab her!"

"How do you know she was stabbed?"

"Because I …" I trail off again, my pulse racing as I realize my mistake.

"Because you?"

"I pulled the knife from Ruth's chest," I say. "I know now that I shouldn't have, but I wanted to help her. I was trying to apply pressure to the wound."

"In addition to the victim's blood over all your clothes," says the detective. "And your own admission that you handled the knife—"

"No, I didn't admit that," I rush out, panicked. "I was just explaining—"

"You also entered Ms. Rice's home when, according to you, she wasn't expecting you," says Detective Francois, "and wouldn't have allowed you entry had she known you were coming."

"I didn't break into her house," I say, my voice imploring. "The door was open."

The detective gives me a cold smile. "Ms. Carter, the door to a private residence may be open but that does not mean you have permission to enter said residence."

Clearing my throat again, I say, "I know it was wrong to go into Ruth's house without her permission, but I did, and I found her bleeding from a knife in her chest, which I absolutely did not put there, but …"

"But …?" prompts the detective.

"But I think I know who the killer is …" I say as a memory slams through my mind. Ruth's voice wafting from her cubicle as I stood just outside the partition wall. She'd been talking to someone. The person threatened Ruth. *You don't have to kill me.* "Oh my goodness! I *do* know who the killer is!"

François stares at me.

"I'm pretty sure the killer is the person Ruth was talking to earlier at work," I say, staring at the detective. "I overheard her telling the person that she would do what they told her to do and that they didn't have to kill her. And you know what I think?"

"What do you think?"

"I'll bet Ruth didn't do what the person told her to do and they killed her," I say. "Or, she *did* do what the person said, and they killed her anyway."

"Ms. Carter, you know, what I think?" asks the detective.

"That you're going to arrest the person who threatened Ruth?" I ask, hopeful. "I mean, I realize you don't know who the person is … yet. But, you're a great detective so I'm sure you'll figure out—"

"You know, Ms. Carter, you're right," says the detective, giving me a dazzling smile. "I am a great detective. And I know a murderer when I see one …"

Confused, I ask, "Where do you see a murderer?"

Glaring at me, he says, "I'm looking at her."

Shocked, terrified, and outraged, I shake my head. "No, that's not true. I didn't kill Ruth."

"The evidence speaks for itself," says the detective.

"What evidence?" I cry out. "I explained that Ruth's door was already open when I got there, and I only took the knife from her chest because I was trying to save her life, not take her life, and—

"The reason I had you wait in here for so long was because the forensics department was processing the fingerprints found on the knife," says the detective.

I stare at him, numb and unable to speak, my mouth dry as cotton.

"Your prints are on the murder weapon," he says. "You killed your coworker."

Gasping, I manage to whisper, "But—"

"You're under arrest for the murder of Ruth Rice," says François. "You have the right to remain silent and considering the ridiculous lies you've already told, I think you should stay quiet."

Chapter 16

A warm, gusty breeze lifts my hair from my shoulders and cools the tears streaming down my face.

After spending a night in jail and then making bail an hour ago at three in the afternoon, I walked out of the police station, feeling alone, dejected, and abandoned.

Now I'm back at work.

The first thing I did after I walked through the door was stop by Marty's office. The Managing Editor didn't give me tea and sympathy —though both would have been nice—but he admitted he thought the cops were fools for arresting me.

"I know you didn't kill Ruth," declares Marty. "You wouldn't have done something so horrible. You couldn't have."

Relief floods me. "So, you believe I'm innocent? You don't think I killed Ruth?"

"I don't think you can link two independent clauses together with a coordinating conjunction," says Marty. "So, there's no way I believe that you could orchestrate and successfully carry out a cold-blooded pre-meditated murder."

"Oh …" I say, trailing off. Somehow, I feel as though I've been insulted but I'm not entirely sure. However, it's possible that my boss just accused me of not being able to write a basic sentence.

"Speaking of your writing," begins Marty, shifting in his chair as he grabs a file on his desk.

"What about it?" I ask, both worried and hopeful. Will he tell me it's getting better? Much worse? Although, to be honest, I can't think about writing stories or my career right now. I need to clear my name. Proving that I didn't kill Ruth is the most important thing right now.

"You're going to have to put it on pause."

I'm confused. "On pause?"

Marty clears his throat. "Due to your arrest for the murder of Ruth, Leo Bronson and the paper's legal department feel it would be best if you take a Leave of Absence."

My heart sinks. "A Leave of Absence? But why? I didn't kill Ruth—"

"No one at the *Palmchat Gazette* thinks you did," says Marty. "Leo, Vivian, and I hope that the charges against you will be dropped."

"You hope?" I ask, wary.

Marty sighs, dragging a hand down his flushed face. "Sophia, the evidence against you is rather damning."

"I know that," I agree. "But it's like I explained to Detective Francois, I was trying to help Ruth, not kill her! That's the only reason why I removed the knife and got my fingerprints on it."

"Sophia, I believe you," says Marty. "But, the *Palmchat Gazette* has to distance itself from this situation so as not to seem biased. The optics of allowing you to continue working during an active investigation against you wouldn't be good."

Feeling glum, I nod. "I get it. People don't want to read stories written by someone accused of murder."

"No, they don't," says Marty. "You can come back to work when … or if … you are exonerated."

Discouraged by his use of the word "if", I take a deep breath. "I understand."

"Now, concerning Ruth's murder, the *Palmchat Gazette* has a journalistic obligation to report the story," says Marty. "However, again, in order not to seem biased, we will use an independent news outlet to publish the story about what happened to Ruth and your arrest. Rest assured that no one from the paper will comment."

"I appreciate that," I say, devastated by the thought of having my name in the paper as a murder suspect.

Leaning back in the chair, Marty asks, "So, have you found a lawyer?"

"I'm planning to call Attorney Octavia Constant," I say.

Nodding, Marty says, "Good choice. She gets her clients off by having them find a better suspect."

"She got my coworker Beanie's wife off when she was accused of murder," I say. "And I'm going to take her advice, which I'd already thought to do myself, and find a better suspect. I'm going to clear my name. I didn't kill Ruth. And I'm going to prove it."

Chapter 17

It's been a week since my arrest for murder.

I've spent the last seven days holed up in my apartment, hiding under my covers, lamenting my fate. And drinking lots of tea and eating too many donut holes. Also, I've been talking to my lawyer and my family, mainly my mom and sister.

I should have been trying to clear my name but I couldn't bring myself to do any girl sleuthing. So, I took a few days off to clean up my place, clear my head, and binge-watch a few trashy reality television shows I hate to love.

Now I'm sitting on the chaise lounge on the patio of my small apartment, taking small sips of lemon, mint, and chamomile tea.

I can't believe I was arrested for Ruth's murder. Staring at my wrists, I shudder as I recall the moment when François placed me in handcuffs—something he probably didn't have to do since I was already at the police station—and marched me to be booked, fingerprinted, and photographed for a mug shot.

Fresh terror and panic rip through me. I have a mug shot. I was arrested. Charged with a murder I didn't commit. That I could not have committed, despite the fact that my prints are on the murder weapon. With a trembling hand, I swipe my damp cheeks. What am I going to do? How am I going to prove that I'm not a killer? I can't go to jail. I wouldn't last one hour in Tiverton. I can't spend the rest of my life in a maximum-security prison.

Moaning my sorrow, I take another sip of tea, which I'm determined not to cry in, but I feel the prick of bitter tears. Squeezing my eyes shut, I take a deep breath as a flood of panic travels through me.

"Meow … meow …"

Startled from my distraction, I sit up quickly. My ear attuned, I listen. Was that a … cat? Or am I hearing things? But why would I be hearing a cat? I glance around the patio. I don't have a cat. At once, the Calico I rescued from the Seagrape tree comes to mind. The psycho cat, I think, shaking my head. I'm lucky that one-two punch she gave me didn't leave any scars.

"Meeeeeoooooowwww!"

I freeze, arrested by the plaintive wail. The same desperate, chaotic purring I heard when she was trapped in the tree. The mourning cry that captured my attention, stole my heart, ignited my compassion … and ultimately made a fool of me. Recalling the humiliation of the cat headbutting me in the nose, I swing my legs over the side of the chaise and—

"Meow!" The purr sounds more like a wailing growl.

Before I can stand, I discern something in my periphery. From my left, there's a flash of something flying through the air, and I turn my head.

I screech as a cat leaps toward me …

And lands in my lap.

Instead of jumping up and running for my life, I remain paralyzed, staring at the distinctive black and orange patches across the cat's back. It's the psycho cat. My heart slams. What is this cat doing here? On my patio? Sitting in my lap?

"Meow …"

Swallowing, I lean back, wary of the large, round green eyes staring back at me.

"What do you want?" I ask. "Because I have to tell you I am so not in the mood to be slapped and headbutted."

"Meow ...." Responds the psycho cat, tilting her head.

"Was that an apology?" I ask, quite sure I heard some contrition in that meow.

Purring, the cat tilts her head to the right, continuing to stare at me.

"Did you come back to say you're sorry?" I ask. "Because I'll have you know that I was only trying to help you."

"Meow ..." The cat purrs again.

"How'd you get in that tree anyway?" I ask, tempted to stroke the soft fur behind her ear.

"Meow ... meow ... " says the cat. "Meow. Meow ... meow. Meow."

"I hear you," I say, nodding, as though I can understand every word she's saying. "I know what it's like to get stuck in a situation that you have no idea how you're going to get out of."

The cat tilts her head to the left. "Meow?"

"My coworker Ruth Rice was murdered," I tell the cat. "I went to her house to beg for mercy and instead I found her walking toward me with a knife in her chest."

"Meow ...?" The cat's eyes narrow and I swear I hear doubt in that meow.

"Ruth was alive, barely, when I went to her house," I insist. "I only removed the knife because I wanted to help her."

The cat tilts her head.

"I was trying to stop the wound from bleeding," I say. "I tried explaining that to Detective Francois but he didn't believe me."

"Meow?"

Frowning, I roll my eyes, detecting a dubious tone in the cat's voice. "Okay, so I will admit that the evidence against me appears to be damning. Yes, my fingerprints were on the knife. And Ruth's blood was all over me."

The Calico tilts her head to the right. "Meow?"

"But that was only because she fell against me when I reached out to help her," I say. "Unfortunately, Detective Francois didn't believe that, either."

"Meow …" the cat turns her head into her neck to lick her fur.

"And that's why he arrested me for Ruth's murder," I say, feeling the tears again. "But, I didn't do it. I swear I didn't kill Ruth. I would never have done that!"

"Meeooowww…" says the cat, rubbing her head against my arm.

Detecting a distinct sympathy in her tone, I give the Calico a small smile.

She purrs.

Reaching behind her left ear, I gently stroke her fur and—

The Calico hisses like a hellcat, pointy teeth bared, eyes wild and manic. Screaming, I jump up, my pulse racing as I stumble back. The psycho cat drops to the ground, landing deftly on her feet. But she's not there for long. Before I can get my bearings, she leaps up and clutches my right wrist with her paws, sinking her claws into my skin.

I scream again, this time in terror and pain as the cat growls and hisses.

"Get off me!" I screech. "You crazy cat!"

The cat hisses and growls even louder as I try to push her off with my left hand. The cat maintains her hold. I grab her around the neck, struggling to pull her away. Stumbling to the side, I swing my arm from side to side, hoping the frantic motion will dislodge her, or at least make her dizzy enough to loosen her hold, which seems to have gotten tighter.

"Bad kitty!" I say, trying to move my arm in an up-and-down motion, hoping the cat will fall.

She doesn't.

"Get away from me, you deranged psycho cat!" I turn in a circle, flinging my arm back and forth, praying the cat will let go of me. Instead, something feels like it's sloshing in my head. Trying to stay on my feet, I stumble. My left calf hits something hard. I lose my balance and teeter backward. Crying out, I feel myself falling and there's nothing I can do to stop myself from toppling over. Timber, I think as I hit the chaise, banging my hip before I tumble over the side.

The cat screeches.

She still has me in a death grip.

I use my free hand to push myself up, then grab the mug of tea from the table. I slosh hot tea into her face. Her growl of protest and anger is ferocious. Horrifying. Reminding me that she is, at her very essence, a tiger.

Dropping the cup, I thump her dripping-wet forehead. Hard. Her eyes widen in shock. Then her green eyes narrow and I feel a stinging sharpness slicing into my hand. I yowl and fling the cat away from me. The Calico sails through the air. Landing on her feet, she hisses and growls, then takes off like a rocket, leaving me shell-shocked, gobsmacked, and bleeding.

Shaking, I stare at my bloody hand, cringing at the two tiny punctures piercing the flesh between my thumb and index finger. Unsteady on trembling legs, I walk back into my apartment. In the bathroom, I place my throbbing hand under a stream of cold water, washing blood down the drain. A glance at myself in the mirror above the sink reveals my confusion and shock. Did that just happen? Did that psycho cat seek me out to sink her teeth into me? But why? What did I ever do to her except rescue her from a tree? Something firefighters do all the time and get praised for.

I let out a long, exasperated breath.

The cat gaslighted me. Deceived me. Made me think she was sorry so I would let my guard down. And I did. And she attacked. Crazy feline. I should have known she hadn't come back to apologize. After cleaning the wound with hydrogen peroxide, I slather Neosporin antibacterial cream across the gashes. I find some gauze in the cabinet below the sink and wrap it around my hand.

I open the medicine cabinet and grab a small bottle of pain pills. Shaking two into my palm, I vow to never trust that psycho cat again.

Chapter 18

Tossing and turning, tangled in damp sheets, I flop over onto my stomach. The room seems to be spinning. And unbearably hot. I push the bedlinens from my body.

Immediately, I'm freezing. Why is it so cold in my bedroom? And how did I get into my bedroom? When did I go to bed? I stare at the ceiling fan overhead and try to recall the last thing I remember. My memories are elusive. I roll over onto my right side to look at the clock on the bed table. It's not there. Where is the clock? Maybe on the nightstand on the other side of the bed, I think. I roll over onto my left side. There's the clock. Squinting, I struggle to make out the digital letters. 3:47.

Why am I up at three in the morning? Groaning, I swipe a hand across my forehead. It's sweaty. And blazing hot.

My heart jumps into my throat. Why am I so hot? And why is my hand throbbing? I glance at the gauze wrapped around my hand. My bedroom is dim, except for the light I keep on in my closet, which allows a thin sliver of illumination into my room. Enough to see that blood has soaked through the bandages.

I need to change the gauze. Sitting up, I wipe the back of my neck. Sweat coats my palm. Why am I so sweaty? Is the A/C broken? I glance at the ceiling fan again. It's whirling around at full speed. As I let out a shaky breath, my teeth chatter. Again, I'm freezing. Shivering. Feeling way too dizzy. The throbbing in my hand intensifies, and I glance at it. I scream. To say it's swollen is an understatement. It seems to be three times the normal size. It looks like a hand balloon. Fear grips me. I don't feel well. What's wrong with me?

I stumble out of bed and stagger into the bathroom. Take more pain meds. Next, I head into the kitchen. After turning on the light, I shuffle to the refrigerator and open the freezer. I scoop ice from the bin to put on my hand. Back in the bedroom, I collapse on the bed linens and try to go to sleep.

Two hours later, after more tossing and turning, I feel worse.

I think of driving myself to the emergency room, but my legs are shaking so badly, and my head won't stop swimming. My hand is so swollen, I doubt I could drive with it.

Trembling and worried, I call an ambulance.

Chapter 19

The paramedics show up twenty minutes later.

I can barely walk to the door. Somehow, I manage to grab the knob. My sweaty hand slips, but I concentrate on completing the task, even though doing so gives me a horrible headache, and open the door. The EMTs walk into the foyer. Shaking and shivering, I practically fall into the arms of one of the paramedics.

At once, I feel myself being lifted into the air. Staring at the ceiling, I try to focus on the voices questioning me.

Miss, can you hear me?

I think I can, but I'm not sure even though I tell him yes, but did he hear me? I don't know.

"Can you tell me your name?"

"Sophie …" I whisper, coughing. "Sophie Carter."

Concerned faces hover above me. "Can you tell us what's wrong?"

A searing bright pinpoint of light flickers in front of my eyes, blinding me for a moment.

"What happened to your hand?"

"She's burning up."

Exhausted, I close my eyes. The EMTs converse with one another.

"It's cold," I say, shivering.

"Miss, you have a fever ..."

"Psycho ... cat ... " I gasp.

"What?"

"Bit ... me ..." I whisper.

"Cat bit her."

"I'm going to take a look at the wound, okay?"

I feel the gauze being removed from my swollen, throbbing hand.

"Whoa, that's nasty ..."

"And probably infected."

Infected? My stomach twists. Is that what's wrong with my hand? It's infected. Oh my God. If my hand is infected, then ... does that mean ... I could lose it? No. I can't lose my hand. I need it to write my stories. Well, technically, I suppose that I could write with only one hand, but it would be difficult. Oh, what am I thinking? So what if I lose my hand? I mean, I don't want to lose it, but, if I do ... what does it matter if I don't have a job? I was arrested for Ruth's murder and if I get convicted, my head is gonna swim even worse than it's swimming right now. And trust me, it feels like Michael Phelps is doing a world-record Butterfly stroke in my brain.

"Miss ... can you hear me?"

I nod. "Yeah ..."

"We're going to take you to the hospital, okay?"

Chapter 20

"Miss Sophia …"

Sophia? Again, someone calling me by my full given name. Who's talking to me? Marty? He's the only person who calls me Sophia.

"Sophia, can you hear me?"

The voice sounds weird, almost alien. Was I taken up into a spaceship? Am I being probed? No, no … I don't think so. I was taken somewhere, but not into outer space.

"Sophia, it's Dr. Villalongo …"

The hospital. Now I remember. Somewhat. My hand was throbbing. I had chills and a fever. I called an ambulance. I went to the hospital. Because of my infected hand. Oh, God!

Panicked, I open my eyes. "Did I lose my hand?"

"What?" The doctor standing over me frowns. "Why would you lose your hand?"

"The paramedic said it was infected," I say. "I thought it might fall off."

"No, it's still there," says the doctor. "Take a look."

Biting my lip, I glance down at my injured hand. It's resting on my abdomen, bandaged tightly. The swelling seems to have gone down a bit, but it still throbs. Not so painfully, but enough to cause discomfort.

"How are you feeling?" asks the doctor. "Better?"

"Somewhat, I guess ..." I stare at the doctor, who has a kind face creased with deep wrinkles. "My hand does still hurt."

"Well, it is indeed infected," says Dr. Villalongo. "We are going to give you antibiotics and a fever reducer."

"I still have a fever?" I touch my head. It's not scorching hot anymore, but it feels warm.

"The fever reducer will help," says the doctor, patting my shoulder. "You'll get pain medication, also, which may make you drowsy and help you sleep."

"Okay ..." I say, settling back against the pillows.

"The nurse will be in shortly to give you the medicine."

After the doctor leaves, I sigh and close my eyes. What a night, I think. I got attacked by a psycho cat. Again. Can't forget how that crazy cat head-butted me. Can't believe that Calico put me in the hospital.

Sighing, I tell myself not to dwell on the negative. Sure, things look bad ... well, I guess technically things are bad. Worse than bad. I'm in the hospital and I might go to prison for the rest of my life. But, things can only get better, right? The medicine will work. And once I'm out of the hospital, I'll figure out how to prove that I'm not a cold-blooded killer.

I'll find out who really killed Ruth.

Chapter 21

"Hey … wake up …"

Huh …?

"Hey …"

The voice comes to me at once and at the same time out of nowhere. It's insistent. And female. But I don't recognize it. One of the nurses, maybe. A different nurse, perhaps?

I feel something tap my chin. Then my right cheek. Then my left cheek. What is that? Why would a nurse be hitting my face?

"Will you please wake up? I need to talk to you."

"What?"

Blinking, I open one eye. The overhead lights in my hospital room are off, but it's not completely dark. The bathroom light is on. I asked the nurse to keep it on just in case I need to use the restroom. And because I don't like to sleep in the total pitch darkness.

"I have something to tell you."

Opening my other eye, I stare at the ceiling. Who is talking to me? Doesn't sound like Nurse Kelly, who administered the antibiotics and pain medicine. She was Irish with a thick brogue. So who—

Another tap on my left cheek. Slightly harder. More insistent.

"Your eyes are open, so I know you're awake."

Blinking again, I glance directly in front of me.

A cat sits on my lap.

Not just any cat.

Psycho cat.

The crazed Calico who put me in the hospital.

Terror grips me, sending my slamming heart careening into my throat. I open my mouth to scream but the Calico walks up my body, to my chest, and places a paw over my lips, preventing me.

"Don't freak out and start screaming," says the cat. "I don't have time to calm you down. I need to tell you something. And, yes, it is important."

My terror turns to shock. I move my head from side to side, forcing the cat to move her paw.

"What the—"

"Watch your mouth," admonishes the cat. "There's no need for that kind of language."

My shock turns to confusion. "I don't understand."

The cat tilts her head. "What don't you understand?"

"I don't understand ..." I struggle to articulate my disbelief. "How are you ... talking?"

"I'm using my voice."

"Why are you talking?"

"Girl, is there something wrong with your ears?" The cat asks. "I told you. I need to tell you something."

I take a deep breath and try to focus. "But this doesn't make sense. How can you tell me something?"

"Easy. I just tell you."

"There's no way you can tell me something," I say, frustration churning in my gut. "Cats don't tell people things. Cats don't ... talk."

The Calico tilts her head to the other side. "Girl, how much medication did they give you?"

"Obviously, too much ..." I mumble.

"Listen," says the cat. "What I need to tell you is—"

"Wait." I push myself to a sitting position.

"Why?"

"No." I shake my head.

"You don't want to know?" asks the cat. "Girl, what is your problem?"

I stare at the Calico. "You're a cat."

"And?"

"You're talking."

"Again, and …?"

"Cats don't talk," I say, more to myself than to the Calico.

"And yet I am talking."

I shake my head again. "You can't be."

"Why not?"

"Because cats don't …" I exhale. "Okay, I get it. Now it makes sense. I'm dreaming. Probably some sort of manifestation of my PTSD."

The cat's eyes widen. "Girl, you have PTSD?"

Scoffing, I roll my eyes. "You should know. It's because of you."

"Me?"

I hold up my bandaged hand. "You bit me."

"Bit you?"

"And my hand got infected."

"Infected?"

"Are you going to repeat everything I say?" I ask.

"Listen, girl, about your hand," says the Calico. "My apologies."

"Your apologies?"

"I, um … didn't mean to do that."

I cross my arms over my chest. "Didn't mean to do it?"

"Are you going to repeat everything I say?" asks the cat.

With my good hand, I rub my eyes, praying the psycho cat will be gone when I peek between my fingers.

I curse.

"Language," admonishes the cat.

Psycho-cat is still here.

"Look, girl, what I need to tell you is—"

"No. This is not happening."

"—very important."

"I'm hallucinating," I tell myself.

"No, you're not."

"Or, maybe I'm having a fever dream."

The cat pats my forehead.

"What are you doing?" I screech, horrified that she's going to bite me again. Or headbutt me. Or slap me around. "Get off me!"

"Relax, girl," says the cat, moving back to my lap. "You don't have a fever."

Suspicious, I touch my forehead. It's refreshingly cool. "Okay, maybe it's just a normal dream," I concede. "Point is, this isn't real. You're not talking to me."

"Girl, we have already been over this," says the Calico. "I'm talking to you, okay?"

"No, it's not okay," I protest. "Cats don't talk. It's not possible."

"Well, you want to know what is possible?" asks the cat. "You proving that you didn't kill your coworker Ruth."

I frown. "What? Wait. How do you know I didn't kill my coworker Ruth?"

Tilting her head, the Calico asks, "Girl, what? That medication they gave you was strong."

Frustrated, I sigh. "No, I didn't mean it like that. What I meant was … how do you know I was arrested for killing Ruth—which I absolutely didn't do. I'm not a murderer."

"Sammy Alastair told me," says the Calico.

"Who is Sammy Alastair?"

"The mouse who lives in the women's restroom at the *Palmchat Gazette* offices."

"There's a mouse living in the women's restroom?" I shudder. "Oh my God."

"Relax, girl," advises the cat. "Sammy's a good egg."

"A good egg?" I made a face. "He's vermin. He needs to be exterminated."

"Before you go setting mouse traps, let me ask you this," says the cat. "How many roaches have you seen in the breakroom lately?"

"Roaches in the breakroom?" I frown. "We don't have roaches in our breakroom."

"You can thank Sammy for that."

"Gross."

"Don't throw stones," says the cat. "It's maladaptive."

"Maladaptive?"

"You don't know that word?" asks the cat. "I thought you went to university."

"Of course, I know that word," I say, even though I can't recall the exact definition at the moment so I'm hoping the cat doesn't request it. "I've just never heard a cat say maladaptive."

"Girl, anyway, Sammy's cousin Larry the rat lives in the men's room at the police station, and Larry saw you get arrested and heard the charges," says the cat.

"Are you serious?" I shake my head. "Wait. No. Don't answer that. Of course, you're not serious because this is not real. This conversation is some weird side effect of the coma."

"Look, girl, I'm sorry for hurting you," says the cat. "So I figured I would help you clear your name which, according to Sammy, you desperately need so you won't spend the rest of your life in Tiverton."

Flabbergasted, I stare at the cat.

"If you want to find out who killed your coworker Ruth, you need to find out who killed the dead guy found by that fruit stand in Guavatown."

And with that, the Calico jumps down from the bed, and races across the floor to a chair near the slightly opened window, which she slips out of ...

Confused and terrified, I stare at the window, struggling to come to terms with what just happened to me. Was I really talking to a cat? Was the cat talking to me? Did the cat actually speak? Form words and sentences I could understand?

Or ... maybe I'm sicker than I thought.

Maybe I'm not dreaming.

Maybe the infection travelled to my brain and I've lost all cognitive function.

That is to say, maybe I've lost my mind.

Chapter 22

Cats don't talk …

I know this. And yet—

No. No. NO.

Cats don't talk. And it's not even that cats don't talk, which implies that sometimes they do … the truth is, cats can't talk. That is, they do not have the ability to speak. Which is not to say that cats can't communicate, because clearly, they can. Cats purr. Cats growl. Cats hiss. Whine. Cry. Yowl.

However, they are not capable of speaking English. Vocalizing and voicing words that can be clearly understood by humans. I know this. And yet—

No. No. NO.

Cats don't—

But the cat did speak.

No, the Calico wasn't really speaking. I was in the throes of a fever dream. Except I didn't have a fever. Okay, so, it was just a regular dream. No, it was a nightmare. That psycho cat traumatized me, so I dreamed about her talking to me. I'm sure a therapist would agree. Not that I have a therapist, but maybe I need one, considering that I'm dreaming about talking cats.

Sighing, I open my eyes. Stare at the ceiling. I've been awake for a while. I'm not sure how long, but I was resting my eyes. Maybe afraid to open them. The last time I did, there was a psychotic cat on my lap. But the cat is gone, thank God.

Wait. No. The cat was never here. I was dreaming. Or hallucinating. Or whatever.

I glance toward the window. Light streams through the pane, filling the hospital room with a warm, diffusive glow. The window is closed. Had the psycho cat closed it on her way out? No, cats don't close windows. The window wasn't open. And the cat wasn't in my hospital room.

I was dreaming, I remind myself.

About a cat who had something to tell me.

If you want to find out who killed your coworker Ruth, you need to find out who killed the dead guy found by that fruit stand in Guavatown.

According to the psycho cat, the key to solving Ruth's murder, and thus clearing my name, has something to do with the Guavatown murder. But what, exactly, did the psycho cat mean? No, wait. It doesn't matter what the cat meant. I was dreaming, remember? Gosh, what is my problem? I mean, don't get me wrong, I absolutely want to prove that I didn't kill Ruth. It's imperative that I do, in order to stay out of prison. But why would Ruth's murder be connected to the murder in Guavatown? Well, I don't know if the murders are connected. So why would I dream that they are?

Hmmm …

With supreme effort, I sit up. I'm so tired. Yawning, I wonder why I feel so sluggish and strange. Maybe effects from the antibiotics and pain meds. Dr. Villalongo said they would make me drowsy. But I feel worse than drowsy. Feels like I slept too long. I need to wake up.

I exhale, then reach for the call button and press it.

As I wait for the nurse to come in, my thoughts drift to what happened to Ruth. Discovering her bleeding from what would turn out to be a fatal stab wound still haunts me. Who killed Ruth? Who would want her dead? And is it connected to the strange call I overheard between Ruth and the unknown caller? Once I get out of the hospital, I'm going to start investigating. I know Marty told me not to cover crime stories, but Ruth's death isn't just a story. Her untimely demise could lead to mine. I'm not trying to write about her death. I need to find out who killed her. My freedom is at stake.

"Miss Sophie!" Nurse Kelly barrels into the hospital room, smiling at me like it's her job. "Oh, happy day!"

Confused, I stare at her. Oh, happy day? Why does she seem so enthusiastic to see me?

"Sophie!"

"Mom ...?"

Shock assails me as my mother nearly pushes Nurse Kelly out of the way in her haste to hurry to my hospital bed.

"Oh, my baby! My baby!" cries my Mom as she grabs me into a fierce hug. "Oh, sweetie! My prayers have been answered!"

"Mom ..." I mumble, my words muffled beneath the crush of my mother's embrace. What is she talking about? What prayers?

"Miss Sophia!"

I recognize Dr. Villalongo's booming lyrical Nigerian accent.

"Oh, my baby ..." Her hands cradling my face, Mom steps back.

"Mom? What's going on?" I ask. "Why are you here?"

"Because you're awake, dearie!" says Nurse Kelly, walking to the opposite side of the bed.

"Yeah, I'm awake," I say, gently removing Mom's hands from my face. "Why is that such a big deal?"

Shaking her head, tears brimming in her eyes, Mom says, "Because we didn't know ..."

My heart slams. "You didn't know what?"

"If you would rejoin us in the land of the living!" says Dr. Villalongo with an expansive smile.

"What are you talking about?" I ask, staring at Mom, then Dr. Villalongo, and finally Nurse Kelly.

"You've been in a coma," explains the doctor.

I feel like I've been sucker punched. Twice. "A coma?"

Nurse Kelly says, "Since you arrived at the hospital three days ago."

"Three days ago?" I am agog. Aghast. Flabbergasted. "I've been in a coma for three days?"

Dr. Villalongo says, "You slipped into the coma after we administered the antibiotics. You developed a rare allergic reaction."

"But I prayed and prayed and prayed!" declares Mom. "And you woke up and came back to us!"

As Mom envelops me in another bear hug, I struggle to contemplate what I've been told. I've been in a coma for three days. Good gracious. It's almost impossible to fathom. Hard to wrap my mind around. I'm terrified but relieved.

The idea that I was in a coma completely unnerves me.

And yet, I feel a sense of peace and comfort.

Because if I slipped into a coma the day I came to the hospital, that means I really was dreaming about that strange, psycho cat.

I can rest easy knowing the Calico did not speak to me.

Chapter 23

Driving out of the parking lot of my apartment complex, I sing along to the latest song from CoCo, the global superstar, and Palmchat Islands native. It's called *Sweetie Badness* and I absolutely love it.

It's the perfect song to distract me from my problems. From the predicament looming large in the back of my mind—clearing my name. Finding out who really killed Ruth so I won't end up in prison.

Doing a little shimmy in my seat, I turn onto the main boulevard. The late afternoon traffic, thankfully, isn't so bad. St. Mateo doesn't have a rush hour of densely packed bumper-to-bumper cars inching down the road at a glacial pace. Traffic flows a few miles above the posted speed limits, and most drivers go faster than that.

Singing along with the song, I reflect on how to start the process of clearing my name.

Honestly, I don't have a clue, and yet … something makes me think I should start with the Guavatown murder. It's been a few weeks since the dead body was found behind the fruit stand, and although I haven't really been keeping up with the story, I know the police are still investigating.

However, I don't really know why I think I should look into the Guavatown murder.

Well, no, that's not exactly true.

I know why, but … I don't want to think about it. Doing so makes me feel a bit spooked because the reason I think I should focus on the Guavatown murder is bizarre …

I have a feeling Ruth's death might be connected to the Guavatown murder.

But, I don't want to think about why I think that what happened to Ruth might have something to do with the dead body found behind the fruit stand.

I don't want to think about that crazed Calico cat.

Or what she told me.

If you want to find out who killed your coworker Ruth, you need to find out who killed the dead guy found by that fruit stand in Guavatown.

No. The cat didn't tell me anything. I dreamed that the psycho cat was talking to me. It was a coma dream. I must have dreamed that Ruth's death could be connected to the Guavatown murder. But that makes no sense because—

"Did you clear your name yet?"

Confused, I stare at the radio.

Did you clear your name yet? Strange. I don't remember that being a lyric in the song. And I know all the words. I always learn the words to CoCo's songs. I take great pride because I can sing the parts when she segues into island patois, which most people can't do. I am quite sure there is no line about clearing your name in the song. Why would there be? The song is about—

"Girl, did you hear me? Turn that music down."

Turn that music down?

That's not a lyric from the song.

And that wasn't CoCo's voice.

And yet … something about the voice is familiar. I feel like I've heard that half-sassy, half-sarcastic haughty, demanding tone before.

"Hey … I'm back here …"

My heart thuds. Who is back where?

"In the backseat … "

I check my rearview mirror and then scream.

The psycho Calico cat who attacked me is sitting in the backseat of my JEEP on the passenger side.

But she's not just sitting there.

She's talking to me.

"Did you clear your name yet?"

My heart slams violently in my chest as my mouth goes dry. This is not happening. Not again. No, not at all. Again implies that something happened once before. That the cat spoke to me once before but that's not true. She did not come into my hospital room and speak to me. She couldn't have because I was in a coma. I dreamed that the Calico spoke to me. I was in the throes of some sort of coma fever, and—

Oh my God.

Is that happening to me right now? Have I slipped back into a coma? Am I somewhere unconscious? Did I slump over my desk? Or collapse in the middle of the street? Or—

"Girl, watch out!"

Looking over my shoulder, I stare at the agitated feline, who's standing on her hind legs as she waves her front paws at me.

Confused, I ask, "What?"

"Keep the road!" yells the Calico.

Keep the road?

Suddenly snapping out of what feels like a strange fog, I turn my head back to the front windshield and focus on the road in front of me.

A car is heading straight at me, blaring its horn. Almost too late, it occurs to me that somehow, someway, I must have veered across the two northbound lanes—and the middle goat lane used for merging or turning into traffic—into the southbound lanes.

With a yelp, I yank the wheel to the left to avoid a horrific head-on collision but doing that so quickly and violently causes me to overcorrect. Next thing I know, I'm gunning toward a sidewalk of pedestrians, some walking idly with no care in the world—tourists, probably, while others stride with determined purpose—local

Palmchatters, most likely. One thing they all have in common is they have no idea I'm about to jump the curb and career into them.

"Girl, don't hit those people!" screeches the cat.

Terrified, I do a quick glance over my shoulder as I pull the wheel back to the right, narrowly missing the curb while igniting the ire of a few people, who squeal in fright and protest as they scramble to get out of the way.

Luckily, I avoid a mass casualty.

"And don't hit that truck!" warns the Calico.

Whipping my head toward the road, I gasp. A dump truck is stopped in front of me. Crying out, I slam on my breaks, but it doesn't seem to be helping. Tires screech and squeal in protest but the JEEP hasn't stopped, and if I don't do something drastic, I'm going to plow into the back of the truck. I jerk over into the next lane.

Another horn blares, loud and livid.

In my rearview, I see that I cut someone off.

"Sorry," I squeak, speeding up.

"You should really use an indicator if you're going to change lanes," admonishes the cat.

"Well, I would have but I was too busy trying to make sure we didn't crash into the truck and die instantly."

"Well, you wouldn't have to worry about crashing into anything if you knew how to drive!"

"Excuse me?" I glance in the rearview mirror at the cat. "I will have you know that I am an excellent driver, and—"

"Look out!"

Chapter 24

My gaze flicks toward the windshield again.

A line of cars is speeding toward me.

"So much for being an excellent driver," says the cat. "You're on the wrong side of the road! This is St. Mateo! We drive on the left. This is not America!"

Ignoring the cat and wondering how I got on the wrong side of the road again, I do my best to avoid the cars and the cacophony of honking horns and irate drivers screaming obscenities.

I yank the wheel, and the car swerves left. I drive around a yellow Peugeot only to come head-on with a red Volvo, which I maneuver around but then I'm faced with an old sun-bleached Toyota that nearly hits me but I'm able to circle around it.

Revving my engine, I gun it and shoot into the traffic circle, desperate to get back into the right lane and—

"Oh rats!" exclaims the Calico.

Rats? Oh God, no. Please no. I can't deal with a feisty feline and disgusting vermin. I just can't—

"It's the fuzz!" The cat says.

The fuzz?

And then I hear it …

Sirens. That telltale high-low whine of a police cruiser. Rats, I think, agreeing with the cat's assessment, which is ridiculous since the cat is not even in the backseat. And she's definitely not talking to me. I'm dreaming, I figure.

"You better pull over," says the Calico. "I don't want to be in a high-speed chase. I'll get car sick."

"If you puke in my car ..." I glance back at the cat and see the police car right behind me.

Rats ...

The sirens blare louder, and I angle the JEEP toward a small grocery store. Turning into the parking lot, I pull into the closest space and kill the engine.

"Well, you've really done it now," says the cat. "All that reckless driving. You could have killed someone. I'll bet they're going to take you to jail."

I turn in my seat to glare at her. "If I end up in jail it'll be your fault because—"

"My fault?" The Calico leans back as she stares at me. "Girl, please. You will not blame your bad driving on me. But, why am I not surprised? Just like a human. You never take responsibility for your actions."

"Excuse you?" I stare at the cat, wondering if this is happening. Am I really being chastised by a feline? No, no it can't be happening. I'm dreaming, remember? Cats don't talk.

"Girl, do you need your eyes checked?" asks the cat. "You must be one of those humans who's blind in one eye and can't see out of the other."

"My eyes are just fine, okay?" I tell the feline, offended by her sassy attitude. "And furthermore—"

Sharp, insistent rapping against the driver's window makes me jump. Rats, I think. Powering the window down, I reach toward the glove compartment and open it.

"License and registration, please ..."

"Right," I say, grabbing the documents, and praying the cat is wrong. The last thing I need is to be arrested again. "I have everything right here …"

I turn toward the driver's window to face the officer.

A gasping squeal … or maybe a squealing gasp … escapes my lips.

The officer stares at me, his eyes wide.

I imagine we're experiencing the same shock and surprise because we recognize each other.

"Hi …" I wave, suddenly entranced by the same fluttery feeling in my stomach I felt the first time I saw Officer Noah Cuetee.

The edges of Officer Cuetee's mouth quirk in the most delightful way, bringing out his adorable dimples, but he doesn't exactly full-out smile at me.

"Sophie … um, Ms. Carter," begins Officer Cuetee.

"You can call me Sophie," I tell him. "Unless you have to be formal with me?"

Shaking his head, Officer Cuetee smiles. "Sophie, what's going on? Why were you driving so erratically? Something wrong with your car?"

"No, it was that crazy cat," I say, exhaling. "She was in the backseat, and she startled me when she …"

"When she?" prompts Officer Cuetee.

Hesitating, I bite my lip. I can tell he's waiting, but I can't tell him the truth. Can't tell him that psycho cat was yelling at me about being a bad driver, which I so totally am not. Well, I could tell him … wait, not the part about the cat talking to me, because that didn't happen. And anyway, the cat wasn't in the backseat. I dreamed that. Wait. Am I dreaming now?

I pinch myself.

"Owwww!"

"Why did you pinch yourself?"

Okay, so I'm not dreaming. I clear my throat. "Oh, um … nervous tick. Listen, as I was saying … I totally didn't mean to be driving like a crazy woman, but the cat … I didn't expect a cat to be in my backseat and I don't know how she got back there …"

"Maybe she got in because you drive an open-air JEEP," suggests Officer Cuetee.

"Oh, yeah …" I glance around at the missing roof, remembering that my JEEP is the kind where you can remove the roof and feel like you're driving a convertible with the wind whipping through your hair.

"Well, looks like the cat is gone," says Officer Cuetee, inclining his head toward the rear of the JEEP.

I turn to glance toward the backseat.

The Calico is nowhere to be seen.

Figures. It's her fault I got pulled over and then she leaves me to deal with the fallout.

"Well, I can imagine that realizing a strange cat was in your car could be a bit scaredy …"

Frowning, I ask, "You mean scary?"

"No, um … I meant …" Officer Cuetee chuckles, his expression sheepish. "I was trying to make a joke by saying scaredy … as in scaredy cat, but—"

"Oh, no, yeah, I totally get it," I say.

His grin self-effacing, he says, "It was a bad joke."

"No, it was a good joke," I assure him. "It's just … the cat that was in my backseat is not a stranger to me. She's the same cat who attacked me and put me in a coma."

"A cat put you in a coma?"

"It's a sad and sordid … tail," I say, giving him a smile.

Officer Cuetee just stares at me.

"You get it? A sad … tail … T…A…I…L," I explain. "Like a cat's tail … oh, yikes, bad joke."

"Oh, no, wait, I do get it now," says Officer Cuetee. "That was a good joke. I'm just having a hard time processing how a cat put you in a coma after you made bail. By the way, I don't believe for one second that you murdered your co-worker."

"Thank you," I say, appreciating his support. "As I was saying, it's a long story. One that's best told with donut holes and tea."

Officer Cuetee smiles. "That sounds great. I'm working a double shift today, but how about tomorrow morning."

"Sounds good," I say, and we make plans to meet at Lowercase Tea, a popular teahouse.

"Before I go," says Officer Cuetee, his tone a bit more severe.

"Yeah …" I get the feeling he's going to give me a citation, which I probably deserve.

Instead, he says, "I'll let you go with a warning this time."

Relieved, I say, "Thanks!"

"You haven't heard the warning …"

"What is it?" I asked, entranced by his boyish charm.

"The next time there's a cat in your backseat, don't drive so recklessly …"

Chapter 25

"I wish to be seat-belted, please ..."

Closing my eyes, I groan. I recognize that irritating voice. The sassy tone full of annoying sarcasm. Not again, I think. I open my eyes and glance to the left. The psycho Calico cat is sitting in the passenger's seat, staring at me. When am I going to stop dreaming about this cat?

Yesterday, I dreamed the cat was talking to me from the backseat of my JEEP.

Although upon further reflection, I realize I wasn't dreaming, I was hallucinating. After all, there *was* a cat in my back seat. But she wasn't talking to me then. And she's not really talking now. For some reason, I'm hallucinating again.

"I wish that you would get out of my JEEP," I respond, hoping this hallucination ends quickly. The trauma of the cat's attack must have affected me more than I realized. I wonder if I need therapy, or—

"Girl, did you hear me?" demands the cat. "Please seat belt me."

"Seat belt you?"

"I am liable to lose every one of my nine lives with you behind the wheel," says the cat.

"Will you stop complaining about my driving?" I shake my head. "I am a good driver."

The cat makes a weird hissing noise that actually sounds like a scoff. "You could have fooled me."

"Okay, correction." I turn in my seat to face the cat. "I'm a good driver when I'm not distracted by an annoying feline."

"Yeah, right," the cat says, pawing at the buckle of the seatbelt. "And what happened when you got pulled over?"

"You conveniently disappeared."

"Girl, please. I'm not catching a charge for you," says the cat. "Speaking of which, did that cute cop give you a ticket?"

I feel my cheeks warm a bit as an image of Officer Cuetee fills my mind.

Immediately, I'm transported back in time to this morning, nine hours ago, when we met at Lowercase Tea for donuts and tea. In the cute, quaint little shop, we enjoyed donut holes drizzled with lime glaze and coconut sugar and sampled lemon and wild jasmine tea, a first for both of us.

We sat at one of the bistro tables, and I told him about my horrific experience with the psycho Calico. As he listened intently, he asked questions and appeared riveted. He was so super attentive and sympathetic. And dreamy, as my grandma would say. I don't know how a guy could be so handsome, but he pulled it off.

After my wild cat story, I asked him a few questions about the Guavatown murder. But only because I'm truly interested and not at all because the annoying cat told me that the body found behind the fruit stand is connected to Ruth's death and could help me clear my name.

"The victim's name was Ricardo Miranda," Officer Cuetee told me. "Detective Francois hasn't made an arrest yet, but he's looking at the victim's wife, Marlo Miranda, as a person of interest."

"Interesting," I murmured, wondering how Ruth's murder might be connected to Ricardo Miranda's murder, which I should not have been doing because it meant I actually believed what the crazy cat told me—and I didn't.

I still don't.

I wanted to ask Officer Cuetee more questions but dispatch called him away to a possible road rage incident.

"Are you going to answer me anytime soon?" demands the cat. "Did you get a ticket? Did you go to jail?"

"For your information, I only got a warning."

"You got off easy," says the cat. "That cute cop should have given you a ticket."

Glancing at the cat, I ask, "You think he's cute?"

The Calico's head bobs up and down. "Yes, I do, and so do you."

Alarmed, I ask, "What makes you think I think he's cute?"

"Cats know these things," says the cat.

"Cats know … what things?"

"How humans feel about each other," says the cat. "When I first asked you if the cute cop gave you a ticket, you didn't say anything. Just went into this weird, dopey-eyed trance."

"I did not go into a dopey-eyed trance," I dispute, though the cat might be right. I felt myself blushing when she mentioned "cute cop." Still, I doubt I lost consciousness. Although, maybe I did. Maybe I'm unconscious now. Or most likely dreaming about the cat talking to me again.

"So about clearing your name, sis," says the cat. "Have you done it yet? You better do it before it's too late and you end up in prison."

"Yeah, well, I would be a lot further along in my investigation if I hadn't been attacked by a cat who put me in a coma for three days."

"Girl, I did not attack you …"

Noticing that the cat trailed off and looked away, I say, "You didn't attack me?"

The cat looks at me. "I was going to say that I didn't attack you … for no reason."

"For what reason did you attack me?" I ask. "What did I ever do to you except save you from that Seagrape bush."

"What I meant was … I attacked you because I was under the influence of too much catnip."

I give the cat what I hope is my most suspicious stare. "Too much catnip?"

"You humans blame it on the alcohol all the time," says the cat. "We cats blame things on the catnip."

Rolling my eyes, I say, "This is not happening right now. I am not talking to a talking cat."

"Girl, stop worrying about if we're really talking to each other, or not," says the cat. "You have better things to worry about—like finding out who really killed your coworker."

"For your information," I tell the cat. "I'm starting my own personal investigation into Ruth's murder, which I believe will help me clear my name, right now. I need to talk to Ruth's friend, Zeke Kelly."

"And you think he's going to tell you who murdered your coworker?" demands the cat.

After telling the cat about the conversation I overheard Ruth having when she was threatened by the person she was talking to, I say, "I'm wondering if Ruth told Zeke that someone wanted to kill her. Maybe she told Zeke who threatened her."

"Wouldn't he have told the police?" asks the cat, licking her fur. "And wouldn't the cops have arrested that person instead of you?"

I bite my lower lip. "You have a point, but …"

"But?"

"I still want to talk to him," I say. "He might not know about the threatening call, but maybe Ruth has some other friends that she might have told. I just think I need to find out more about her to find out who wanted to kill her."

"Sounds like an okay start," says the cat. "Although, I think you should ask your coworker's friend if your coworker knew the dead guy behind the fruit stand. I'm telling you, those two deaths are connected."

I stare at the cat. "But how do you know that?"

"Sis, I got sources," says the cat. "And that's the word on the curb. I don't have all the details. That's what you need to find out. Your coworker's friend might be able to help."

Sighing, I say, "Yeah, but there's a problem."

"Which is?"

"I know that Zeke Kelly is staying at the Neptune Inn and Suites," I say, recalling the information I wrote in my notebook when I interviewed the tourists who'd found the dead body in Guavatown. "But I don't know which room. I've called the motel a few times and they've connected me to Zeke's room, but he never picks up the phone. And the motel clerk refuses to tell me which room Zeke is staying in for privacy reasons."

The cat stares at me. "What's the name of the motel again?"

"Neptune Inn and Suites," I tell her. "Why?"

"I know somebody at that motel who can give us the information."

"What?" I frown. "Who?"

"Timmy the rat ..."

I frown at the Calico. "Timmy the rat? Are you serious?"

"Girl, rats gonna rat," says the cat. "They always have information."

Starting the JEEP, I say. "Fine. Let's go ..."

"Wait ..." The cat places a paw on my right hand, which is wrapped around the gear stick.

"What?"

"Girl, I was serious when I said I want to be seat belted."

Chapter 26

"Zeke Kelly is in room twenty-four?" I ask, wary, and yet curious. "Are you sure?"

"That's what Timmy said," says the cat, settling into a loaf on the passenger seat of my JEEP.

Twenty minutes ago, based on her insistence that some rat she knew could help me out, I drove to the Neptune Inn and Suites. Feeling as though I was losing my mind, or suffering from coma-related PTSD, I drove into the small parking lot, avoiding potholes as I pulled into a narrow space in front of the main office. Declaring that she would be back in two shakes of a goat's tail, the cat leaped out of the window and scampered around the building, out of sight.

She returned, leaping back into the JEEP, to inform me that Zeke Kelly is staying in room twenty-four.

"But how does Timmy know?" I ask.

"Girl, the owner of this place is an old guy who doesn't trust computers," says the cat. "He writes everything down by hand, including the motel guest registry. Timmy read the guest registry. Zeke Kelly's name was next to room twenty-four."

"Interesting," I say, not sure if I want to believe the cat, or not. After all, I'm still not convinced she's really talking to me. This conversation could be a side effect of the coma. "Wait. The rat can read?"

Jumping to all fours, the cat says, "Apparently. Anyway, I gotta go. Don't forget to ask Zeke Kelly if your coworker knew Ricardo Miranda."

And with that, the feline leaps out of the JEEP.

Strangely galvanized by the cat's words, which are probably just a weird figment of my imagination which is giving me subconscious motivation, I exit the car. As a gusty, warm breeze wafts over me, carrying the scent of sea salt and hibiscus, I head toward room twenty-four, determined to get information to clear my name.

Chapter 27

"How did you get out of jail?"

Blinking, somewhat confused even though I know the answer to Zeke Kelly's question, I stammer, "Oh, well, um, you see …"

"You killed Ruth!" Zeke says, his red-rimmed eyes haunted as he glares at me. "You should still be behind bars!"

Despite Zeke Kelly's opinion, I'm not in jail because I made bail, but just because I made bail doesn't mean I'm off the hook. I need to clear my name, which is why I have to talk to him. However, judging from his scowl, and his belief that I'm a cold-blooded murderer, I'm not sure he'll be willing to help me.

Nevertheless, I have to try.

Clearing my throat, I say, "I'm guessing you read the article about me being arrested for Ruth's murder."

"Why did you kill her?" asks Zeke, standing in the doorway of his motel room. "I know you weren't friends, but—"

"How do you know that?" I ask.

"Ruth told me," says Zeke Kelly.

"When?"

"When I told her you were asking questions about the dead body found behind the fruit stand in Guavatown," says Zeke. "She said you were rival reporters. And that you were jealous of her."

"That is not true!" I insist. "I mean, no we weren't friends or even friendly coworkers, or even polite to each other, I suppose, but ... I was not jealous of her."

"Unless you were," says Zeke Kelly, his narrowed eyes full of suspicion. "Is that why you murdered Ruth? You wanted to get rid of the competition?"

"Get rid of the competition ..." I trail off as my mouth goes dry. "I did not want to get rid of Ruth. You have to believe me. I could not have killed her!"

"Then why did the cops arrest you?" asks Zeke Kelly, eyes burning with pain and rage.

Swallowing, my heart slamming, I say, "Because my fingerprints were on the murder weapon—"

"Which means you killed her!"

"No, I can explain," I say, my tone pleading. "I was only trying to help Ruth. She was walking toward me with a knife in her gut, so I pulled it out ... that's how my prints got on the knife."

"Or maybe they got on the knife when you plunged it in her," suggests Zeke, eyes narrowed with suspicion.

"Look, I will admit the evidence against me looks bad," I say. "But I didn't kill Ruth, I'm trying to find out who really murdered her so the real killer doesn't go free, and Ruth can have justice."

His lips pressed into a thin, grim line, Zeke Kelly looks away from me, saying nothing.

Clearing my throat, I say, "Listen, can I ask you something?"

Zeke Kelly gives me a wary look. "What?"

"Do you know if Ruth ..." I trail off, unsure how to phrase the question. "Um ... before Ruth died, I heard her on the phone talking to someone who threatened her."

"Threatened her?"

Nodding, I say, "She told this person that they didn't have to kill her."

Zeke Kelly's expression is haunted. "Did you tell the police this?"

"Yes, but I'm not sure the detective believed me," I say. "That's why I was wondering ... did Ruth tell you about somebody threatening her?"

"No, she never said anyone was threatening her, but ..."

"But?" I prompt, sensing Zeke Kelly knows something.

"Ruth was working on an explosive story," says Zeke Kelly. "Something she hadn't told her editor about because it was so dangerous. She was going to write about some pretty bad characters. People who didn't want the story published and they threatened her. So she got a gun."

"A gun ..." I echo.

"Ruth told me the gun was for protection because she didn't live in the best neighborhood," says Zeke. "But, I don't think she was worried about burglars. I think she was afraid of the people who didn't want that explosive story published."

"Did she tell you the names of these dangerous people?"

Shaking his head, Zeke says, "She told me she couldn't tell me. Said she had to protect her sources. If somebody was threatening her, it might have had something to do with the story she was working on."

"Did you tell the cops about Ruth's dangerous story?" I ask.

Zeke says, "Ruth has always worked on dangerous stories. We met when she lived in South America. She used to do articles on drug dealers and arms smugglers. She's been threatened before, but she never let that stop her. She moved to this island to take a break from writing about the bad guys."

"But she covered crime," I point out.

Nodding, Zeke says, "Because she couldn't help herself. When she left South America, she told me she was heading to a beautiful island where she would write about lifestyle topics—travel, food, arts, and entertainment."

"Interesting," I say, finding it ironic that Ruth initially wanted my assignment, while I wanted hers.

"But when she moved to the island, her editor talked her into writing crime stories because he was so impressed with her previous stories. And Ruth realized crime reporting was in her blood. She couldn't give it up. Not even for blue skies, white sand, and sunshine."

Saddened by Zeke Kelly's mournful lament, I glance away for a moment. Despite my animosity with Ruth, learning about her life before she arrived at the *Palmchat Gazette* makes me wish I could have gotten to know her better. If I could have managed to convince her I wasn't pathetic and undeserving of my job, she might have become an invaluable mentor, providing tips and tricks about investigative reporting.

"You said she wrote about drug dealers," I say. "Could one of them have threatened her?"

"I suppose it's possible, but I doubt it," Zeke Kelly says. "If you're telling the truth and you didn't do it, then … I have no idea."

Somewhat dejected, I say, "Well, thank you for talking to me."

Zeke shrugs. "No problem. Oh, since you're here, I can ask you … did your editor decide not to put my name in the story about the dead body behind the fruit stand?"

Recalling that I was in a coma when the story was first published, I say, "Oh, I didn't write it after all."

"Are you going to write the follow-up stories now that Ruth … can't?"

"I don't think so," I say, deciding not to tell him that I'm on a leave of absence. "I haven't really been following the story, but …"

"But?"

Recalling what the cat told me, I ask, "Do you know if Ruth knew Ricardo Miranda, the guy who was found dead behind the fruit stand?"

Zeke frowns. "I have no idea. I don't think so. Why do you think Ruth knew him?"

"Oh, um, I'm not even sure …" I clear my throat. "I should probably be going. Have a good day."

Pivoting, I walk quickly back to my JEEP, wishing I'd never listened to that crazy cat. There is no connection between Ruth and the dead guy behind the fruit stand. Why did I ever think that? Because the cat told me. How ridiculous is that.

A cat *told* me.

Felines don't talk.

I need to remember that.

Chapter 28

Drinking dragon fruit tea with strawberry glazed donut holes, I stare at the article featured on the *Palmchat Gazette* website.

Three days have passed since I spoke with Zeke Kelly, who told me Ruth was investigating a story about dangerous criminals. An investigation that might have gotten her killed. I have no proof, but it's a good possibility. After all, someone threatened Ruth. It might have been some heinous thug who didn't want her writing an expose article about his criminal shenanigans.

Sighing, I prop an elbow on the breakfast bar.

It's around nine on a gloomy, overcast morning, one tourists hate because it brings the possibility of rain and the cancellation of tours and excursions. Thinking of tours makes me recall the walking tour in Guavatown I never got to review. And that has me pondering the dead body found behind the fruit stand, which draws my attention back to the article.

SUSPECT ARRESTED IN GUAVATOWN MURDER

If you want to find out who killed your coworker Ruth, you need to find out who killed the dead guy found by that fruit stand in Guavatown.

I shake my head, trying to ignore the cat's words. Which the cat didn't even speak. Because the feline wasn't talking to me. Actually, the last time I saw the Calico was when I spoke to Zeke Kelly. Good riddance, I think. But that's not true. As I've continued my investigation into Ruth's death, without much progress, unfortunately, I have found myself thinking about the cat.

Wondering where she is. What she might be up to. If I'll see her again.

Which is ridiculous, I know.

Back to the article.

The story is brief, a no-nonsense account, detailing how the cops arrested Marlo Miranda, the wife of the victim. Officer Cuetee told me that Marlo Miranda was under suspicion for the murder of her husband, so I'm not shocked she was arrested.

If you want to find out who killed your coworker Ruth, you need to find out who killed the dead guy found by that fruit stand in Guavatown.

I take another sip of tea, contemplating what the cat told me. Not that she told me anything, because she didn't speak to me. Cats don't talk, remember? Besides, Ruth didn't know Ricardo Miranda, so how could their deaths be connected. Doesn't make sense.

And yet …

Something—and, honestly, I don't know what—makes me think I should have a talk with Marlo Miranda.

Chapter 29

"I did not kill my husband," insists Marlo Miranda.

After deciding I wanted to talk to Marlo, I drove to the St. Mateo jail and told a tiny, white lie. Pretending to be writing a story for the *Palmchat Gazette*, I was able to secure a jailhouse interview.

Behind the glass partition—which is scratched and smudged with the fingertips of previous inmates and visitors—the main suspect in the murder of Ricardo Miranda glares at me with wild, angry green eyes. As she clutches the telephone, I take in her disheveled blonde hair done up in a haphazard top knot, sallow skin, raccoon eyes, and pursed lips in a puckered sneer.

"I loved that man," says Marlo. "Probably more than I should have. More than life itself. I would never have murdered him. I never wanted to be in this world without him!"

I'm wary of her impassioned declaration, which is believable, even though it's a bit melodramatic. She's definitely doing the most, pulling out all of the stops to be convincing, but I'm not exactly sure I'm convinced.

"Why did the police arrest you?" I ask. "What evidence do they have?"

Exhaling, Marlo rubs her bloodshot eyes. "Apparently, Ricky was shot twice in the back of the head."

"Gruesome," I say, making a few notes on my legal pad.

"With a Glock nine-millimeter," says Marlo. "I also have a Glock nine-millimeter, but I can't seem to find it. Because of that, Detective Francois arrested me. He's convinced that I shot Ricardo, then ditched the gun so I could get away with murder."

"The evidence seems somewhat circumstantial," I say. "I mean, there're probably other people on the island who own a nine-millimeter."

"That's what I told Detective Francois," says Marlo. "But, I also don't have an alibi, so there's that."

Nodding, I say, "You have any idea who killed Ricardo?"

"I have no idea," Marlo says, her expression as glum as her tone. "I wish I did."

"Well, before I go," I say, disappointed at another seemingly dead end. "Do you know if Ricardo knew a woman named Ruth Rice?"

"Ruth Rice … " Marlo tilts her head to the side, as though contemplating the question. "That name seems familiar …"

"It does?" I ask, hopeful.

Marlo gives me a shrewd look. "Didn't I see her name in the paper? She was killed, wasn't she?"

Realizing why Marlo found Ruth's name familiar, I try not to feel dejected. "Um, yes, unfortunately, she was murdered."

"Well, to answer your question, as far as I know, Ricardo didn't know her," Marlo says, her gaze quizzical. "Why do you ask? Do you think he did? Why would he know her? Did she interview him? No, Ricardo would have told me if his name was going to be in the paper."

"I was told that they might know each other," I say, kicking myself for listening to that cat, who wasn't even really talking to me. "But that information wasn't true …"

Chapter 30

"Have you found out who really killed your coworker yet?"

Nearing choking on the sip of mint tea I just drank, after shoving another chocolate glazed donut hole into my mouth, I sputter and cough, rising to a sitting position on the chaise lounge on my patio. Swinging my legs down to the concrete, I stare at the Calico, who walks effortlessly along the railing of my balcony.

Several hours have passed since my visit to Marlo Miranda at the St. Mateo jail, during which I, unfortunately, didn't do any girl sleuthing, despite my desperation to clear my name. Instead, I made tea, grabbed a box of donut holes, and went out onto the patio to enjoy the mid-afternoon sunshine.

I was pretending that I didn't have a care in the world, that my life isn't in shambles, and that there isn't a murder charge hanging over my head when the feisty feline showed up out of the blue.

"Well, for your information," I say, coughing again as I place my mug of tea on the little table next to the chaise. "I looked into what you told me … you know, how if I want to find out who killed Ruth, then I need to find out who killed the man found dead behind the fruit stand in Guavatown?"

Bobbing her head, the cat leaps from the railing onto the lounge. "So have you done that?"

Shaking my head, I say, "You were wrong about that. The person who was arrested for killing Ricardo Miranda—the dead man found behind the fruit stand—is Marlo Miranda, his wife. But I don't think she killed Ruth."

"Why not?" asks the cat, licking her fur. "Because she says she didn't."

"Well, I didn't exactly ask her," I say, biting my lower lip.

"Why not?"

"Well, if I had asked her, and if she did kill Ruth, then she wouldn't have admitted it to me," I say. "But, I asked her if Ruth knew Ricardo because I was trying to determine if there was some connection between Ruth and Ricardo. Some reason why Marlo would have killed both of them. And Ricardo and Ruth didn't know each other."

The cat gives me a look. "How do you know that?"

"Well, because Marlo Miranda told me that Ricardo didn't know Ruth," I say, feeling as though, somehow, I've dropped the ball, or missed a chance.

"And you believed her?" asks the cat. "A woman who was arrested for killing her husband?"

I grab my mug and take a gulp of tea. "Well, when you put it that way … maybe she did lie to me."

"Girl, if the cops think she killed her husband—"

"Well, that's the thing," I say, interrupting the cat. "I think the police rushed to judgment. The evidence against her is pretty circumstantial."

"As far as you know," says the cat.

Glancing at the cat, I say, "Marlo Miranda told me about the evidence against her. Maybe she left some things out. Or, maybe the police have some other evidence she doesn't know about. Like her DNA at the crime scene, or something like that."

"Exactly," agrees the cat.

I pop another donut hole into my mouth and chew thoughtfully.

"Still, I can't imagine why she would kill Ruth. I mean, I can imagine her having a motive for killing her husband. Maybe he was cheating on her?"

The cat says, "Or doing his business in her litter box."

"Um, yeah, I'm not sure about that," I say.

"Girl, here's what I'm sure about," the cat tells me. "You need to find out if there's a reason why Marlo Miranda wanted your coworker dead."

Chapter 31

A bittersweet longing fills me as I slip into my cubicle at the *Palmchat Gazette* and sit down at my desk.

It's a few minutes after six in the morning, super early, but it's the best time to sneak into the office unnoticed. I'm planning to use the newspaper's research software to find out more about Marlo Miranda. At least, that's what the talking cat who showed up on my patio yesterday thinks I should do. The talking cat who may or may not actually be talking to me. I should have ignored her. Should have chalked her appearance up to lingering PTSD from the coma I suffered, because she attacked me. And yet, I found myself strangely happy to see her … which I don't want to examine or analyze.

Nevertheless, here I am taking her advice.

You need to find out if there's a reason why Marlo Miranda wanted your coworker dead.

Granted, I'm not sure how I'm supposed to do that, but I figured I would start with a background search of Marlo Miranda. Maybe, just maybe, I might find out that Marlo knew Ruth Rice. Maybe they met in South America. Or maybe Ruth cut Marlo off in traffic. Or perhaps Ruth wrote an article that infuriated Marlo to the point of homicide. Who knows?

After turning on my computer, I access the personal information database and type in Marlo Miranda's name.

Minutes later, I'm staring at the screen, shocked by what I see …

A petition for divorce filed by Ricardo Miranda.

The document was filed with the St. Mateo Clerk last month, and the document contains very interesting information. The petitioner, Ricardo Miranda, claimed that he made the painful decision to file for divorce due to the fact that his wife of the past six years, Marlo Miranda, had become increasingly jealous and bitter, making it impossible for him to reconcile the differences between them.

Additionally, the legal filing detailed that Ricardo believed Marlo had caused violent harm to a female neighbor, who Marlo believed Ricardo was having an extra-marital affair with, though Ricardo denied that claim.

Marlo filed a counterclaim, contesting the divorce, pleading that the marriage could be saved, and asking a judge to agree to a trial separation and order that they attend marriage counseling. In response, Ricardo's attorney filed a motion asking the judge to deny Marlo's pleas, reiterating that Ricardo was no longer in love with Marlo and was in no way interested in saving the marriage, which he believed was irrevocably damaged.

As I click my mouse to print the divorce documents, my mind whirls with questions and speculation. Marlo didn't mention the impending divorce from her husband. I wonder if the police know that Ricardo thought she was jealous, bitter, and violent. Could that be the reason why she was arrested despite the circumstantial evidence against her?

Standing, I collect the documents, fold them in half and shove them into my cross-body purse.

Of course, the information about Ricardo divorcing Marlo is intriguing, and certainly gives her a motive for Ricardo's murder—if she can't have him then no one can—but it has nothing to do with Ruth. Unfortunately, I didn't find any connection between Marlo and Ruth. Which is not to say that there isn't a connection between them, but I couldn't find it.

Marlo was born in the Palmchat Islands, went to university in England, then returned to St. Mateo, married Ricardo, and settled into a life as a stay-at-home wife. Ruth was in South America during that time, so it's unclear how the women would have crossed paths.

While I'm more inclined to believe that Marlo did kill her husband, I don't think she had a reason to murder Ruth. Once again, I feel foolish for listening to that talking cat, who probably wasn't even talking to me. The Calico is convinced that Ruth's killer is the same person who killed Ricardo Miranda, but I don't think that's true.

My money—not that I have much—is on the story Ruth was writing about the dangerous criminal. I need to find out more about the article she was writing. More specifically, I need to find out who she was writing about. What dangerous criminal was the subject of her investigation. If Ruth found out something that could put the criminal behind bars, he might have killed her to keep her quiet.

Leaving my cubicle, I navigate the maze of six-foot-high cubicles. As I approach Ruth's former workspace, images of Ruth spiral through my mind. I reflect on all the snarky things she said to me. And the times she sneered at me when we happened to be in the ladies' room at the same time. And then there were the times when she ignored me in the breakroom.

Ruth didn't like me, and I didn't like her.

But when I think about what happened to her, sadness invades me. No, we weren't friends, but her death has shaken me to the core. It was heinous and horrible. I want to find her killer, and not just because I'm worried about going to prison for something I didn't do. Ruth deserves justice.

Hurrying past Ruth's cube, I check my watch, thinking that I might stop at my favorite tea shop and—

"Sophie? Is that you?"

Chapter 32

Recognizing Candace's voice, I cringe, kicking myself for getting caught. While I'm on leave of absence, I'm not supposed to be at the paper. I don't know what Marty will do if he finds out I've been here, and I'm hoping Candace won't tell him.

"Sophie ..."

Exhaling, resigned to my fate, I turn. "Hi ..."

Standing just outside the entrance to Ruth's cube, Candace frowns. "What are you doing here? I thought Marty fired you."

"Fired me?" I ask, walking toward her. "No. He didn't fire me. Why would you think he fired me?"

"Because you killed Ruth," Candace says, stepping into Ruth's cubicle.

Following her, I say, "But I didn't kill Ruth."

"Well, I don't expect you to admit it," says Candace.

Shaking my head, I watch as Candace tosses items from Ruth's desk drawer into two cardboard boxes on the floor against the left cubicle wall.

"Anyway ... what's going on here?" I ask, eager to change the subject.

Candace flings a pair of headphones into a box. "Marty volunteered me to clean out Ruth's cube."

"Really ..." I say, biting my lip, wondering if there might be something in Ruth's cubical about the story she was writing. Maybe some notes on the dangerous criminal. Something that might reveal the identity of this person.

"I'm boxing up her stuff and a friend of hers is going to come by and get it," says Candace, dropping more items into the box—a thesaurus, a tiny lamp, a paperweight shaped like an egg, a thin shawl, a mug, and a can of unopened tuna.

"Well," I say. "I'll get out of your way so—"

"Hey, Sophie ..." says Candace, her voice lowered.

"Yes?" I ask, curious about her conspiratorial tone."

"Look, I know Ruth wasn't the nicest person, but you didn't have to kill her."

I blink, staring at Candace. "But I didn't kill Ruth."

Candace says, "But Marty said your fingerprints were on the murder weapon."

"I can explain why my prints are on the murder weapon," I say, praying I won't have to tell this horrible story to a jury at my trial one day. "When Ruth came walking toward me, with the knife protruding from her chest, I removed it because I wanted to stop the bleeding. I was trying to help Ruth. That's why my prints are on the knife. I didn't kill her."

Her left eyebrow arched, Candace gives me a circumspect look. "I expect you to deny killing Ruth, but the evidence against you is pretty damning, don't you think?"

"No, I don't think that," I dispute, disconcerted by Candace's compassionate tone, which doesn't match her suspicious gaze. "I mean, yes, the evidence is bad, but ..."

"Sophie, I mean no offense," begins Candace, reaching out to grab my hand. "But, is it possible that you may be delusional?"

"What do you mean?" I ask, slowly extracting my hand from Candace's grasp.

Tilting her head, Candace says, "You can't possibly believe a jury is going to believe your story. It sounds quite farfetched."

Taken aback, I say, "But it's true."

"You may believe your story is true," says Candace. "But believing doesn't make it so. And I don't think you should waste your time trying to prove something that isn't true. I think you should do the right thing."

"The right thing?" I stare at Candace.

"You should admit your actions and take responsibility for them," says Candace. "Tell the police the truth."

Frustrated, I say, "I did tell them the truth. Detective François didn't believe me."

Candace tilts her head, then says, "Sophie, once again, no offense, but something just occurred to me."

I'm afraid to ask, but I do. "What?"

"Perhaps you have selective amnesia," says Candace. "Maybe you don't remember murdering Ruth because after you stabbed her in a fit of violent, jealous rage, you were so horrified by what you'd done that you blocked the horrible events from your memory."

"Huh?" I gape, wondering if Candace has lost her mind.

"The mind will protect itself from traumatic events that might cause a psychotic break," says Candace. "Listen, I know a really good hypnotist."

"A hypnotist?"

"He can help you recover the memories you've repressed."

"But I haven't repressed any memories," I say.

"I'm sure you have," says Candace. "And when you get those memories of killing Ruth back, you can come clean and start to heal."

Flabbergasted, not sure what to say, I stare at Candace, perplexed by her doubt of me. It never occurred to me that Candace, or any of my coworkers, for that matter, would think that I killed Ruth.

"Anyway ... I need to go to the ladies' room," Candace announced. "I had an extra cup of coffee this morning."

As Candace heads off, I walk further into Ruth's cube. Propping my forearm on the back of Ruth's ergonomic chair, I decide not to take

Candace's doom and gloom to heart. After all, I have nothing to worry about. I don't need a hypnotist to help me recover repressed memories of killing Ruth because I don't have any repressed memories of killing Ruth. Because I didn't kill Ruth. I'm going to find out who really killed her and clear my name so I won't have to worry about spending the rest of my life in Tiverton. And since I do have to clear my name, I glance down into the banker's boxes filled with Ruth's things. Could there be a clue in the box? Something that might help me identify the dangerous criminal she was secretly investigating for her story? Maybe a note scribbled on a torn piece of paper? Or—

Staring into the box, I spy, among the hodgepodge of random items, what appears to be a smartphone.

Odd.

Maybe it belongs to Candace, I think. Although, why would Candace put her phone in the box of Ruth's things? I know, I know, it doesn't make sense. But neither does the idea of Ruth leaving a smartphone in one of her drawers or overhead bins.

Still, staring at the phone, I can't help remembering Ruth's conversation with the person who threatened her. Could Ruth have been talking to her killer? And if the killer is the dangerous criminal she planned to expose, then that means the dangerous criminal called Ruth. Meaning, the dangerous criminal's contact information might be on Ruth's smartphone.

Before I realize what I'm doing, I bend over, reach into the box, remove the phone, and—

"Hey, Sophie ..."

I freeze for a second, then shove the phone into the pocket of my eyelet blazer and turn to Candace, hoping she didn't see me.

Staring at me with slightly narrowed eyes, Candace says, "I have to warn you ..."

Worried, I ask, "About ... ?"

"The ladies' room," says Candace. "I think I saw a rat in there ..."

Chapter 33

"Marlo was very jealous … and really, for no reason," says Emily Foster, Marlo Miranda's next-door neighbor, a slender, perky blonde dressed in over-sized leisure wear.

Following the discovery in Ruth's cubicle yesterday evening, I went home and examined the smartphone Candace must have tossed into the bankers' box. Driving home, I convinced myself that I had to take the phone. I had to find out if Ruth talked to her killer on that phone. And if she had, I would give the phone to Detective François, so he could trace the number. Hopefully, he'd determine the location of Ruth's killer so he could be arrested.

Unfortunately, I wasn't able to access Ruth's phone.

Not surprisingly, it was locked. And, I soon discovered, it can only be unlocked with Ruth's face. Since Ruth is dead, I'm never going to see her face again. The thought was sad and sobering.

I had to make myself a steaming mug of hibiscus tea with lemon and lavender donut holes so I wouldn't feel so hopeless and depressed. I was trying to cheer myself up, sitting on the patio, watching the sun set, when the Calico showed up.

"What's the tea, sis?" she asked.

"Hibiscus," I answered, taking a sip.

"No, I mean with clearing your name," said the feisty feline. "Did you find a connection between Marlo Miranda and your coworker Ruth? Did Marlo have a reason to kill Ruth?"

Shaking my head, I said, "There is no connection between them. Marlo was telling the truth when she said she didn't know Ruth. However, Marlo did lie to me about her husband."

"What do you mean?" asked the Calico, leaping from the balcony railing to the chaise, where she settled into a loaf next to me.

After another sip of tea, I said, "Ricardo Miranda was divorcing Marlo."

"When I asked about the tea, girl, that's what I meant," said Callie. "Give me the details."

"Apparently, according to Ricardo," I began, "Marlo is very jealous and violent. He claimed in his divorce petition that Marlo attacked a woman that she thought Ricardo was flirting with."

"Girl, that sounds like homicidal envy to me," said the cat. "Wasn't your coworker Ruth cute?"

Nodding, I said, "Very pretty."

"Isn't it possible that Ricardo Miranda flirted with her, and Marlo found out, then killed Ruth?" asked the cat.

I wasn't sure about that possibility.

Killing a woman because your husband flirted with her seemed like an overreaction, but Callie was convinced that people had been killed for less.

"You humans are always flying off the handle about something," the cat told me.

"Okay, let's say you're right," I said. "How on earth would I find out if Ricardo ever flirted with Ruth? The only people who could tell me are … dead."

"Girl, the neighbors could tell you."

I glanced at the cat over the rim of my mug. "What neighbors?"

"Marlo Miranda's neighbors," the cat said. "Girl, cats are curious and neighbors are nosy."

"That's true," I allowed.

"Nosy neighbors know all the tea," Callie insisted. "You need to talk to them."

I wasn't convinced of that, but I decided to humor the cat with the intention of proving her silly theory wrong. And so, after researching Marlo Miranda's address, I drove to her neighborhood, and I started knocking on doors. Most of which went unanswered until I came to the home of Emily Foster, who was happy to talk to me about Marlo, a woman who, in Emily's opinion, "should have been locked up long ago."

After introducing myself and telling a little white lie about working on a story for the *Palmchat Gazette*, which I know I shouldn't have done, Emily and I took a seat in the worn, wicker chairs on her patio.

I ask Emily, "Why do you say Marlo had no reason to be jealous?"

Holding a large orange water bottle, which she takes frequent sips from, she says, "No one was interested in Ricardo except Marlo. I mean, the man was an Oompa Loompa."

"An … Oompa Loompa?" I ask, not quite sure about her reference.

"A Munchkin," she says. "Like those little people in the Wizard of Oz. Very short. And with a face only a mother could love."

"Interesting," I say, then ask, "Did Marlo ever accuse you of flirting with Ricardo?"

Scoffing, Emily says, "She accused every woman on this block. Every woman in this neighborhood. She threatened any woman who talked to him to stay away from her man. She even yelled at the Widow Carpenter, who lives at the end of the block, when Ricardo offered to help the old lady with her groceries."

"That's terrible," I say, becoming even more convinced that Marlo did kill her husband.

"You know what's worse?" asks Emily, taking another sip from her orange bottle. "The way Marlo yelled and cursed when that reporter came to talk to Ricky."

A jolt passes through me. "A reporter came to talk to Ricky? When? What reporter?"

"A few weeks before Ricardo was killed," says Emily, tapping the straw attached to her water bottle against her bottom lip. "I forget the reporter's name but she was the one who died recently."

My heart slamming, I say, "Was the reporter … Ruth Rice? Does that name sound familiar?"

Nodding, Emily says, "That's her. She got killed by her coworker."

Guilt rushes through me, and I glance away, focusing on the overgrown bougainvillea climbing along the side of the porch, until I quickly remember that I'm not guilty.

"Anyway, Marlo threatened the reporter," says Emily. "I was watching when it happened. Marlo told the reporter to stay away from Ricardo or she would kill her."

Chapter 34

"Girl, aren't you glad I told you to talk to those nosy neighbors," says the cat as she jumps onto the chaise lounge on my patio.

Moments ago, I was sitting on the plump cushions, drinking apple infused tea and cinnamon dusted donut holes as I contemplated my conversation with Marlo Miranda's neighbor, when the Calico showed up.

Shaking my head, I say, "I can't believe what she told me."

"She told you that Marlo Miranda has a motive for killing your coworker," the cat says, licking her fur. "Marlo was crazy jealous of Ruth because Ricardo was talking to her, so Marlo killed her."

After another sip of tea, I say, "Yes, but ..."

"But what?" The cat stares at me.

"I get that Marlo is a jealous woman," I say. "There are at least two witnesses to her envy—her husband, who outlined her jealousy in his divorce petition, and her neighbor, who was confronted by Marlo. Nevertheless, it still seems very extreme to me that Marlo would kill Ruth because she had a conversation with Ricardo."

"Maybe it depends on what the conversation was about," says the feline. "Did the neighbor know?"

I shake my head. "She had no idea."

"Maybe Ricardo was flirting with your coworker," suggests the Calico. "Marlo saw her husband flirting and went after Ruth."

Thinking about Ruth and Ricardo's conversation, I say, "But what if Ricardo wasn't flirting with Ruth?"

"Maybe Marlo thought he was," the cat says. "But she was mistaken."

"That's possible, but—"

"Girl, why are you going over and over this?" asks the cat. "It's obvious that Marlo Miranda is a jealous psycho."

"But, is it?" I ask, tilting my head as I pop a donut hole in my mouth.

The cat hisses at me.

"Okay, okay …" I hold up my hands. "Maybe you're right."

Girl, I know I'm right," the cat says. "And I also know that you need to get proof that Marlo killed your coworker."

"Maybe I should talk to Marlo again," I say, scratching my chin. "I can ask her a few pointed questions then confront her with the evidence of her violent jealously. And then, maybe, just maybe, she'll be so guilty that she'll break down and confess to the crime."

The feline hisses at me again. "Girl, be so for real, okay? Do you think your life is a mystery novel?"

A strange shiver passes through me. "Well, no, of course not. And, okay, so Marlo probably won't come clean to me. But maybe I can trick her into incriminating herself."

"Girl, do you look like a magician?" asks the cat. "Here's what you need to do. Go to your coworker's house."

"What?" I balk. "Why?"

"You need to find proof that Marlo Miranda was in your coworker's house," says the cat. "When Marlo killed Ruth, she must have left behind some DNA."

"Don't you think the cops would have found it?"

"Girl, the cops weren't looking for it," the feline says. "That detective is convinced you killed your coworker. He's got the knife with your prints on it. And you were in your coworker's house when the cops came. Why does he need to look for any more evidence?"

Finishing my tea, I say, "You're right."

"Girl, I know I'm right," the feline tells me. "So let's go."

I frown at her. "Where?"

"To your coworker's house."

"Now?"

"Girl, do you want to clear your name, or not?" demands the cat. "Come on, let's go!"

Chapter 35

"Well, what are you waiting for?" asks the cat.

I glance down at her. "Well, the last time I walked into Ruth's house, I found her bleeding from a stab wound before she collapsed and died."

Twenty minutes after leaving my apartment, I parked my JEEP on the curb in front of Ruth's house. The cat and I hopped out, then made our way up the walkway to the porch. Admittedly, I was excited and hoping to discover a clue to clear my name, but now that I'm at Ruth's door, I'm not so sure this was a good idea.

"Girl, that was then, and this is now," says the Calico. "The door is open, right?"

Staring at the drooping yellow crime scene tape draped across the front door, I say, "Probably. But I'm sure the cops don't want me going inside and traipsing around, disturbing things."

"You think the cops are coming back here?" asks the Calico. "That detective who arrested you has already closed the case. As far as he's concerned, you're the killer, so why does he need to come back here and look around."

Biting my lower lip, I sigh. "I suppose you have a point."

"Of course, I have a point," says the cat.

Crossing my arms, I say, "Nevertheless—"

The cat moves around my ankles and then disappears between the crack in the front door.

"No, wait, don't …" Shocked, I glance around again. Now what? "Why did you go inside? Kitty … kitty, come back. I don't think this is a good idea …"

Seconds pass. And then minutes.

Sighing, I rub my eyes. I should just turn around, go back out to my JEEP and go home. That's what I should have done instead of allowing that psycho cat to trick me into looking for clues to prove that Marlo Miranda killed Ruth. What was I thinking? First of all, I'm not even sure I believe that Marlo killed Ruth. Okay, sure, Marlo is jealous and her neighbor saw her confront Ruth for talking to Ricky, but … was Marlo envious enough to kill Ruth? Honestly, I'm more interested in what Ruth and Ricardo talked about. Did Ruth and Ricardo know each other? If so, how did they meet? And suppose the cat is right and Marlo did kill Ruth. Do I really think I'm going to find Marlo's DNA at the crime scene? The only thing that could clear my name is some secret interior surveillance that captured Marlo killing Ruth on video, which I doubt there is. Why didn't I have another mug of tea like I'd planned? This is what I get for listening to the advice of a talking cat who probably isn't talking to me and is just one of the terrible effects of being in a coma.

Looking over my shoulder, I glance at my JEEP.

I really should leave but, for some reason, I can't bring myself to leave without that stupid psycho cat. Which makes no sense. That crazy Calico put me in the hospital. I was in a coma because of her. And now, because of the trauma she inflicted on me, I'm hallucinating that she's talking to me.

"Kitty … kitty …" I call out, anxious about stepping over the threshold since I can hardly see two feet in front of me. "Where are you?"

"Where have you been?"

The sassy demand has me jumping out of my skin. Shrieking my shock, I whirl around. The Calico perches on the arm of a sectional couch shaped like the letter E.

Clutching my chest, I glare at the feline. "Kitty! You scared me!"

The cat stares at me, eyes narrowing. "Who is … Kitty?"

I stare back at her, wary of her tone, which seems to have gone from sassy to sinister. "Um … you're Kitty …"

"Kitty?" Standing, the cat hisses at me. "Who told you that? My name is not Kitty. That's what you call some cat that you expect to just come to you when you call her, but I am not a cat who will be summoned, okay?"

I lean back, afraid she might pounce on me again. "Okay …"

The cat sits again, curling her hind legs into her body. "Anyway … my name is Callie."

"Callie …" I say, liking the sound of it. "Callie … the Calico. That's so cute."

The feline glares at me, growling.

I hold up my hands. "Callie … got it. I'm Sophie."

"I already know that," says Callie.

"Okay, now that I know your name," I say. "Tell me this: Why did you go into the house?"

"Why didn't you follow me into the house?"

"Maybe because entering a crime scene is probably against the law," I say.

"Girl, this is no time to be a scaredy cat," says the Calico.

Scoffing, I say, "I'm not scared. I just don't want to be arrested again."

"We're not leaving without looking for clues to clear your name," says Callie. "The way I see it, this is the best time to look around. The cops won't be showing up."

I shake my head. "I am not going to go snooping around in a crime scene."

"You're not snooping around," says Callie. "You're looking for evidence to prove that Marlo Miranda killed your coworker, which will keep you out of prison, and you have every right to search for that evidence, in my opinion."

"I didn't ask for your opinion," I say, my eyes sweeping the living area.

"What's going on over here on this desk," asks the cat, running ahead of me, using the furniture as her own personal parkour course as she leaps between the flat surfaces until she lands on the desk.

Approaching the desk, which seems to be made of quartz, the color of river stones, I take in the desktop computer, a small bonsai tree, a cordless phone sitting in a base, a small clock, and a Lucite desk set.

"Look at that blinking light on the phone," says the cat, balancing precariously on the armrest of the chair behind the desk. "Does that mean someone left your coworker a message?"

Frowning, I say, "Yes, but ... who would have called her?"

"Maybe someone who doesn't know she's dead," says the cat.

Shuddering at the thought, I say, "That's awful."

"See what the message says," Callie tells me.

"You think I should?" I ask. "That's sort of an invasion of privacy, don't you think?"

"Girl, your coworker is dead," the cat says. "She doesn't have any privacy to invade anymore."

"True, but ..." I sigh. "We're supposed to be looking for evidence that Marlo Miranda was in this house, not checking phone messages."

"Girl, what if Marlo called your coworker," Callie says. "Didn't you tell me that you overheard your coworker talking to someone who threatened her?"

Nodding, I say, "Right, but ... you think that might have been Marlo?"

"Marlo has a history of confronting and threatening people," Callie says. "If she called your coworker at work, she might have called her at home."

"But would she have left an incriminating message?" I ask, doubtful.

"Marlo doesn't seem like the kind of human who tries to keep her emotions under wraps," the cat says. "She confronted people in public, where anyone could see her, which is how you found out that she was violent. She doesn't strike me as someone afraid to leave a threatening voice message."

Tilting my head, I say, "You have a point."

"Girl, I know I do," the cat says. "Now, check the messages."

Sighing, I shoo her away and when she leaps from the armrest to the bookshelf tucked into the corner of the alcove, I pull the chair back and sit down at the desk.

Fifteen minutes later, after listening to twenty-one of the twenty-eight unretrieved voice messages on Ruth's phone, I look at the cat and say, "I don't think Marlo called Ruth."

So far, most of the messages were from telemarketers. There were seven hang-ups and three from the Indian takeout place around the corner. The owner was calling to alert Ruth of new menu items, including a spicy goat curry which sounded wonderful, and which I might try for dinner.

"Girl, you gotta keep listening," Callie says. "If she didn't call, fine, but at least you'll know for sure."

Sighing, I press the button to retrieve the next message.

With seven messages to go, I'm hoping they're all hang-ups or wrong numbers. I need more tea. And I need to visit the ladies' room, although I'm reluctant because—

"Hello! Are you tired of not being able to sleep because mosquitoes and jungle flies get in your house and bite you all night?"

Confused, I frown. Huh?

As the message continues, I realize it's a telemarketer hoping to sell me island bug spray, which promises to be all-natural and won't harm the environment, and that's great, but …

"Six messages to go," I announce, deleting the island bug spray company.

I access the next message.

"Hey, Ms. Rice … it's Ricardo Miranda …"

"What?" I gasp.

The cat looks at me. "Is it a message from Marlo?"

"No …" I say. "It's from Ricardo Miranda."

"Marlo's husband?" Callie asks. "What is he saying?"

"Shhhh …" I say. "I'm listening."

Ricardo Miranda continues, "… um, I don't think we can't meet anymore. It's too dangerous. If we get caught, we'll both be killed … I'll try to call you later. Bye."

A chill passes through me. "Oh my goodness …"

"Girl, what did he say?" asks the cat.

I tell her, then say, "I wonder why they were meeting."

"Isn't it obvious?" asks Callie. "They must have been fooling around. And Ricardo must have known that Marlo found out."

Nodding, I say, "So he tried to warn Ruth … "

"But he was too late," the cat says. "Marlo killed them both."

"I think you might be right."

"This might be the proof you need," says Callie.

"I want to replay the message and write down exactly what Ricardo says," I say, grabbing the crystal knob of the pencil drawer. Hoping to find a pen and paper, I yank it open, and—

I gasp. "Oh … my … gosh!"

"What is it?"

Staring down into the pencil drawer, I can hardly believe my eyes. There's only one item in the drawer.

A black gun…

"Is that what I think it is?"

Nodding, I say, "It's a gun … but why is it in this drawer?"

"Your coworker must have put it there, right?" asks the feline leaping onto the desk, landing near the computer.

"Yeah," I say, biting my top lip. "But I wonder why the cops didn't find it?"

"Didn't I tell you they didn't look for any more clues after they arrested you," says the cat. "The better question is, why did Ruth have a gun?"

"Ruth's friend told me that Ruth got a gun," I say, recalling the conversation. "He thought it was because Ruth was working on a dangerous story."

"Or maybe your coworker had a gun to protect herself from Marlo Miranda," says the cat, jumping to the floor.

I bite my lower lip, then ask, "You think?"

"Girl, you heard Ricardo's message," says Callie. "He warned your coworker that she could be killed."

Shaking my head, I say, "I know, but—"

A crashing sound vibrates the walls.

Startled, I glance down at the Calico, whose ears are standing at attention.

"What was that?" I ask, my heart slamming.

"That was all the reason we need to get out of here," says the cat, trotting to the couch and jumping up onto the cushion.

I glance at the cat. "You're right. Let's make like a tree and leave."

"What?" asks the Calico.

"It's something my grandma says," I say. "I think—"

"Behind you!" the cat yells.

"Behind me?" I shake my head. "No, it means—"

"No, girl, behind you!"

Confused, I turn … Two St. Mateo police officers stand just inside the doorway, their guns pointed at me. "Freeze!" one of them commands. The other officer orders, "Don't move!"

Chapter 36

Wringing my hands, I glance around the small, sterile, cold interrogation room at the St. Mateo police department.

Exhaling, I rub my eyes and check my watch. I've been in the room for half an hour. Just like when I was interrogated before, I think Detective François is making me wait on purpose. Again, he wants me to squirm. Using the passive-aggressive interrogation techniques so I'll spill my guts all over the stainless-steel table.

But I have no guts to spill.

Well, I do have guts, of course, but … anyway, the point is … this is not like the last time when I was in this cold, oppressive, little room.

The door opens, and I jump.

Detective François enters the room, his scowl smug and sinister.

"Ms. Carter," says the detective, striding toward the table.

As he approaches, my heart slams, my pulse races, and my mouth goes dry.

"Um … yes …" The reluctant affirmation escapes my mouth as a squeak.

"Do you want to explain what you were doing in Ruth Rice's

home, which happens to still be an active crime scene, and thus off limits to the public ... and the press?" asks François.

I gulp and nod. "Well, you see ... I was looking for clues ..."

"Clues?"

"Evidence to clear my name," I say. "To prove that I didn't kill Ruth Rice."

The detective takes a seat across from me. "A jury of your peers will determine, based on the overwhelming, compelling evidence against you, whether or not they believe you killed Ruth Rice."

"I'm sort of hoping that I don't end up in court," I say. "I'm trying to get the charges against me dropped because I didn't kill Ruth. But ... I think I know who did."

The detective glares at me. "Is that right?"

"Actually, you know the killer, also," I tell him. "She's already in jail."

François says nothing, just stares.

Determined not to let his deafening silence discourage me, I continue, "The person who killed Ruth is the same person you arrested for the murder of Ricardo Miranda—Marlo Miranda."

"And how did you come to that conclusion?"

"Well, I found out that Ricardo Miranda was divorcing Marlo because she's jealous and violent," I say. "And so I talked to one of Marlo's neighbors who told me that Marlo confronted Ruth about talking to Ricardo."

"When did Ruth and Ricardo speak?"

"I'm not sure," I say. "But it was a few days before Marlo killed Ricardo and Ruth."

"What did Ricardo and Ruth talk about?"

Reluctant, I say, "Well ... I don't really know that, either, but ... "

"But?"

"Well, you remember I told you that, before Ruth died, while we were at work, I overheard her talking to someone who threatened her. Ruth told that person they didn't have to kill her."

"Go on," instructs the detective, though he doesn't seem in the least interested in my theories.

Nevertheless, I continue, "I am quite sure that person was Marlo Miranda."

"Are you now?"

Ignoring the detective's condescending smirk, I say, "Well, while Callie and I were at Ruth's house—"

"Callie?"

"My cat," I say, then shake my head. "Well, technically, she's not my cat. She's a cat I know."

"A cat you know?"

Giving the detective a sheepish grin, I say, "Anyway, I listened to the messages on Ruth's phone, which, actually Callie told me to do, and—"

"Wait a minute," the detective interrupts me. "Callie told you to listen to the phone messages? The cat you know ... that Callie?"

Realizing my brain fart, I struggle to swallow the knot in my throat. "Oh, um ... I just meant ... the cat ... jumped on the phone ... probably because she saw the blinking red light and you know how cats are about red lights, always chasing them, and—"

"Get to the point, Ms. Carter," demands the detective, his expression stern.

Clearing my throat, I saw, "Yes, right, of course. Well, anyway, I saw the blinking light indicating that there were messages on the phone, so I decided to listen to them and that's how I heard a message from Ricardo Miranda to Ruth."

The detective glares at me. "And what did the message say?"

"Ricardo was warning Ruth that they couldn't meet anymore or they might be killed," I say. "Callie thinks that Ricardo and Ruth were having an affair, which I sort of find hard to believe because Ruth was beautiful and Marlo's neighbor said Ricardo wasn't the most handsome guy, but—"

"The cat thinks Ricardo Miranda and Ruth Rice were having an affair?"

Flustered, mentally kicking myself for another flub, I shake my head. "No, no, sorry ... I meant, I think they were having an affair and Marlo found out and she killed them."

"And what proof do you have that Marlo killed Ruth?"

"Proof?" I echo, feeling a bit befuddled. "I just told you. Marlo threatened Ruth—"

"You don't know that for sure," the detective says. "Sure, you overheard your coworker telling someone not to kill her, but you don't really know who she was talking to, do you?"

"Well, no … but, I figure it has to be Marlo."

"Because she's jealous and violent?"

"And because Marlo confronted Ruth about talking to Ricardo," I say, trying to temper my exasperation.

"According to a neighbor of Marlo Miranda's, right?"

Nodding, I say, "Right."

"And what makes you think this neighbor was telling the truth?"

"Why would she lie?" I ask.

"Ms. Carter, there are an infinite number of reasons why people don't tell the truth."

"Yes, that's true, however," I say, "I don't think the neighbor was lying because Ruth had a gun."

Francois gives me a sharp look. "A gun?"

Hopeful, I nod. "I found it in her desk drawer. I think she had it to protect herself from Marlo Miranda. Unfortunately, it didn't do her any good."

Eyes narrowed, his gaze vicious, the detective says, "Ms. Carter, do you know what's not doing you any good, at the moment?"

"Well, actually, I don't think there's anything not doing me any good, but—"

"I'm stunned your lawyer got you out on bail, but your freedom is not guaranteed," says the detective. "Bail can, and will be revoked, if my officers catch you snooping around Ruth Rice's home again."

"I wasn't snooping," I protest. "I was trying to—"

"I'm warning you, Ms. Carter," says Francois. "You will end up back in jail until your trial!"

Chapter 37

"That detective suspects you went back to your coworker's house to get rid of evidence you left behind."

Gasping, I drop my purse on the breakfast bar and spin around. I stare toward the foyer, but all I see is the door I just closed. I recognize the voice of that sassy, psycho cat, but I don't see her. Not that I want to see her. After everything I've been through today, the last thing I'm in the mood for is a talking cat who can't really be talking to me. I got home from the police station. I'm still shaken and shell-shocked from Detective François' grueling interrogation, which felt more like an inquisition.

"Down here …"

I glance at my feet.

The cat trots between my ankles and then leaps up onto one of the chairs at the table in the small nook off the galley kitchen.

"How did you get in here?" I ask.

The cat jumps from the chair to the top of the table and sits next to the fake hibiscus flower centerpiece.

"I followed you inside," says the cat. "You held the door open wide as you walked in."

Rolling my eyes, I lean against the breakfast bar. "What do you want?"

"I came to tell you that the detective thinks you went back to your coworker's house to get rid of evidence you left behind."

Panic blooms within me for a moment, but I ignore it. "How do you know that?"

"You're not the only one with sources at the police station," says the cat. "Oh wait. You don't have any sources at the police station."

"Yes, I do …" I dispute, even though I think she might be right.

The cat tilts her head at me. "You're talking about Officer Cuetee?"

"Absolutely," I say. "Who's your source? Some rat in the men's room?"

"A lizard in the supply room."

"A lizard in the supply room." I shake my head. "Why am I not surprised?"

"Anyway, the lizard is tight with one of the Belgian Malinois on the K-9 unit," says the cat. "The dog told the lizard that the detective is certain you were looking for evidence you left behind."

"You and I both know that's not true," I say. "And we also know that Ricardo Miranda called Ruth to warn her about his psycho wife, Marlo, and Ruth obviously took the warning seriously, because she got a gun—"

"Which didn't do her any good," says the cat. "Although it should have. Usually, when someone brings a knife to a gun fight, they end up with a bullet in the head."

"Not necessarily," I say.

The cat gives me a look.

Somewhat offended by her blatant judgment, I'm quick to defend my position. "People don't always get shot in the head during gun fights. Sometimes they're shot in the gut. Or the chest. Or the left pinky toe. Or the—"

"Girl, you know what I mean," hisses the feisty feline.

Shrugging, I say, "Yes, but … " I trail off, thinking about what the cat said.

Callie licks her fur, then says, "Anyway, I think you owe me an apology."

"An apology? For what?"

"I told you that if you wanted to find out who killed your coworker, then you needed to find out who killed the dead man found behind the fruit stand in Guavatown," she says. "And I was right. Marlo Miranda killed her husband, Ricardo, and your coworker, Ruth."

"Yeah, but … " I trail off again, biting my lip.

The cat gives me another look. "But what?"

"But I'm thinking about something you just said," I tell her.

"Something I just said about what?" asks the cat. "You know I say a lot of things."

"Because you're a talking cat."

"A talking cat who only talks to you," says the cat.

I drop down into the chair I jumped up from moments ago. "Are you serious?"

"Listen, here's what I know," says the cat. "You're the only human I can talk to. You're the only human I understand. You're the only human who understands me."

"Are you serious?"

"You already asked that," says the cat.

"So, that means … " I try to come up with a scenario. "Let's say Officer Cuetee and I were talking, and you overheard us … you would understand what I was saying …"

"But I would have no idea what he was saying," says the cat. "You would have to translate for me. And, if I said something to you, it would just sound like me meowing to him …"

"But I would understand every meow you were meowing?"

The cat bobs her head.

"Interesting," I say.

"Don't forget your train of thought, sis," advises the feline. "You were thinking about something I just said, remember?"

"Right," I say. "You were talking about bringing a knife to a gun fight."

"What about it?"

"Well, if Ruth got a gun to protect herself from Marlo, because Ricardo warned her about his crazy, jealous wife, then … why didn't Ruth use the gun when Marlo came at her with a knife?"

"Girl, who knows?" asks the cat. "Maybe the gun didn't have any bullets. Or maybe your coworker didn't know how to shoot a gun. Or maybe she did fire a few rounds, but her aim was off."

"Valid points," I conceded. "But—"

"But nothing, girl," says the cat. "As far as I'm concerned, you've solved the murder of Ricardo Miranda and your coworker."

"Seems that way," I say. "I'm just not sure."

"Girl, you can be sure about this," begins the cat. "Ricardo Miranda called Ruth to warn her about his vengeful, violent wife who he planned to divorce. Ricky knew Marlo was unhinged. Remember, she'd attacked women before."

I nod. "True."

Callie says, "When Marlo saw Ruth, your beautiful coworker, talking to Ricardo, she was so envious that she snapped. First, she shot Ricky to death and then she killed Ruth."

Chapter 38

"Dutiful … what a cool name," I say to Officer Cuetee as Dutiful, the Belgian Malinois who happens to be Officer Cuetee's K-9 partner and one of Callie's sources at the St. Mateo police department, runs around the dog park at Golden Beach with dozens of other canines.

Officer Cuetee and I are sitting next to each other on a bench a few feet from the chain-link fence surrounding the enclosure. This morning, as I drank Hibiscus tea, nibbled on donut holes drizzled with a brown sugar glaze, and ruminated about how to find proof that I didn't kill Ruth, Officer Cuetee texted. He would have a break around two o'clock and would be taking his K-9 partner to the dog park.

Naturally, I agreed to join him, and now here we are.

It's a glorious, sunny afternoon. The kind of Caribbean day that tourist post photos online for likes and comments from people who wish they were here. Even though it's hot, it's not too humid. The blue sky is streaked with white cottony clouds. Every once in a while, a pleasant sea breeze lifts my hair from my shoulders.

"It's the perfect name for him," says Officer Cuetee. "Because that's what he is—dutiful. Reliant. Dependable …"

"There's nothing cool about being obedient," says Callie, curled up in the grass near my feet. "But, that's a dog for you. Canines can always be counted on to do what they're told."

"Unlike cats ..." I remark, picking up on the sarcastic scorn in Callie's tone.

The Calico turns her head to glance at me. "Don't hate me because I'm independent."

"Cats are ... different," says Officer Cuetee.

Callie's ears prick up. "What did he say?"

Bending over, I pretend to tie my shoe and whisper to the cat, "Didn't you hear him?"

"I heard him," says Callie, "But it just sounded like a bunch of weird, discordant sounds. I can't understand him. I can't understand any other humans but you, remember?"

Unfortunately, I do remember that. And I also remember that I don't believe in talking cats and yet I'm re-tying my shoe so I can talk to a talking cat that's probably not even talking to me.

Callie slaps her paw against my fingers. "What did he say?"

"He said cats are ... delightful," I say, deciding not to get the feline riled up.

The cat's eyes narrow. "Why don't I believe you?"

Rolling my eyes, I raise up, lean back against the bench, and focus on the cute officer. "So ... I think I might have figured out who killed Ruth Rice."

Officer Cuetee frowns. "Who?"

"I think Marlo Miranda did it," I say, glancing toward the Belgian Malinois who jumps around with a German Shepherd and two Doberman Pinchers in what seems to be a game of tag. "That's my theory, anyway."

Although, technically, it's Callie's theory. I'm just going along with it, for now, because it seems plausible. I keep ruminating on Callie's conclusion but I'm not convinced. I'm still thinking about Marlo bringing a knife to a gun fight. I don't believe that Ruth wouldn't have used the gun to protect herself. I also wonder why Marlo, who had a gun, which she supposedly used to shoot Ricky, didn't use the same gun to kill Ruth. It would have been easier for Marlo to shoot Ruth.

Killing a person with a knife is risky … and personal. Which makes me wonder why Marlo didn't stab Ricardo, the man who betrayed her? And I haven't forgotten what Ruth's friend said about the dangerous story she was working on. What if Ruth got the gun to protect herself from some South American criminal she wrote a story about?

"Why do you think Marlo Miranda killed Ruth Rice?" asks Officer Cuetee.

"Well, Callie thinks that—"

"Who is Callie?" interrupts Officer Cuetee.

"This is Callie," I say, waving a hand down toward the cat. "The Calico … Callie the Calico."

Officer Cuetee smiles at the cat. "Callie the Calico. That's cute."

"Isn't it?" I agree. "When she first told me, I—"

"When she first told you?" Officer Cuetee frowns. "Who is … she?"

Mentally kicking myself for misspeaking again, I say, "Oh, um, the—"

"What is he asking about me?" The cat wants to know. "Don't put my business in the street! I expect to have my privacy respected."

Ignoring the cat, I focus on Officer Cuetee. "I have no proof of this, but I think—"

"Girl, forget about what *you* think," the cat tells me. "Tell the cute officer why you believe Marlo Miranda killed her husband and your coworker. Then he can tell the detective and you can clear your name."

"I was about to do that," I say out of the side of my mouth.

"About to do what?" asks Officer Cuetee, who obviously heard me.

"Oh, um, I just meant … " I clear my throat. "It's possible that Marlo was jealous of Ruth and killed her because she thought Ruth and Ricky were fooling around."

Officer Cuetee nods. "Romantic rivalry is a powerful motive. A woman scorned …"

"Yes, but … " I sigh. "I'm not so sure."

"Girl, I know you are not about to bore Officer Good Looking with your hare-brained theory," says Callie.

I glance down at her. "I don't have a hare-brained theory."

"You don't have a theory at all," hisses the feline.

"What's that about a hare-brained theory?"

I shake my head. "Marlo Miranda is a good suspect. I'm just not sure she killed Ruth. Especially since a friend of Ruth's told me that she was working on a story about some dangerous people. And I wonder if maybe these bad guys she was planning to write about maybe have—"

"Girl, do you want to clear your name, or not?" demands the cat. "You're not supposed to be clearing Marlo as a suspect. You're supposed to be convincing Officer Good Looking that she's the murderer!"

"Your cat seems to be trying to get your attention," remarks Officer Cuetee.

"Yes, she can be a little annoying at times," I say. "But I'll deal with her later."

Seconds later, a paw slaps at my ankle. Twice.

Gasping, I glance down. "Excuse you?"

"Don't ignore me," says Callie.

"I'm not ignoring you," I say. "We'll talk later, okay?"

Officer Cuetee laughs.

"What?" I ask, entranced by his dimples.

"Just kinda cute how you talk to your cat like you can really understand what she's saying."

For a second, I freeze.

"What did he say?" demands Callie. "Is he talking about me? You better warn him not to get on my bad side. I don't care how cute he is —and he is very cute—I will scratch those pretty blue eyes right out of his head!"

"Aw, she's a noisy little thing, isn't she?" Officer Cuetee bends over slightly, reaching his arm toward Callie.

"No ... " I grab his wrist before he makes the mistake of trying to pet her.

He frowns at me. "What is it? I was just going to scratch behind her ears."

"What is he saying?" asks Callie. "Tell me!"

"Um, she doesn't always like to be touched," I say, giving him a quick smile before I glance down at Callie. "Will you calm down? What's got you so upset?"

"Girl, don't tell me to calm down," warns Callie. "And you know why I'm upset. I know he's probably casting aspersions on my character and you're letting him do it. Some human you are!"

"Will you chill out," I whisper through gritted teeth. "He is not talking about you."

Hissing, Callie narrows her eyes and then turns her back to me.

Sighing, I roll my eyes and then turn back to Officer Cuetee.

His gaze is wary. "Everything okay?"

I give him a bright smile. "She's just being irritating."

A paw slaps my ankle again.

"Anyway …" I say. "Even if Marlo did kill Ruth, I still have to find proof that she killed her, which I haven't exactly done."

"Girl, tell him about Marlo being violently jealous and attacking women for even thinking about taking to Ricardo," the cat says. "And tell him that Ricardo called Ruth and warned her about his crazy wife. That's all the proof you need."

Reaching down to my foot, I pretend to scratch my ankle again so I can tell the cat, "Actually, I need more proof than that."

"More proof that what?" asks Officer Cuetee.

"Oh, well, it's just that the proof I have about Marlo killing Ruth is circumstantial," I say, then divulge the information about Marlo's violent tendencies and Ricardo's dire warnings.

"Finally!" exclaims Callie, licking her right paw. "It's about time you told him! Now can we please get out of here? These dogs are giving me hives."

I stare at the annoying feline. "Hives?"

"Canines always aggravate my allergies," announces the cat.

"How do you have allergies?" I ask. "You are an allergy."

Eyes narrowed, the cat hisses at me.

"Sophie …?" asks Officer Cuetee. "Is your cat okay?"

"She's not my cat," I tell him, making a mental note: Don't talk to the cat and Officer Cuetee at the same time. "And she's okay, but I think all the dogs are getting on her nerves. Maybe we should go."

"Well before you do," says Officer Cuetee. "There is one thing I can tell you about the investigation."

"What?"

"Ruth's fingernails were scraped," says Officer Cuetee. "Apparently, she scratched her attacker, so François is hoping to get a DNA match."

"If the CSI team finds Marlo's DNA beneath Ruth's nails, that could be the proof I need to clear my name," I say, excited, my hopes rising. "Detective Francois will have to drop the charges against me."

"Sophie, I hate to tell you this," says Officer Cuetee.

Wary, I ask, "What?"

"Unfortunately, Detective François is convinced the crime lab will find *your* DNA beneath Ruth's fingernails."

Chapter 39

The crime lab will find your DNA beneath Ruth's fingernails.

Officer Cuetee's words swirl in my mind, making me feel anxious, nervous, panicked, and a bit frustrated. Since I arrived at my apartment an hour ago, I've been pacing my living room, which isn't large at all, so it doesn't take me very long to go from one end to the other and back again.

I can't believe Detective François believes the crime lab will find my DNA beneath Ruth's fingernails. It's ridiculous. Ruth didn't scratch me. Detective François is wrong about me. I didn't kill Ruth.

After making myself a steaming mug of orange and lavender tea, I take a quick sip and then head out onto the small back porch connected to my apartment. The sun will be setting soon. I figure I'll enjoy the last rays of the day and watch the orange globe descend into the horizon, leaving behind an ombre of pink and purple hues.

I walk to the wooden railing and lean over it.

"You know what they say about people who drink alone, don't you?"

That sassy sarcasm makes me roll my eyes as I glance over my shoulder.

Callie sits on the chaise lounge, curled up, making herself comfortable.

Shaking my head, I face the Calico. "You again?"

"You know you missed me," says the cat, licking her fur.

It's been a few days since I've seen the feisty feline, and while she was nowhere to be found, and I was desperately trying to think of how to prove that Marlo Miranda killed Ruth and Ricardo, I realized that I did miss the sassy Calico. Not that I was worried about her, though. I figured she was off somewhere being independent, making her own rules, or whatever.

Not having her around was very peaceful.

Dealing with her sarcastic sass is beyond annoying, especially since I'm still not sure she's really talking to me. I mean, what am I thinking? Of course, Callie isn't talking to me. Because of my fever and the coma, and the trauma that psycho cat put me through, I'm just imagining she's talking. For some reason, my mind is tricking me into thinking I can understand her meowing. It's probably some weird PTSD symptom. I am sure with the passing of time—and maybe some therapy—I'll stop thinking the crazy Calico is speaking to me.

"Girl, what are you drinking?"

"Jasmine and elderberry tea."

The cat makes a face. "Girl, do you want me to gag?"

"It's great for the immune system."

"Girl, forget about your immune system," says the cat. "You need to figure out how to prove that Marlo Miranda killed your coworker."

"I've been thinking about that," I say. "I keep thinking about when I heard Ruth on the phone with someone who was threatening her."

"It was probably Marlo," Callie says.

"That's what I'm thinking," I say. "I need to prove that Marlo called Ruth, and I think I could do that because I have Ruth's phone."

"You should be able to find Marlo's number in Ruth's call log," says Callie. "That's your proof."

Nodding, I take another sip of tea. "The problem is that, although I have Ruth's phone, I can't get into it. It can only be unlocked with

Ruth's face. She had biometric protection instead of a password. And, since Ruth is dead, I don't have her face to unlock her phone."

"Can't you use a photo of her?"

"That did cross my mind," I admit. "But when I researched using a photo to unlock a phone, I found out that it doesn't always work."

"Girl, you should at least try."

"I would if I had a photo of Ruth, but I don't," I say. "We weren't friends. So, we never took any pictures together, or … ohmigoodness!"

"Girl, what is it?" demands the cat, jumping to all fours, back arched.

I jump up from the stool. "The *Palmchat Gazette* website! There's a page highlighting the staff. All of our photos, along with bios, are on that page."

"Well, don't just stand there," Callie says. "Get your coworker's photo from the website."

Excited and galvanized, I finish my tea, put the mug on the counter and hurry into my bedroom to get my laptop.

Half an hour later, my excitement has been replaced by disappointment.

"Where's your coworker's picture?" asks the cat, staring at the laptop screen. I've got the *Palmchat Gazette* website pulled up, and I'm on the staff page. Marty's photo is at the top, followed by a few other senior reporters. I'm on the bottom row, but I don't mind too much. The photo is rather fetching. But it's not cute enough to temper my frustration.

"It's gone," I say, focused on the second row of photos, where Ruth's photo should be … but it isn't. "The paper must have removed it after she was murdered."

The cat says, "Guess it makes sense. She doesn't work there anymore."

"But that photo was the only chance I had to get into Ruth's phone," I grumble, closing my laptop. "What am I going to do now?"

Callie says, "Girl, who took the staff photo of your coworker?"

I glance at the Calico. "Clark took the photos. Wait … why did you ask me who took the staff photos?"

"Because the photographer might have copies of the photos he took," says the cat.

Smiling, I say, "You might be right."

"Girl, I'm always right!"

Chapter 40

"How did you get Ruth's phone?" asks Clark, sitting at the kitchen table across from me.

Yesterday, after the cat suggested that Clark, who'd taken Ruth's staff photo, might have a digital copy of the photo he took, I gave him a call, explaining my predicament. Clark wasn't able to come to my place because he was working, but he agreed to stop by my apartment before he headed into work this morning.

Somewhat sheepish, I say, "Well, I sort of ... found her phone."

Taking a sip of his coffee, Clark gives me a smirk. "Found her phone?"

"It was in a box in her cube and I ..."

"You found it in a box in her cube?" Clark says, nodding, looking as though he's suppressing a laugh.

Exhaling, I shrug. "Okay, so I took it. I know I shouldn't have, but I was thinking about the person who threatened her—"

"Wait," Clark stops me. "Someone threatened Ruth? When? How do you know that?"

I take a sip of tea, then tell Clark about the day I overheard Ruth talking to someone who threatened her. "Obviously, I only heard Ruth's side of the conversation but she told whoever she was talking to that the person didn't have to threaten her. And I'm wondering if Ruth was talking to this person on her phone—"

"The phone you found in her box?" teases Clark.

Wishing he'd be serious, I say, "Right. That's why I need to get into Ruth's phone. I need to check the phone log to see if I can find out who threatened her. I need to check the calls Ruth made on the day she was threatened. Then I can research the numbers and maybe come up with some names to give Detective Francois."

"Well, I've got the photos I took of Ruth," Clark says, pulling out his phone.

Trying not to get my hopes up, but unable to temper my excitement, I hurry out of the kitchen and into my bedroom, where I retrieve Ruth's phone from my bedside table drawer.

Ten minutes later, in the breakroom, Clark says, "Bingo ..."

My heart hammering, I stare at him. "Bingo? What does that mean?"

Clark looks up and smiles, waving Ruth's phone. "It means we're in ..."

"Wait. What?" For a second, I'm flabbergasted. "You got into Ruth's phone?"

Clark smiles. "I did!"

"I can't believe it worked!"

"Well, it did," says Clark.

"Let's check the call history log," I say.

Clark presses an icon. "Okay let me ... oh, shoot ..."

"What?" I ask, worried that the phone will automatically lock itself despite the fact that Clark reset the phone, so it won't lock again.

"I opened Ruth's text messages," says Clark. "I hit the wrong app."

"Does she have any texts?" I ask.

"Yeah, but not very many," says Clark, frowning. "You want to see what they say?"

"Sure, but let's check the call log first," I tell him.

Clark taps the screen, then swipes up a few times, frowning. "Hmmm ..."

"What is it?"

"Lots of calls to South America," says Clark. "I recognize the country code because my parents did missionary work there."

"Missionary work?"

"I'll tell you about it some other time," Clark says. "But it seems as though Ruth used this phone to call someone in South America."

"Well, that actually makes sense," I say, recalling what Ruth's friend Zeke Kelly told me. "Ruth used to work in South America."

Clark nods. "That's right. I think Candace mentioned that."

"She probably had friends there that she stayed in contact with," I say.

"What date was it when you heard Ruth being threatened?" Clark asks.

I tell him, then ask, "Does she have any calls on that day?"

Brows furrowed, Clark says, "Several. Two different South American numbers."

Grabbing my own phone, I open a notetaking app. "Tell me the numbers. One of them just might be the person who called Ruth and threatened her. Maybe I can trace the numbers."

"Yeah, you should be able to …" Clark trails off, then continues, "Wait a minute …"

"What?" I ask.

"I was wrong … looks like someone else did call Ruth on the day you heard her being threatened. A Palmchat Islands number. Actually, a local St. Mateo number."

"I wonder who it was," I ask.

Clark recites the number, then says, "The same St. Mateo number is also in Ruth's text message log. Ruth received a message from the St. Mateo number a few days before Ruth was killed."

"What does the message say?" I ask.

Clark reads: "*'You need to stay away from my husband … or else.'* Interesting. Any idea who the message is from?"

After a slow sigh, I say, "If I had to guess, I would say … Marlo Miranda."

Clark says, "Let's find out if you're right."

Nodding, I say, "We can trace the number."

"We can do better than that," Clark says. "Let's call her."

Frowning, I say, "I think Marlo is still in jail."

"Then we'll leave a message," says Clark, dialing the number, then pressing the 'Speaker' button.

My heart pounds in a mixture of fear, excitement, and indecision as the line rings. Seconds later, the voice mail is activated. "Hey, It's Marlo … leave me a message.".

Chapter 41

"I think I found proof that Marlo Miranda killed Ruth," I announce, hardly able to contain my excitement, or even enjoy my tea, a blend of apple, honeysuckle, and caramel.

His expression curious, Officer Cuetee stares at me. "You did?"

We're sitting across from each other in a booth at With a Capital Tea, a tea shop near the beach that has a coastal hippy vibe. After spending most of the night contemplating the developments in my quest to prove my innocence, namely that Marlo Miranda called Ruth on the day she was threatened, I woke up with renewed vigor and hope, anxious to share my news.

Which, after a sip of my delicious tea, I do, explaining how Clark and I were able to access Ruth's cell phone and investigate her texts, call log, and voice messages.

"So," I start my conclusion, "it's very possibly, highly likely, in fact, that Ruth was talking to Marlo Miranda the day when I heard her being threatened. She was telling Marlo that she didn't have to kill her. And you know what else?"

Officer Cuetee pops a donut hole drizzled with dark and white chocolate ganache into his mouth and asks, "What?"

"Clark and I were able to confirm that Marlo also sent threatening texts to Ruth," I say. "Ruth had text messages warning her to … stay away from my man, or else … and I suspected Marlo sent them and as it turns out, the number associated with those texts was Marlo Miranda's number. So you see—"

"Marlo Miranda had a motive for killing Ruth Rice," says Officer Cuetee, looking contemplative as he scratches his chin, then stifles a yawn.

"Which is what I told Detective Francois, but he didn't believe me." I take a sip of tea, savoring the flavors as I take a moment to gawk at the officer. I know I shouldn't be shallow, especially when we're discussing crucial evidence that could prove I'm not a stone-cold killer, but he's so handsome, I can't help it.

Officer Cuetee yawns again. "Sorry. Well, actually, he might believe you, considering the latest developments in Ruth's murder case."

"The latest developments?" I ask.

"Remember I told you the CSI techs were testing the blood and skin found beneath Ruth's fingernails?" asks Officer Cuetee, then covers his mouth as he yawns a third time.

Amused, I ask, "Wait. Am I boring you? You keep yawning."

"No, sorry about that," he says, sheepish. "I had a late night. Had to break up a bar fight. One of the guys flicked cigarette ash into another guy's drink."

"Rude."

Officer Cuetee nods. "Yeah, so the guy punched him a few times. Wasn't much of a fight. The victim – cigarette guy – went to the hospital and we arrested the guy who punched him. Anyway … what was I saying?"

"Oh, the CSI techs were testing the skin beneath Ruth's nails," I remind him.

"It was an indication that she'd probably scratched her attacker."

Sighing, I say, "And you said Detective Francois expected to find my DNA under her nails, but he won't."

"You were right," says Officer Cuetee, stirring his cinnamon and pear blend. "He didn't.."

For some reason, my heart starts to slam. "Whose blood and skin was it?"

Officer Cuetee says, "It was ... Marlo Miranda's DNA."

Chapter 42

"So, I was right," announces the sassy Calico. "I told you that the person who killed your coworker was the same person who killed the guy they found behind that fruit stand in Guavatown."

Twenty minutes ago, the cat showed up on my patio while I was relaxing with a cup of vanilla and jasmine tea. I told her about my conversation with Officer Cuetee, and the new developments with Ruth's murder case.

"Yeah, you did say that," I tell the cat. "And you were right."

"Is that detective going to drop the charges against you?" Callie asks, licking her fur.

"Not exactly," I tell her. "My lawyer says this is good for my case and creates reasonable doubt, but it isn't enough to get the charges against me dropped."

"That's stupid." The cat hisses. "He's got all the evidence he needs to arrest Marlo Miranda. She's got motive, means, and opportunity."

"You and I know that," I say, taking another sip of tea. "But Detective Francois seems stuck on the fact that my fingerprints were on the murder weapon."

"Girl, that detective sounds like a dingbat," Callie says. "It's a wonder any crime gets solved on this island with his faulty logic."

"I agree," I tell the cat. "Which is why I have to take matters into my own hands."

The cat gives me a look. "What does that mean?"

"I need to talk to Marlo Miranda," I say. "The evidence against her is compelling. She sent threatening texts to Ruth. She left a threatening voice mail. And she called Ruth on the day that I overheard her being threatened. It's likely that Ruth was talking to Marlo that day when she said, you don't have to kill me. But despite all that, I think Detective Francois is going to drag his feet. I need to give him compelling evidence. I need to give him Marlo Miranda's confession to the murder of Ruth."

"Good idea, girl," says the cat. "You think Marlo will come clean?"

"I'm not sure," I admit. "It won't be easy to get her to spill her guts. But maybe I can trick her into incriminating herself. If so—"

"Okay, let's go ..." says the cat, rising to all four feet.

I stare at her. "Go ...where?"

"Let's go talk to Marlo Miranda."

"Now?"

"Why not?" asks the cat. "The sooner you talk to her, the sooner you can make her confess to the murder of your coworker and clear your name!"

Chapter 43

"I didn't kill Ruth Rice," says Marlo Miranda as she tosses feed to the dozen or so chickens clucking and scratching the dry, dusty soil with their three-toed feet.

Marlo's last attempt to be granted bail worked and she was released from jail a couple of days ago. We're in her backyard, a large clearing of dirt surrounded by tropical trees and bushes.

"Marlo, I want to be honest with you," I say, glancing at the chicken coop along the back fence. A few feet away, surrounded by poultry netting, are a handful of chicks, squeaking and squealing. The chick's excitement may be due to Callie, who made her way over there after circling and weaving through the chickens, a few of which she hissed at. "I know that you sent Ruth a threatening text message. And that your DNA was found beneath Ruth's fingernails."

"Okay, I'll be honest with you." Marlo delves a hand into the bag of feed and tosses it toward her chickens. They scramble and squawk, wings flapping and fluttering as they pick at the crumbled grains with their beaks. "Yes, I did send Ruth that message. But not because I wanted to kill her. I wanted her to stay away from my husband. She was calling him every other day, at all times of the day and night. And I wanted her to know that I knew she was doing. I knew she was trying to steal Ricardo from me, because who wouldn't want Ricardo? He was the most perfect specimen of a man …"

Recalling the description of Ricardo that Marlo's neighbor gave me, I'm inclined to disagree, but I don't interrupt Marlo as she continues.

"And, yes, I did allow my jealousy to get the best of me," admits Marlo. "And I shouldn't have done what I did …"

"You mean, you shouldn't have killed Ruth Rice?" I ask, hopeful that Marlo will accidentally incriminate herself.

Waving a dismissive hand, Marlo says, "No, that's not what I mean! What I shouldn't have done was … go to Ruth Rice's house the day she was killed."

"So you were there," I confirm, my mind racing, wondering how I'll get her to come clean, or if I can, as it seems she's sticking to her story about not killing Ruth.

"Only because Ruth asked me to come," says Marlo, tossing more feed.

Confused, I stare at her. "What?"

"On the day she was killed, Ruth called me and asked if I would meet with her at her house," Marlo says. "She needed to talk to me about something very important. And I assumed she was going to confess that she'd been in love with Ricardo and tell me that before he was killed, they were going to run away and be together. I won't lie, if that had happened, I probably would have strangled her, but that wasn't what she wanted to talk about."

"Why did she want to see you?" I ask, my attention drifting toward the sassy Calico, who is now near the coop, hissing at three hens who cluck and flutter vigorously.

"Ruth wanted to know if Ricardo had told me anything about a news story she was working on," says Marlo, frowning.

"A news story?"

"Ruth told me that she'd been writing a secret expose about some dangerous criminals," Marlo explains. "And she said the reason she'd been calling Ricardo so much was because he was helping her."

"Helping her how?" I ask, recalling Ruth's friend, Zeke Kelly, who told me about the story Ruth had secretly been working on.

"Ruth claimed that Ricardo was her confidential informant." Marlo swipes a palm across her damp forehead.

"Did you know Ricardo had information on criminal activities?"

"Of course, I knew nothing about that," Marlo says. "Ricardo hadn't told me anything about helping Ruth with a story. Ruth was very nervous and worried that day. She told me that I needed to be careful. She said that the people she'd been investigating were ruthless and if they suspected that Ricardo had confided in me, they might come after me … just like they'd come after Ricardo."

My heart slams. "What?"

"Hey, your cat's not dangerous, is she?"

"Hmmm…" I follow Marlo's gaze to the chicken coop, where Callie and the hens continue to congregate.

"You need to get her away from my hens," warns Marlo.

"Oh. Um. She's not my cat," I say.

"Not your cat?" Marlo scowls, eyes narrowed. "She walked into my house with you."

"Yes. That's true, but …" I clear my throat. "We have a … complicated relationship."

"Complicated relationship?"

"What I mean to say is … she's not dangerous at all," I tell Marlo, which of course, is a complete lie, considering Callie's psychotic tendencies, which I suffered firsthand. "Anyway … I want to get something straight. Ruth told you that the dangerous criminals she'd been investigating came after Ricardo?"

Scowling, Marlo says, "She told me those crooks might have killed Ricardo because he'd been helping her. And that's when I lost it."

Confused, I ask, "You lost it?"

Marlo shrugs. "I attacked her …"

Chapter 44

"I didn't do as much damage as I could have." Marlo reaches into the feed bag and then scatters more grain on the ground. "I slapped her a few times. Kicked her. Scratched her. And that's how my DNA ended up under her fingernails, which I told the detective when he questioned me. But Ruth wasn't a helpless victim. She punched me. In the gut, of all places. And then when I was doubled over, the wind knocked out of me, and trying to breathe, do you know what she did?"

"Um … she karate chopped you in the back of your neck?" I ask, glancing toward the chicken coop. The hens are still squawking, and Callie is bobbing her head. For some reason, I get the feeling that the cat and the chickens are having a conversation. Which makes no sense because chickens don't talk. And neither do cats, I remind myself. But, Callie does talk. To me, at least. Although, I have no proof the cat is really talking to me since—

"I thought she might do that," says Marlo. "Or maybe give me an uppercut to the chin. But no. She hustled me out after the guy called out her name."

"A guy called out her name?" I ask. "What guy?"

Marlo shrugs. "I have no idea. I didn't see him. I just heard him call her name and then she told me I had to leave. She said, you can't be here. If he sees you, he'll kill you."

"And you have no idea who she was talking about?"

"I wasn't going to stick around to find out," Marlo says. "I left through the back door, and made my out through the backyard, which I also told the detective when he questioned me about my DNA under Ruth's nails."

"So, on the day Ruth died, someone was in the house with her?" I ask, contemplating this new development.

Marlo nods. "Some guy. After I found out that Ruth had been killed, I probably should have gone to the cops immediately and told them about the guy in her house, but I didn't want to look like a vengeful, jilted wife who'd killed her husband, then attacked his mistress. Then I read that the police arrested you, so ..."

Exasperated, I say, "But I didn't kill Ruth."

"Yeah, and I didn't kill Ricardo," says Marlo. "But the cops think I did because they believe my gun was used to murder him. And your fingerprints were on the knife used to kill Ruth, so you must have done it, but you say you didn't."

Sighing, I say, "We're kind of in the same predicament."

"I didn't kill Ricardo and you didn't kill Ruth," says Marlo. "But someone did. I think it was the same person. And whoever it is plans to get away with murder by blaming us for his crimes."

Fifteen minutes later, I'm in the JEEP, with the Calico, heading back to my apartment.

"By the way," I say to Callie as I navigate the curving roads through Marlo's neighborhood. "You weren't trying to attack those hens, were you?"

She glances over at me and hisses. "Chicken? Girl, please. I prefer tuna. And, for your information, I was getting information for you."

"What kind of information?"

"On the day that Marlo was arrested," says Callie, "a man jumped the fence into the backyard and broke into the house."

"How do you know that?" I ask, turning onto the main road that leads back to my neighborhood.

"The hens told me," says the cat. "One of the hens went up onto the back porch and saw him through the screen door, which was open. He was looking in a box that was on the kitchen table."

"What was he looking for?"

"How should I know?" says the cat. "But the hen says he almost set her on fire."

Alarmed, I ask, "What?"

"Apparently, he was smoking," says the cat. "The hen followed him into the house since he'd left the screen door open. She walked inside and flew up onto the table. He yelled at her to get away and then flicked his cigarette at her. The cigarette was still lit and it landed on her and her feathers almost caught fire."

"That's terrible," I say, braking at a traffic light.

"Girl, she's fine," says the cat. "Now tell me what happened with Marlo. Did you get her to confess that she killed your coworker?"

"Not exactly ..."

"Well, what exactly did you talk about?" Callie demands. "The two of you were over there yapping for a long time. If she wasn't confessing, what was she saying?"

After giving Callie the details about my conversation with Marlo, I say, "But now I'm wondering if maybe Marlo didn't kill Ruth."

The cat hisses at me. "Girl, don't tell me you believed that story about Ruth telling her to leave before some guy killed her?"

"It could be true," I say, accelerating around a traffic circle.

"And it could be goatwash," says the cat, licking her fur. "Something she made up to hide her guilt. She wants you to think that Ruth was killed by the guy who was in the house with her."

"But what if Ruth was killed by that guy?" I ask, making the turn onto the main boulevard that runs through downtown St. Mateo.

"Girl, you don't even know who the mystery guy is," says the cat.

"Maybe it was the person Ruth was writing the secret expose about," I suggest. "Marlo told me that Ruth said Ricardo was her confidential informant and the dangerous criminals she was planning to expose might have killed him. What if the dangerous criminal showed up at Ruth's house to kill her so she wouldn't publish the expose?"

"Well, if that's true," says the cat, licking her toe beans, "then you have to find out about the story Ruth was working on. Who is the dangerous criminal she was going to expose?"

Nodding, I ask, "And how do I find out?"

Chapter 45

How do I find out the name of the dangerous criminal Ruth was going to expose...

The next morning, ruminating on the question that's remained in my head since I talked to Marlo Miranda yesterday, I stare at the bowl of tropical fruit on the countertop of the breakfast bar in my kitchen.

I woke up early, roused from a fitful sleep, anxious to escape strange dreams about guavas and rice. During my shower, I stood under the hot stream of water and thought about what the dream meant. Now, admittedly, initially, I thought I'd dreamed up a new recipe—guava rice. Sort of like mango rice, a Palmchat Island staple. But I'm not sure guava and rice would work together the way mango and rice blend so deliciously, so I figured there had to be another interpretation of the dream.

While toweling off, I concluded that the dream had something to do with the murders of Ruth Rice and Ricardo Miranda. I dreamed of rice because that's Ruth's last name. And I dreamed about guavas because Ricardo's body was discovered behind that fruit stand in Guavatown.

Obviously, it was some kind of stress dream. If I don't discover who killed Ruth—who I believe is the same person who killed Ricardo —then I might spend the rest of my life in jail.

The question remains: Who is the criminal that Ruth planned to expose?

And how do I find out?

Walking into the kitchen, I grab a mug from the cabinet and a box of tea strawberry infused tea, which I plan to have with kiwi-glazed donut holes.

As far as I know, the only people who know the identity of the dangerous criminal are Ruth Rice and Ricardo Miranda. Both of whom are dead. Both of whom were killed by the same person, which I'm certain of …

And I'm equally certain that the person who killed Ruth and Ricardo wasn't Marlo Miranda, despite the evidence against her, which makes her look guilty. I don't think Marlo shot Ricardo. She was too head over heels in love with him to kill him. And I believe Marlo when she insisted Ruth was still alive when Marlo left her house.

I grab the tea kettle, cross to the sink and fill it with water.

Something I keep thinking about is how Ricardo became Ruth's confidential informant. He must have had information about the person Ruth was investigating. Which means Ricardo must have known the dangerous criminal. But how? Did Ricardo and the criminal have some sort of connection? Maybe a more thorough investigation of Ricardo Miranda might yield clues as to the identity of the criminal. Maybe I need to find out more about Ricardo.

Setting the kettle on the stove, I resolve to do more in-depth research of Ricardo. Something in his background might—

My phone rings.

Heading into the living room, I grab it from the coffee table and answer.

"Hi, um … is Sophie Carter available?"

"This is Sophie Carter," I say, curious, not recognizing the voice.

"Ms. Carter, this is Zeke Kelly, Ruth's friend … I'm not sure if you remember me, but—"

"Oh, yes, of course, I remember you," I say. "How are you? What's going on?"

"Um, I was hoping that we could talk," says Zeke. "I need to see you. Could you come to my motel room? It's important."

Curious, I ask, "Could you tell me what it's about?"

"Ruth's murder," says Zeke. "I think I know why she was killed ..."

Chapter 46

Twenty minutes later, I'm knocking on the motel room door of Zeke Kelly.

As I wait, staring at the peeling paint on the weather-beaten wood, a gusty wind blows my curly coils across my face. It's a blustery, overcast day in St. Mateo. The sky is a swirling mix of grays, from slate to nickel to gunmetal with a low cloud deck. The sharp briny scent of impending rain mixes with the saltiness of the sea, a foreboding fragrance that makes me worried and wary.

Driving to Neptune Inn and Suites, I kept ruminating about what Zeke Kelly told me about Ruth's murder. I think I know why she was killed. What does he mean by that? How did he find out? What is he going to tell me? Zeke didn't want to talk over the phone, so I was forced to dress quickly and hurry out of my apartment.

Now that I'm here, I'm anxious and reluctant, but also hopeful.

Maybe, just maybe, what Zeke tells me will be a significant clue, something I can share with Detective Francois, something that will convince him to drop the charges against me and—

The motel door swings open abruptly.

Zeke Kelly stares at me, his expression frantic and furtive, eyes darting, but his manic nervousness isn't the only thing I notice about him.

His face looks gaunt and mottled.

There's a purplish bruise around his right eye, his bottom lip is split, and a faded yellowish-greenish bruise appears smeared across his left cheek.

"Oh my God ..." I gasp, shocked by his injuries, taking a slight step back.

"Looks worse than it is," says Zeke, stepping back, ushering me into his motel room. "Hurry and come in."

I step over the threshold and immediately have to clear my throat. The smell of cigarettes permeates the room, making my nostrils flare as my eyes water from the thin haze of smoke.

"You weren't followed, were you?" Zeke asks, grabbing a pack of cigarettes from the bed table.

"Followed?" I echo, frowning. "Who would have followed me?"

Zeke lights the cigarette with shaking fingers, then takes a long drag before exhaling a stream of smoke toward the ceiling. "You probably weren't. You wouldn't have known if you had been."

Shaking my head, I say, "I don't understand."

Pacing in front of the bed, Zeke takes another drag on the cigarette, then says, "You remember I told you Ruth was working on a secret expose?"

I nod. "About some dangerous criminal."

"Yeah, well, that dangerous criminal decided to use my face as a punching bag," Zeke says.

"What happened?" I ask.

Zeke says, "The guy was waiting for me in my motel room when I got home from dinner a few nights ago. Don't know if he broke it or bribed the motel clerk. Doesn't matter. He started asking me questions about the story Ruth was working on."

"What kind of questions?" I ask.

"Wanted to know what Ruth had found out about the man she was investigating," Zeke says, then takes another quick puff. "Wanted to know were her files were. I told him I had no idea. Of course, he didn't believe me. He knew Ruth and I were good friends, and that she must have confided in me. But she didn't. Ruth told me she was working on an explosive story, but she specifically said she didn't want me to know the details so I wouldn't become a target."

"But you did become a target," I say, grimacing inwardly at Zeke's horrible bruises, thinking of how he must have suffered, how confused and afraid he must have been.

"Thought the guy was going to kill me," Zeke says. "He beat me until I passed out. I woke up the next afternoon."

Alarmed, I ask, "Did you go to the emergency room? You might have a concussion."

"I didn't leave this room," Zeke says. "I haven't left since it happened and I'm not going to, but ..."

"But?" I prompt.

Finishing the cigarette, Zeke flicks it into a small trash can beneath the desk against the wall. "The guy threatened me. Told me he'd kill me if I didn't find the information Ruth had collected during her investigation. He said the information is on a jump drive."

"A jump drive?"

Zeke drops down onto the edge of the bed. "I have no idea where it is. I thought it might be in the box of stuff that your coworker gave me, but I've gone through those boxes a hundred times and it's not in there. I have no idea where it could be."

"Maybe it's somewhere in Ruth's house," I suggest.

"I thought of that," Zeke says. "But her house is still considered a crime scene so it's not like I can get inside."

"But if you tell the police—"

"I can't go to the police," Zeke says, eyes wide with fear. "That guy will kill me if I do. He said he would know if I went to the cops. He's watching me. Oh God ... I'm so stupid!"

"What do you mean?" I ask, venturing toward the bed.

His gaze tortured, Zeke says, "I shouldn't have asked you to come over her. He's watching me! He probably saw you enter my motel room."

Ignoring my apprehension, I say, "Well, even if that's true, he doesn't know why I'm here."

Reaching for the pack of cigarettes again, Zeke says, "I've made you a target, too."

I push away my worries, and sit on the opposite end of the bed. "I can take care of myself. What I'm most concerned with is finding out who killed Ruth. You said you knew why she was killed—"

"The guy who beat me up killed her," says Zeke, lighting his cigarette. "He wants that jump drive. He killed Ruth so she wouldn't expose his boss."

"Who is his boss?"

Zeke blows smoke away from me. "I have no idea. Some powerful drug lord, probably. He sent a henchman to get rid of Ruth and destroy the information Ruth discovered about him."

"How does he know that Ruth put the information on a jump drive?"

Zeke shakes his head. "Don't know that, either. Maybe he's just assuming she did."

Sighing, I say, "Listen … if some drug lord sent a hitman to kill Ruth, then the police need to know—"

"No cops!" Zeke jumps up and starts to pace again. "That guy will kill me if—"

"Okay, okay," I say, trying to keep him from crashing out. "I won't call the police"

Zeke stares at me. "But there is something you can do."

"What?"

Exhaling, Zeke says, "Can you search for the jump drive in Ruth's cubicle at the newspaper? Maybe she hid it there."

"She might have," I say, thinking it's entirely possible. "But if I find it …"

"Then you have to give it to me," says Zeke, stark, cold fear in his gaze. "And I'll give it to the henchman, so he can destroy it."

Hesitant, I ask, "But what if I don't find the jump drive?"

Zeke Kelly looks away. "Then I'm a dead man."

Chapter 47

Callie sniffs me, then gags. "Girl, you smell like a chimney!"

Sighing, I grab the collar of my shirt and bring it to my nose. The cigarette smoke from Zeke Kelly's motel room still lingers, long after I left, which was several hours ago.

After telling the cat about my meeting with Zeke, she asks, "Did you search your coworkers cubicle?"

Pouring boiling water into my mug of cinnamon tea, I sigh. "Yeah, I did …"

Breathing in the warm, spicy smell of my tea, I reflect on what happened after leaving Zeke Kelly's motel room. First of all, I stepped outside and took a massive deep breath, thankful to be free from the oppressive cigarette smoke.

Driving to the Palmchat Gazette, I was anxious and apprehensive. Part of me keep thinking about the henchman who killed Ruth, wondering if he was, as Zeke suspected, following me. Wondering if I might be run off the road, dragged from my JEEP, and forced to spill my guts about why I'd visited Zeke Kelly.

I kept checking my rearview and both side view mirrors until I drove into the employee parking lot of the *Palmchat Gazette*. Thankful that it was the weekend, and I probably wouldn't run into many of my coworkers, I entered the building. Honestly, I was only worried about seeing Marty, or Candace—who I suspect may still think I killed Ruth — but if I did, I had a story prepared. I planned to tell them that I wanted to look for a bracelet that I thought I'd left in one of my drawers.

Fortunately, neither Marty nor Candace was in the office.

I was able to sneak into Ruth's old cubicle and snoop in peace.

Licking her foot, Callie says, "Girl, don't keep me in suspense. What happened? Did you find the jump drive?"

Staring at the tea bag seeping in my mug, I shake my head. "I didn't even find a paperclip. Her cube was spotless. It looked as though no one had ever worked there."

"So now what are you going to do?"

I walk to the breakfast bar and pull out a stool. "I'm not sure. Zeke Kelly doesn't want me to tell the cops about the jump drive, but I think I have to. I think it might be in Ruth's house."

"Girl, we need to search Ruth's house again," says Callie.

I shake my head. "We can't do that."

The Calico hisses at me. "We did it before."

"It's a crime scene," I remind her. "And remember what happened the last time we searched Ruth's house? Oh. Wait. You probably don't because you left when the cops showed up."

Licking her leg, the cat says, "Girl, I can't get arrested. If I end up with a record, then I won't be able to ..."

Curious as to why the feisty feline trailed off, I ask, "Won't be able to ... what?"

"Nothing," says Callie, jumping down from the kitchen table. "Anyway, what time is it?"

"I glance at the digital clock on the stove top. "Almost six o'clock. Why?"

"Girl, I gotta go."

"Wait. Where are you going?"

"Not that it's any of your business," says the cat, "but I got a date."

"A date? With who?"

"You don't know him, sis," says Callie. "I don't even know him."

"I don't understand."

"It's a blind date," says the cat. "My friend Manny—she's a Manx—fixed me up with him. Some tomcat she knows. Apparently, he's got a thing for Calicos. We'll see."

"Well, let me know how it turns out," I say as the cat scampers away, slipping out of my apartment through the half-opened patio door.

Staring after her, sipping my cinnamon tea, I'm wondering about why she trailed off about having a police record, then changed the subject. Although, I have no idea why I'm wondering. After all, cats can't be arrested. It's ridiculous. And yet—

My phone rings.

Thankful to be pulled away from my odd musings, I grab it and answer. "Hello?"

"Hey, Sophie … " says Officer Cuetee. "It's Noah."

"Hey, what's up?"

"Just wanted to give you some … " Officer Cuetee pauses, then says, "… not so great news."

My heart plummets. "Don't you have any good news that you can give me before the bad news?"

"Remember the gun you found at Ruth Rice's house?" he asks.

"Yeah, it was in her drawer," I say. "Her friend Zeke Kelly says she had it because she was afraid due to the story about some dangerous criminal she was working on."

"Well, the gun was registered to Marlo Miranda," Officer Cuetee says.

"So Marlo was telling the truth about someone stealing her gun," I say. "But I can't imagine Ruth stealing it."

"Fingerprints on the gun belonged to Ruth Rice and Ricardo Miranda," he tells me. "Detective Francois thinks that Ricardo might have given Ruth the gun."

"That makes sense," I say. "Ruth and Ricardo were working together on Ruth's secret expose. Ricardo was her confidential informant. Ricardo probably gave the gun to Ruth for protection."

"Interesting thing is that the gun was never fired," Officer Cuetee says. "Ballistics showed that Marlo's gun was not the gun used to shoot and kill Ricardo."

"So, Marlo didn't do it," I say, though I suspected as much.

Officer Cuetee says, "Also, there's some video surveillance from one of Ruth's neighbors that shows Marlo entering and then leaving Ruth's house. Ruth is seen walking out into her backyard as Marlo leaves."

"That's what Marlo told me when I talked to her," I say.

"That means Ruth was alive when Marlo left her house," says Officer Cuetee. "Sophie, I know you were looking at Marlo as a suspect in Ruth's murder, but Detective Francois has cleared Marlo for the murder of Ricardo. And he doesn't think Marlo had anything to do with Ruth's death either."

Sighing, I say, "So the bad news is …?"

Officer Cuetee says, "Detective Francois still likes you for the murder of Ruth Rice."

Chapter 48

Officer Cuetee's bad news was disappointing, but not at all surprising.

I already speculated and concluded that Marlo Miranda probably hadn't killed Ruth.

From my conversation with Zeke Kelly, I'm convinced the dangerous criminal's henchman killed Ruth, and Ricardo Miranda, because they uncovered damning evidence against him. Evidence that might have put him behind bars. Evidence the henchman is still looking for, that he thinks Ruth saved on a jump drive. A jump drive that's missing. And the henchman believes Zeke Kelly knows where the jump drive is, even though he doesn't.

Thinking about Zeke's bruised face, I shiver.

I know I promised Zeke that I wouldn't tell the cops about the henchman who nearly beat him to death, but I think I have to. The police can provide Zeke with protection while they look for Ruth's jump drive. I'm sure Detective Francois would like to get his hands on evidence he could use to put away a vicious criminal.

I need to talk to the detective.

Despite his suspicions of me, I have to explain to him that Ruth's murderer is a psychotic henchman, who also killed Ricardo Miranda, and works for a dangerous criminal Ruth planned to expose.

Exhaling, I take another sip of tea.

The problem is, I don't know the identity of the henchman or the dangerous criminal. There's no proof that Ruth was working on a criminal expose, or that Ricardo was working with her as an informant. Sure, Ricardo may have given Ruth a gun and left a message on her phone warning her that it was too dangerous for them to meet, but it's so vague. The danger Ruth and Ricardo faced was never explicitly stated and thus, it could have been about an increase in neighborhood crime.

Finishing my tea, which I should have paired with vanilla glazed donut holes, I put the mug down.

If I'm going to convince Detective Francois that Ruth and Ricardo were murdered by some crook's henchman, I need solid proof. I need evidence that clearly shows Ruth was investigating a criminal who silenced her—for good.

I need to find Ruth's jump drive.

I'm sure it'll have detailed notes about her investigation and her plans for the story. And I'm thinking the jump drive might be in Ruth's house. Which means I'll have to sneak into Ruth's house again and—

My phone rings.

Startled, I reach for it … but my phone is not on the breakfast bar. Frowning, I slide off the stool and glance at the kitchen table. No phone. The ringing continues. Where is my phone? I check the kitchen, wondering if I sat it down on the counter or near the sink, when I filled the tea kettle with water. But the phone isn't in the kitchen.

As the ringing goes on, I stand still, trying to determine where the sound is coming from. The living room, maybe? I take a few steps into the living area, but then the ringing stops abruptly.

"Shoot …" I mumble.

Sighing, I glance toward the couch, and the love seat, then scan the area around the coffee table, and—

"There it is …" I say, grabbing it from the end table.

The blinking light indicates that whoever called left a message, which I access.

"Hi Sophie ... it's Marlo Miranda. Give me a call ... or better yet, can you come over to my house? I think I know who killed Ruth and Ricardo ..."

Chapter 49

"I don't understand why she couldn't just leave the killer's name on the message," hisses Callie, curled up on the passenger seat of my JEEP.

"Me either," I tell the cat, who showed up on my patio as I was about to leave the apartment and head to Marlo Miranda's house.

After listening to Marlo's message, I tried calling her back a few times but she didn't pick up, so I decided I wouldn't waste anymore time, and just head over to her place.

"She must have found out the name of the henchman," says the cat.

"Or maybe she knows the name of the dangerous criminal," I say. "Either way, she's got to tell Detective Francois."

"Wonder why she didn't call the police first," says the cat. "You humans are very strange."

"Well, maybe she didn't think the cops would believe her," I suggest, turning off the main road and onto the narrow two-lane street leading to Marlo's house. "I certainly understand that. Then again, she said she thought she knew who killed them."

"Girl, who cares what she thinks?" asks Callie. "Either she does, or she doesn't. I hope she's not going to waste your time with circumstantial evidence because I have other things I could be doing."

Braking at the red traffic light, I give the cat a lot. "Other things like what?"

"Other things like none of your business," the feisty feline tells me. "I swear, you humans are so nosy."

Scoffing, I say, "And you cats are too curious."

Callie hisses, but doesn't dispute my observation.

Fifteen minutes later, my heart slams and my pulse races as I pull into Marlo's driveway. Callie and I get out, then head up the stairs onto the porch. I knock on the door, anxious to find out what Marlo knows.

Exhaling, I glance over my shoulder. Late afternoon sun bathes the small bungalow in a warm, coppery glow as a gentle, hibiscus-scented breeze swirls through the air.

"Girl, is she going to answer the door, or not?" asks the cat, sitting near my feet. "We've been waiting forever."

Sighing, I roll my eyes at the Calico. "It hasn't been forever ..."

But, it has been a few minutes, which I do find odd since Marlo was eager to see me.

"It's been long enough ..." Callie says before she leaps off the porch.

"Callie! Callie ..." I glance around the porch. "Where are you ..."

The cat scampers around the side of the house.

"Going ..." I sigh, throw up my hands, and turn back to the front door. Knocking again, I call out, "Marlo? Are you in there? It's Sophie ..."

Several minutes later, I pinch the bridge of my nose. Where is Marlo? Why isn't she answering the door? Especially when she specifically asked me to come to her house. Especially when she claims to have bombshell information about Ruth's murder that could—

"Girl, let's go," says the cat, scampering up the steps, followed by a hen, who seems madder than a wet goat, fluttering her wings and squawking loudly.

"What?" I ask, keeping an eye on the flustered hen, who's skittering around the porch, feathers flying as her wings flap chaotically. "Why do we need to leave? I haven't talked to Marlo yet. And what's up with this hen?"

Callie hisses at the hen, who responds with even louder squawking.

"She says that Marlo is lying on the floor in the kitchen," Callie tells me. "And she won't get up."

"What?" My heart sinks. "Are you serious? Is Marlo okay?"

"Girl, I don't know," Callie says.

"Oh my gosh …" I murmur, dashing down the porch steps and running around the house. Slipping through the gate, I enter the backyard. Each and every one of the hens and all of the chickens are in a tizzy, running around like … well, like chickens with their heads cut off.

I glance at the kitchen door, which is wide open.

My pulse takes off as I make my way toward the house, careful in my approach, hoping that everything is okay, that Marlo is okay, even though I have a terrible feeling that …

Standing just outside the back door, I stare into the kitchen.

Like the hen told Callie, Marlo is on the floor, lying face up, not moving …

And I know she's not breathing, I know Marlo is dead.

Because she's been shot in the head…

Chapter 50

"Ms. Carter, why did you go to Marlo Miranda's house?" demands Detective Francois, scowling at me from across the table where I'm sitting in the small, stifling interrogation room.

After finding Marlo's dead body, and admittedly freaking out a bit, I managed to get myself together and called the police. While waiting, Callie and I tried to calm the hens down, and I did a cursory glance of the kitchen. The galley-shaped space was neat and clean—except for a cigarette butt beneath the small table across from the sink. Something about the discarded butt seemed out of place. I didn't remember seeing Marlo smoking when I'd talked to her, but that didn't mean she wasn't a smoker. When the cops showed up, I gave them my statement, and mentioned the cigarette butt, suggesting that it might have belonged to her killer.

I'm not sure the cops took my suggestion seriously, which is why I'm anxious to tell the detective.

"Marlo wanted to see me," I start. "She left a message on my phone saying she knew who had killed Ruth and Ricardo. I went to her house to find out what she knew so I could pass the information on to you and you could drop the charges against me and clear my name."

His gaze shrewd, the detective asks, "And who did she say killed Ruth and Ricardo?"

"She didn't get a chance to tell me," I say, shaking my head. "She was already dead when I showed up at her house."

"Or maybe," begins the detective. "You showed up at Marlo's house, she confronted you with evidence proving that you killed Ruth, and then you killed her so she wouldn't expose you."

Shocked, I gape at the detective. He's the grandson of a world-famous lawman, renowned for apprehending a ruthless, sadistic serial killer, but I swear, he doesn't seem to have inherited any sense of logic or reasoning.

"Detective Francois," I say, tempering my frustration. "Marlo was shot to death. I don't own a gun."

"But Marlo Miranda does," says the detective. "That gun you found while you were snooping around in Ruth Rice's house belonged to Marlo Miranda."

Biting my lip, I remain quiet, not revealing that Officer Cuetee already gave me that information. I don't want to get him into trouble.

"After we processed the weapon," the detective continues, "we returned the gun to Mrs. Miranda. So, it was in her possession when you visited her this evening."

"You think I shot Marlo with her own gun?"

"It's possible."

Sighing, I say, "I didn't kill Marlo. But I think I have an idea of who did."

His expression dubious, the detective says, "I'm listening."

Somewhat hopeful that he's at least willing to consider my theories, I say, "Ruth was working on a story about a dangerous criminal. Ricardo Miranda was helping her—"

"Miranda was a reporter?"

I shake my head. "No, he was Ruth's confidential informant."

"What was he informing Ruth Rice about?"

"I'm not exactly sure," I admit. "But it must have had something to do with the story she was working on. Maybe Ricardo Miranda knew the dangerous criminal."

"And who is the dangerous criminal?"

Sheepish, I say, "I don't know that, either, but—"

"Why am I not surprised?"

I clear my throat, deciding to take a different approach. "Did the police happen to mention to you that there was a discarded cigarette butt under the table in Marlo's kitchen."

The detective tilts his head. "And what if they did?"

"Are you going to process it?" I ask, using his nomenclature.

"Why? Don't you want me to?"

"I absolutely want you to process it," I say.

"What if I find your DNA?"

"You won't," I assure him. "Because I didn't touch that cigarette and I didn't smoke it and leave it there because I don't smoke. But, I think maybe the killer smokes. And you know what?"

Detective Francois seems slightly amused. "I'm sure you'll tell me."

"I think the killer broke into Marlo's house," I say, recalling what Callie told me about the hen whose feathers were almost burned. "It was the day Marlo was arrested."

The detective frowns. "How do you know this?"

"Oh um …" I hesitate, knowing that I can't tell him a talking cat told me. "I have a confidential source. But, I think the smoker who broke into Marlo's house is the same person who killed her. And I think it has to do with the story she was working on about the dangerous criminal and …"

The detective's eyebrows raise. "And?"

"And … I wasn't supposed to mention this, but one of Ruth's friends was beat up," I say, hoping I can keep the details vague and not betray Zeke Kelly's confidence. "The dangerous criminal sent a henchman to get rid of Ruth so she wouldn't write the story. I think that person killed Ricardo Miranda, too, because he was Ruth's confidential source. And then the henchman got rid of Marlo because she must have discovered his identity."

"Ms. Carter," the detective says. "I think I've heard enough."

"So, you believe me?" I ask. "You think that Ruth, Ricardo, and

Marlo were killed by the same person and it all has to do with the story Ruth was working on?"

"I've heard enough of your silly theories," the detective says. "You expect me to believe that some henchman came to this island and killed three people to stop a story from being published?"

"I think that's what happened," I tell him, confident in my theory.

"You want me to investigate your theory?" The detective glares at me. "Then prove that this mysterious henchman exists. Get me a name …"

Chapter 51

"Girl, wait a minute … " Callie puts a paw up. "Isn't Francois the detective?"

Nodding, I say, "Yes."

The cat and I are out on my patio. It's a nice morning, warm and sunny, and I was taking advantage of the cool ocean breeze when, out of nowhere, the cat jumped up on my railing. Not that I was shocked, or anything. The Calico usually shows up unannounced, from parts unknown, but I don't mind.

"Then why do you have to find out the name of the henchman?" asks the cat, licking her fur. "Shouldn't he be doing that?"

"Well, he would …" I say, trying not to feel glum. "…if he actually believed that there is a henchman, but he doesn't. He thinks the henchman is part of my silly theory. But I know I'm right."

"Then you need to find out who the henchman is," says the cat, as though it's the easiest thing in the world to do.

"Yeah, but how do I do that?" I sigh. "Where do I even start?"

"From the beginning," says the feline. "Let's go over how you think things led to your coworker getting murdered."

"Okay," I say, sitting my empty mug on the little round table next to the chaise. "I believe that Ruth was working on a story about a dangerous criminal. Ricardo Miranda was her confidential informant so he must have had information about the dangerous criminal. Somehow, the dangerous criminal found out about Ruth's investigation, so he sent a henchman to kill Ruth and Ricardo …"

"What?" asks the cat as I trail off.

I stare at the Calico. "Remember when I overheard Ruth talking to someone who wanted to kill her? You know, she said, 'you don't have to kill me', or something like that. Anyway, I thought she could have been talking to Marlo Miranda, but now I wonder if she was talking to the henchman?"

"You still have your coworker's phone, right?" Callie asks.

Nodding, I say, "I need to check the call log again, and do a reverse look-up on the phone numbers."

"And you think the henchman killed Marlo, too?"

"Because she must have discovered his identity," I say. "But he killed her before she could tell me. And I think he left that cigarette butt under the table."

"Probably the same man who almost set that hen on fire," says Callie.

"Right," I say. "But other than checking Ruth's phone again, I'm not sure how I'll figure out who the identity of the henchman."

"You need to find that jump drive," says the cat.

"If only I could," I say. "I'm sure it has all of Ruth's notes. That's why the henchman wants it."

"Well, if the guy who killed Marlo is the henchman, then he killed her because of that jump drive."

Frowning at the cat, I ask, "What do you mean?"

"I talked to the hens yesterday," says the cat. "They're devastated and worried about where they'll go now that Marlo is dead."

"I'm sure they are," I say. "But maybe they can go to another farm."

The cat licks her fur. "Maybe. Anyway, the hens told me that the day before the man killed Marlo, he demanded that she give him the jump drive."

"Are you serious?"

Bobbing her head, Callie says, "Marlo told him she didn't know anything about the jump drive, but the man didn't believe her. The man told her to find the jump drive, or else he'd kill her … just like he killed Ruth and Ricardo."

Chapter 52

If only hens could talk, I think as I copy the numbers from Ruth's call log onto a green spiral notebook.

The cat left an hour ago to meet some friends down at the marina —"You don't know them, sis," she told me. "They're alley cats."—and I'm still reeling from what she told me about the man who killed Marlo.

All I can think is that the dangerous criminal's henchman murdered Marlo Miranda.

He wants Ruth's jump drive, and he'll do anything to get it … and by anything, I mean he'll kill to get it. He's already killed three people, and I can't help thinking that I need to warn Zeke Kelly. The henchman beat Zeke to within an inch of his life after demanding the jump drive.

Worried, copying the last number, I can't help wondering if the henchman will pay Zeke another visit. And if he does, he might kill Zeke. I grab the mug of tea I made after the Calico left and take a sip. It's suddenly occurred to me that the henchman may have decided to get rid of anyone who he thinks might have information about Ruth's story—whether they do, or not. He might have killed Marlo because she was Ricardo's wife and he probably thought Ricardo had confided in her. Which, unfortunately, is plausible. Spouses often share information. To curtail Marlo's violent tendencies, Ricardo might have told Marlo he was Ruth's confidential informant so she wouldn't be jealous. Of course, Marlo claimed to know nothing about Ricardo helping Ruth with the story, but the henchman wouldn't have known that.

I sigh and take another sip of tea.

I need to share the information about the henchman killing Marlo with Detective Francois, but I don't see how I can do that. He's going to want proof. And what can I tell him? That a talking cat I know found out from one of Marlo's hens?

Shaking my head, I stare at the numbers I wrote down.

I don't recognize the area or country codes, so I do a quick search on my phone and find out that most of the numbers are from Brazil. In fact, Ruth called one of the numbers several times the day she was killed.

I frown, biting my lip.

Zeke Kelly told me that Ruth was a reporter in South America, so it's possible she could have been calling a friend or associate. But ... what if she was calling someone in connection with her investigation of the dangerous criminal? What if she was calling a source? Or ... could she have been calling the criminal?

Anticipation grips me. My heart pounds in a mixture of fear, excitement, and indecision. I want to call the Brazilian number but I'm not sure I want to talk to a ruthless criminal. What on earth would I say to him? *Hi, my name is Sophie Carter. I'm a reporter with the Palmchat Gazette and I have a few questions for you about Ruth Rice, but before we get started, can I have your name and the spelling of it, please?*

Rolling my eyes, I pick up Ruth's phone, dial the digits, and hit the 'Speaker' button.

My heart slams, and I'm thinking that I'm making a mistake, that this is not a good idea, and I should disconnect the call before—

"Ruth? Are you okay? Why didn't you call me back?"

Chapter 53

"Ruth? What? Um …" My heart slams as confusion grips me. "Wait … this isn't Ruth …"

A pause, and then, "Who is this?"

"Oh, um …" I clear my throat. "My name is Sophie Carter and—"

"What are you doing with Ruth's phone?" The man asks with a heavy accent which I'm assuming is Brazilian. "Where is Ruth?"

Exhaling, I say, "I actually found Ruth's phone. As I said, my name is Sophie Carter and I used to work with Ruth at the *Palmchat Gazette—*"

"You're from the *Palmchat Gazette?*" asks the man, his voice slightly less accusing and suspicious, more curious. "You're calling from St. Mateo."

"Yes, I am," I confirm. "Ruth was my coworker—"

"*Was* your coworker?"

Wincing, I bite my bottom lip. Whoever I'm talking to is obviously someone who knew Ruth well and is concerned about her. Someone who was expecting a return call. I don't want to be the person to tell him why Ruth never called him back but I know it can't be avoided.

"How do you know Ruth?" I ask, stalling. "Why was she supposed to call you back?"

"My name is Hector Garza," the man tells me. "I'm the editor of the paper where Ruth used to work here in São Paulo. Ruth had been calling me recently about a story she was working on."

"Something about a dangerous criminal?" I guess.

"She had a lead about a story she'd covered while she was working here," says the editor. "Please tell me, where is Ruth? I'm worried about her. The last time we spoke, she feared her life might be in danger."

Following a sigh, I say, somewhat reluctantly, "I'm afraid that … Ruth was right to be afraid."

"What do you mean?" the editor demands.

"Ruth is …" I stop for a moment, then force the word out, "… dead."

"Dead?" whispers Hector Gomez. "Ruth is … dead? Are you serious?"

"Unfortunately, yes," I say.

"How?" Hector asks. "What happened to her?"

"She was … murdered."

"Murdered?"

"I think she was killed because of the story she was working on about the dangerous criminal," I say.

"Do the police know who killed her?" Hector asks. "Has anyone been arrested."

"Um, yes …" I clear my throat. "But … the person who was arrested didn't kill Ruth. I think she was murdered by a henchman who was sent by the dangerous criminal."

"A henchman?"

I hear the incredulity in Hector's tone but I don't let it discourage me. "Mr. Gomez, you said that Ruth feared for her life. I think it's because the dangerous criminal warned her not to write the story. And when Ruth continued the investigation, a henchman was sent to get rid of her."

Hector Gomez expels a resigned sigh. "I told Ruth to be careful. I warned her that El Zapata was deranged and ruthless."

"El Zapata?" I echo, shuddering. "Is that the dangerous criminal?"

"He's a South American drug lord who was arrested and put on trial for heinous crimes," Hector explains. "He might have been sent to prison for the rest of his life but he orchestrated the deaths of several key witnesses. As a result, he was acquitted due to lack of evidence."

"No wonder Ruth was afraid," I say.

"However, one of the witnesses managed to escape Brazil," continues Hector. "He was one of El Zapata's bodyguards, a man who secretly videoed the witness assassinations and put the video of those murders onto a jump drive."

"A jump drive?" I ask, my pulse starting to race.

"I believe Ruth had that jump drive," says Hector.

"She did," I tell him. "The henchman is looking for it. He's killed two other people in his search for it and nearly beat another person to death."

"If El Zapata knows about that jump drive," says Hector, his tone ominous. "He won't stop until he gets it and he'll kill whoever he has to in order to possess it. That jump drive could destroy him and his criminal empire."

My hands trembling, I ask, "So you think Ruth got the jump drive from the bodyguard?"

"I think that was the lead she told me about," says Hector. "I didn't ask her for details, but—"

"So, if I could find the bodyguard," I say, thinking out loud. "Then he could tell the police that El Zapata knew about the jump drive and likely sent a henchman to kill Ruth."

"I don't think that's the best thing to do," says Hector. "You need to go to the police."

"I have gone to the police," I tell him. "I gave them my theory about the dangerous criminal and the henchman, but they don't believe me. They want more proof of my claims."

"Look, I'll be honest with you," Hector says. "Ruth left Brazil because she tracked down the bodyguard who escaped. She tracked him to St. Mateo, so she got a job at the newspaper there, with the intent of convincing the bodyguard to be her confidential informant."

A jolt passes through me. "Confidential informant? What is the bodyguard's name?"

"Let me see ..." Hector sounds as though he's typing on a keyboard, for a few seconds, then he says, "The bodyguard's name is Luis Inez Eduardo. But when he fled to St. Mateo, he changed his name to ... Ricardo Miranda."

Chapter 54

He changed his name to … Ricardo Miranda…

The next morning, ruminating on what Ruth's former editor, Hector Gomez, told me about Ricardo fleeing Brazil, I stare at the bowl of tropical fruit on the countertop of the breakfast bar in my kitchen.

Considering what I've learned, I need to figure out what to do. Part of me wants to go to Detective Francois, but without the name of the henchman, will he believe me? I could tell him about El Zapata, and Hector Gomez could corroborate the story.

Also, if I tell Detective Francois that Ricardo changed his name, then he could confirm that Luis Inez Eduardo was once a bodyguard for the notorious drug lord, El Zapata. After talking to Hector Gomez yesterday, I did some research of El Zapata. Calling him a ruthless criminal is an understatement. Many of the articles I found about El Zapata had been written by Ruth Rice. Her stories were riveting and informative, and I found myself swept up in her clinical narratives that detailed El Zapata's crimes. There was even an article about the bodyguard who fled the country—Luis Inez Eduardo. Ruth's story outlined how Luis Inez Eduardo—Ricardo Miranda—was rumored to have witnessed the executions of several witnesses scheduled to testify against El Zapata. The prosecution believed Luis Inez Eduardo had evidence of the brutal slayings and left Brazil to avoid his own execution.

I grab an orange and start to peel it.

It's clear, to me, at least, that Ruth tracked down Ricardo Miranda, formerly Luis Inez Eduardo, and convinced him to share the evidence of the witness executions with her. My guess is that Ruth hoped to kill two birds with one stone. She would write an award-winning exposé about El Zapata's deadly scheme to avoid justice while also making sure that the drug lord got what he deserved—life behind bars.

But, somehow, someway, El Zapata learned about Ruth's plan and sent a henchman to kill her.

I pull the wedges of orange apart and pop one in my mouth, wishing it was orange-infused tea with orange-glazed donut holes instead.

The problem is, what's clear to me might not be clear to Detective Francois. He might not be willing to consider my theory, despite the new information I've learned.

Standing, I walk into the kitchen and grab a small bowl to put the orange slices in.

Detective Francois remains convinced that I killed Ruth because my prints were on the murder weapon. If I can't convince him to realize that El Zapata's henchman had more of a motive to kill Ruth than I did—and the truth is I didn't have a motive to kill her—then I might spend the rest of my life in jail.

Exhaling, I turn and—

A man stands several feet away from me. Dressed in all black, he wears a black nylon mask that covers his entire face, making it impossible to see what he looks like.

My heart shoots into my throat, robbing me of speech. I can't even scream. All I can do is stand rooted to the spot, paralyzed, and terrified. Confusion rocks me to the core. I don't understand. Who is this man? Why is he in my house? How did he get in? What does he want? What is he going to do to me?

"Give me the jump drive ..."

"What?" I squeak.

"The jump drive ..." he rasps.

He wants the jump drive? What? I'm confused. I have no idea what he's talking about. I don't have a jump drive. What—

It dawns on me. The jump drive. He wants Ruth's jump drive. The jump drive that contains the evidence against El Zapata.

"Give it to me ..."

I shake my head. The henchman, I think. This is the henchman El Zapata sent to silence Ruth. The person who killed Ricardo and Marlo. The man who beat Zeke Kelly to within an inch of his life.

The masked man lunges at me.

Screaming, I stumble back, glancing over my shoulder as I stagger into the galley kitchen. Desperate and terrified to escape, I realize too late that I've backed myself into a corner. Rational thought is impossible. All I can think is—

"Are you deaf?" growls the masked man, advancing toward me.

"Am I deaf?" I frown at him. What kind of question is that? "No, I'm not deaf. Why would you think I'm deaf?"

"Because I told you to give me the jump drive, but you haven't done it," he says. "So I have to wonder if you didn't hear me because you're deaf."

Shaking my head, I say, "I don't have the jump drive."

"Oh, I think you do," says the man. "It was in Ruth's stuff. I know you took it out!"

The man advances toward me.

I take another step back, glancing around the kitchen. I should be able to find a weapon, shouldn't I? Maybe a knife. A fork. A spoon. Or—

"Give me that jump drive or I'll put a hole in your head!"

Arrested and paralyzed by the vicious threat, I glance toward the man.

My heart sinks.

He's pointing a gun at me.

"Now give me the—"

"Why should I?" I ask. Yes, of course, I know it's crazy to try to hold a conversation with this dolt, but I need to stall for time. I can't let him kill me.

"Lady, didn't you hear me when I said I would shoot you?" asks the masked man.

"Yes, I heard you," I say. "As we established, I am not deaf, but …"

"But what?" asks the man, exasperation in his tone.

"But why do you want the jump drive?" I ask.

"Don't you worry about why I want it," he tells me. "Just give it to me."

"I don't know why you think I have the jump drive," I say. "But, I don't."

"Lady, did you understand what I meant when I said I would put a hole in you?"

I gasp. "Yes, I understood. Nevertheless, I would like to know why you want the jump drive. Or, if you prefer not to tell me that, then why do you think I have it? Are you El Zapata's henchman? Did he send you to get the jump drive because it has evidence of his crimes and he wants it destroyed? Did you kill Ruth and Ricardo and Marlo? Did you attack—"

"No more questions," he shouts, cocking the gun.

I gulp at the distinctive click.

"I am going to count to three," he says. "And when I do, you better—"

"Oh, don't bother counting. Fine. Here, you want the jump drive, it's yours!" I reach into the pocket of my fluffy robe and pull out the small hair clip I'd stashed there after I removed it from my corkscrew curls. I toss it over the breakfast bar, hoping the clip sails far enough away for me to escape before the attacker realizes it's a hair clip and not the jump drive he demanded.

The masked man curses, then scrambles into my small living room, chasing the hair clip.

Taking advantage of his preoccupation, I grab the rolling pin from the cabinet drawer where I store it and dash out of the kitchen.

Diving over the coffee table, the masked man drops to his knees in front of the loveseat, where the hair clip landed. I run up behind him, holding the rolling pin over my head, and—

The masked man jumps up and spins around, facing me.

Screaming, I swing the rolling pin down, hoping to connect with his head, but he raises his arm to block the blow, and I end up crashing the apparatus against his hand, dislodging the gun. As the firearm slides across the hardwood floor, I swing the rolling pin again. Grunting, the masked man grabs the opposite end and yanks it away from me.

Shoot, I think as the man swings my weapon toward me.

Yelping, I duck as the rolling pin swishes through the air. Afraid of getting my block knocked off, I tumble onto my side and scoot away.

The masked man flings the rolling pin toward me.

I screech and hold my arms over my head, fearful of where the rolling pin might fall, then lunge toward the gun. As I grab the firearm, I feel the masked man right behind me. Turning, I point the weapon at him, my arms outstretched and locked, hands trembling. "Get out!" I screech. "Get out of her before I blow your head off!"

Hands lifted high, the masked man stumbles backward to the front door, the turns, flings it open, and sprints out.

Following several deep breaths, I manage to stand, then drop the gun on the couch. On wobbly legs that feel like mush, I walk to the door, close it, and lock the deadbolt.

Trembling, I slide to the floor.

Chapter 55

An hour later, a host of cops and crime scene techs swarm my small apartment.

I called the police once my heart stopped pounding, my pulse stopped racing, and my mind stopped spinning with nightmarish scenarios of what could have happened to me. Ten minutes after I dialed 911, the cops were pounding on my door. I flung it open and was face to face with Officer Cuetee. I was so happy to see him that I burst into tears and nearly collapsed in his arms.

Now, we're standing on my back patio.

As the crime scene guys finish dusting for fingerprints and searching for evidence, Officer Cuetee soothes me with his comforting presence. He and his partner have already gotten the details of the harrowing attack from me. I couldn't tell them much, other than the attacker wore all black, including a black mask. Not a lot to go on, but Officer Cuetee assured me they would find the guy. His partner didn't share his belief but provided realistic encouragement regarding finding the perpetrator.

"I'm going to go inside the apartment and see if the crime scene guys have found anything else," says Officer Cuetee. "I'll be back in a second."

As Officer Cuetee turns from me, a chill passes through me, even though it's a typical balmy morning, and I rub my arms.

"What's going on? Are you okay? What's with all the fuzz?"

Startled by the voice, which I recognize, I turn toward the railing. Callie, the sassy, sarcastic Calico, perches on the ledge.

"All the fuzz?"

"Cops," says the cat.

Shaking my head, I roll my eyes. "Nobody calls cops the fuzz anymore."

"Who cares what people call them? What are they doing here?"

"Speaking of that, what are you doing here?"

The cat explains that she came for an update on the Ruth Rice murder case.

"I wanted to find out how you're progressing in the investigation, but you seem to be otherwise engaged," says Callie. "Was that Officer Cuetee I saw?"

"Yes, that was him," I say.

The cat's eyes narrow. "He wasn't trying to get fresh, was he?"

"Trying to get fresh?"

The cat hisses, then says, "Was he trying to shoot his shot?"

"Not exactly …"

"You sound disappointed?"

"No, no, no," I say, not exactly convincingly. "He's here because I called the police."

"What happened?"

I tell the cat about my harrowing ordeal.

"Was it the henchman?" asks Callie. "The same guy who killed Ruth, Ricardo, and Marlo?"

"I'm pretty sure it was …"

"Oh my God, he came to kill you!" The cat leaps onto the chaise lounge and paces back and forth. "And I wasn't here to scratch his eyes out."

"Where have you been?" I ask.

The cat stops pacing to stare at me, then says, "Well, not that it's any of your business and not that I owe you an explanation, but …

well, I've been spending time with that tomcat. Remember I told you about him?"

"You did," I say. "How are things going? Is it getting serious between you two?"

"Serious? Sis, please!" The cat tilts her head. "I mean, don't get me wrong, he is super cute. And he's totally falling in love with me, but …"

"But …?" I prompt, sitting on the edge of the lounge.

"But I'm not sure I'm in the mood for a serious relationship."

"But you like him, right?"

The cat purrs. "Yeah, I do. Still …"

"Well, if he likes you and you like him," I say, "then don't you want to see what might happen between the two of you?"

"Uh … Sophie …?"

Panic floods me as I curse under my breath. I was so enthralled and enthusiastic about that psycho cat's love life that I forgot about the cops. I can't believe I let Officer Cuetee catch me talking to a cat. Wait. I can't believe I'm talking to a cat. No, wait. I'm not talking to a cat. Well, no, I was talking to the cat, but the cat wasn't really talking back to me, I was just imagining—

"Sophie?"

Jumping to my feet, I pirouette to face Officer Cuetee.

"Were you talking to someone?"

"Oh. Um …"

"What is he saying?" asks Callie.

I say, "No, I wasn't talking to anyone …"

"You shouldn't lie to the cops," says Callie. "You were talking to me."

Officer Cuetee frowns. "But, I heard you—"

"Thinking out loud," I blurt out. "I was just … "

"Thinking about what might happen between the two of … who?"

A paw slaps my ankle. "What is he saying?"

"Nothing …" I say, shocked that Officer Cuetee heard so much of my conversation with Callie.

"Don't tell me nothing." Callie hisses. "I may not be able to understand Officer Dreamboat, but I can tell he's saying something."

"I mean … no one," I say to Officer Cuetee as I try to ignore that sassy cat. "Um … so, are the crime scene guys finished?"

"I'm not sure," he says. "But you have to leave, anyway."

"Leave my apartment?"

"Speaking of leaving," announces the cat. "I need to go."

"Date with the tomcat?" I ask.

"Something like that," says the cat as she turns and trots away.

"What did you mean when you said … date with the tomcat?" asks Officer Cuetee.

Swallowing, I blink a few times. "Thinking out loud again. Sorry. What were you saying about me having to leave my apartment?"

"Well, technically, your apartment is still an active crime scene."

"If I can't go home, where am I supposed to go?" I ask, alarmed. "I don't have any family in St. Mateo, or any close friends, or—"

"You have me," he says.

I stare at him, momentarily transfixed by the concern on his handsome face. "I do?"

Officer Cuetee smiles. "You can stay at my place tonight."

"I can?"

Slipping an arm around my shoulder, he says, "Come on, let's go …"

Chapter 56

"Thanks again for letting me stay here," I tell Officer Cuetee, and then take a sip of the steaming turmeric and ginger tea he made for us after we arrived at his place.

"It's no problem," he says. "Considering everything that's happened to you, I didn't want you to worry about where you were going to stay tonight."

"I appreciate it," I say, sneaking a glance at him over the rim of my mug, slightly mesmerized by his dreamy cuteness. Or, am I entranced by his cute dreaminess? Hmmm … not sure it matters. I clear my throat. "Anyway, I am grateful for your kind hospitality."

Officer Cuetee chuckles. "I just wish there was more hospitality to extend to you."

"What do you mean?"

Leaning back in his chair, Officer Cuetee glances around. "My humble abode isn't that big."

Well, he's right about that. Officer Cuetee lives in a bungalow. It's a cute place, but it's pretty small. And when I say small, I mean it's only about five hundred square feet. On one side, there's a kitchen and the table where we're sitting. On the other end is a couch that pulls out to a queen-sized bed. A door behind the couch leads into the bathroom.

"Well, it's big enough for you," I tell him. "And it's decorated really nice."

"You can thank my older sister for that," he says. "All these finishing touches and the furniture placement and the color schemes are her doing. I was fine with the ratty old couch I slept on when I was in college. It was lumpy and the fabric was frayed, but it was free. Friend of mine found it near a trash bin behind a restaurant. Somebody had dumped it illegally."

I laugh and make a face. "It was probably a biohazard."

"We gave it a good scrubbing and sprayed it with disinfectant," he says. "But, I actually am glad my sister told me to get rid of it. Wouldn't have wanted you to have to sleep on it. The pull-out bed is much nicer."

After another sip of the fragrant tea, which would pair nicely with honey and lemon glazed donut holes, I glance over my shoulder at the couch. "Where are you going to sleep?"

Officer Cuetee shrugs. "Floor will be fine for me."

"The floor?" I shake my head. "No, you can't do that. I don't want to put you out of your own bed."

"Then where will you sleep?"

"I'll take the floor."

Officer Cuetee shakes his head. "You're not sleeping on the floor."

Putting my mug down, I say, "We can share the bed."

His eyes widen for a second, and then he smirks a bit, but not in an overly smug way. "Are you okay with that?"

"Oh. Well. Um …" I trail off, not sure if I am, or not. "It's not like we have a choice. Neither of us wants the other to sleep on the floor, so …"

I take another gulp of tea.

Officer Cuetee nods. "So we'll have to sleep together."

His innuendo, delivered with casual aplomb, almost makes me do a spit take, but I manage not to spew tea all over him. Instead, I swallow the warm brew and launch into a coughing fit.

"Are you okay?"

"Just need …" I stop to cough and then clear my throat. "Some water."

"I'll get you a bottle."

When Officer Cuetee rises from his seat and walks to the refrigerator, I take a moment to collect myself, which I desperately need. *We'll have to sleep together.* I know he didn't mean that literally, but the thought of being with him, in that way, is threatening to send me into a tizzy, as my grandma would say. Seriously, I don't have time for butterflies, warm fuzzies, and inappropriate fantasies. I was almost killed tonight. Attacked by a man who demanded that I give him a jump drive. A man who I believe was the henchman El Zapata sent to kill Ruth Rice and Ricardo Miranda. I don't care how handsome Officer Cuetee is, I can't get caught up in his *dreamboatery.*

Back at the table, Officer Cuetee sits and pushes a bottle of water toward me.

"Um, so, I was thinking …" I open the bottle of water and take a quick sip.

"About?"

"The man who attacked me," I say. "I think he's a henchman who works for a notorious South American drug lord called El Zapata."

Officer Cuetee frowns. "El Zapata?"

After a sigh and another fortifying sip of water, I tell Officer Cuetee about the conversation with Hector Gomez, Ruth's former editor at the newspaper she worked for in Brazil … and how El Zapata was arrested and was going to be tried but he killed all of the witnesses who were supposed to testify against him … and how one of his bodyguards videoed the murders, then fled the country, afraid that El Zapata would kill him, too … that bodyguard was Luis Inez Eduardo … who came to St. Mateo and changed his named to … Ricardo Miranda.

"Ruth had been writing stories about El Zapata before she moved to St. Mateo," I say. "She came here because she tracked down Ricardo Miranda, El Zapata's former bodyguard. Ricardo agreed to become

Ruth's confidential informant, providing her with information for her expose on El Zapata."

His expression grim, Officer Cuetee says, "And El Zapata found out about Ruth's investigation so he had her silenced … permanently."

Nodding, I say, "And the henchman killed Ricardo Miranda and Marlo, too. He even beat up Ruth's friend, Zeke Kelly. He's looking for a jump drive that Ruth had which contained damaging information about El Zapata."

Officer Cuetee frowns. "Why did El Zapata's henchman think you had the jump drive?"

Shaking my head, I shrug. "I don't know."

"Could he have thought that Ruth had given it to you?"

"Maybe, but that doesn't make sense," I say. "Ruth and I were not friends. There's no way she would have given the jump drive to me."

"The henchman may not have known that," says Officer Cuetee. "You and Ruth were coworkers so he might have thought she'd told you about the story she was writing."

"I suppose so," I concede. "But the question remains—how do I prove that the henchman killed Ruth, Ricardo, and Marlo?"

"I think you need to—"

Guttural, insistent barking interrupts Officer Cuetee.

I jump a bit. "What …?"

Rolling his eyes, Officer Cuetee exhales. "Duty calls. Literally."

"I don't understand."

"Dutiful. My dog," he says. "He's in the shed out back."

"Dutiful lives in a shed?"

Officer Cuetee stands. "It's bigger than this place. Anyway, he lets me know when he needs to go out."

I rise to my feet. "I'll come with you. It'll be nice to see Dutiful again."

About fifteen minutes later, Officer Cuetee and I stand near a cluster of shoulder-high Oleander bushes surrounding a small clearing behind the bungalow. Twenty feet away, the Belgian Malinois does his business as we wait.

"So, about the henchman," says Officer Cuetee. "You said he beat up Ruth's friend?"

"His name is Zeke Kelley," I say, glancing at the handsome officer. "He was the person who first told me about the story Ruth was writing, but he didn't know any details. And now I'm thinking that the henchman must have thought Ruth told Zeke Kelly about the jump drive, but he knew nothing about it."

"Zeke Kelly needs to come down to the station and file a complaint," says Officer Cuetee. "When he does that, he can give his statement to Detective Francois."

Sighing, I say, "He doesn't want to go to the cops. The henchman threatened him, told Zeke he would kill him if he went to the police. Zeke is terrified to leave his motel room."

Officer Cuetee says, "Maybe I can talk to him. You need him to corroborate your story about the henchman sent to get rid of Ruth."

"I'm thinking maybe Hector Gomez can talk to Detective Francois," I say.

"Good idea," says Officer Cuetee. "And I'll talk to Detective Francois about El Zapata. He's probably heard of him."

I nod, my attention distracted by a stray dog ambling toward Dutiful. The mutt barks at Dutiful, and the Belgian Malinois responds with his guttural growl. The mutt responds with another round of barks, which elicits more barking from Dutiful.

"I wonder what they're talking about," I muse out loud.

Officer Cuetee chuckles. "You think they're talking."

Nodding, I say, "Animals can communicate with each other."

"Yeah, I know," says Officer Cuetee. "But ... not like humans."

"Actually, that's not true," I say.

"It's not?"

"Um ... I just meant ..." I clear my throat. "How do we know, you know, what they may or may not be saying as they bark at each other ..."

"True, but, I don't think they're communicating like you and I are communicating, you know," says Officer Cuetee. "I don't think they have the same cognitive abilities as humans. They're not barking in complete sentences."

"Yeah, you're probably right," I say, even though I'm not sure and part of me believes that the Belgian Malinois and the stray dog do have humanistic cognitive abilities. After all, Callie talked to the chickens in Marlo's backyard. She talked to that disgusting rat who allegedly lives in the woman's bathroom at the *Palmchat Gazette*. She even talked to the Belgian Malinois.

Or, did she?

Now that I think about it, I didn't hear Callie talking to any of those animals. So how could I know how they were communicating? Or, if they were communicating? That is, how do I know Callie was being honest with me? Furthermore, how do I know Callie is really even talking to me?

I don't believe cats can speak.

And yet Callie does talk to me.

Or, does she?

Chapter 57

"How did you get in here?" I ask Callie as she makes herself comfortable on the table in Officer Cuetee's bungalow.

When Officer Cuetee's alarm went off at five a.m., I woke up easily, feeling rested and refreshed, despite my current predicament. I'd expected to spend the night tossing and turning, plagued by haunting nightmares of being attacked and spending the rest of my life in prison. But my dreams were surprisingly sweet—

"I slipped in when Officer Good-looking stepped out to take Dutiful to do his morning business," says Callie, licking her fur. "You were in the bathroom doing your morning business."

Rolling my eyes at the cat's uncanny perceptiveness, I say, "Wait. How did you know I was here?"

"Dutiful told some stray dog to get word to me that you were here," says Callie.

"A stray dog?" I ask, recalling the mangy mutt Dutiful barked at last night. The canine cacophony led to my debate with Officer Cuetee about whether, or not, animals could communicate with each other in the same way humans communicate.

"Did the cops arrest the guy who attacked you?"

I shake my head and take another sip of tea. "Unfortunately, he got away."

Callie jumps to all fours. "He got away? Why am I not surprised? The cops on this island can't catch a clue. Did you tell the cops it was the henchman?"

"I gave them my statement and told them I had an idea who had attacked me," I say, popping another donut hole in my mouth. "But I didn't have a name. I could only tell them it was a henchman who worked for a ruthless drug lord named El Zapata."

The cat gives me a look. "El Zapata?"

"Did I tell you about him?" I ask.

"No, girl, give me the tea."

After I spill the tea about talking to Ruth's editor, and everything he told me about El Zapata, I say, "The cops told me they'd give the information to Detective Francois, but who knows if he'll believe me."

The cat stares at me. "Girl, that detective does not seem to be the sharpest tool in the shed, as you humans like to say. I'm sure if you explain it to him like he's stupid, he'll understand."

"The problem is that I don't know the henchman's name," I say. "So, technically, I have no proof that he attacked me, however …"

"However?" prompts the cat, licking her fur.

"There are people who can corroborate my story about the henchman," I say. "Ruth's old boss and her friend both know that El Zapata targeted Ruth because she'd written stories about him in the past. And her old boss knows that Ricardo Miranda's real name was Luis Inez Eduardo. He was one of El Zapata's bodyguards who witnessed several gruesome murders orchestrated by the drug lord before he fled Brazil. Even so, I'm not sure what Detective Francois will think."

"Maybe Officer Cuetee can talk to the detective," suggests the cat. "Where is he?"

"He's in the bathroom," I say.

"Doing his morning business?" asks the cat.

I make a face. "I think he's taking a shower. Getting ready for work. And he's already promised to talk to Detective Francois for me."

"See that he does," says Callie, jumping down onto the chair opposite me, and then leaping to the floor. "Make sure you keep me posted."

"You're leaving?"

"I also have morning business," says the cat. "But, not that kind."

"What kind of morning business do you have?" I ask.

"The kind of morning business that's none of your business," Callie says. "The kind of morning business you don't need to worry about considering that you need to focus on proving you're not a killer."

The Calico trots to the door and I follow to let her out.

When she's gone, I feel a bit forlorn and curious. I wish she would have stuck around to curl up in my lap as I wasted the day lamenting my bad luck. Although, I doubt she would have curled up in my lap. Callie is fiercely independent, which I do like about her. And I suppose—

"Sophie?"

Startled, I turn from the door to face Officer Cuetee.

I open my mouth to speak, but when I see him, I have no words.

Still damp from the shower, Officer Cuetee wears a towel around his waist and nothing else, revealing what I'd always suspected was beneath that police uniform—a body to die for, muscles that take my breath away, and—

"Who were you talking to …?"

I swallow, then hurry back to the table, trying desperately not to gawk at him. "Oh. Um … yes, I was … talking to the cat …"

"Talking to the cat?"

"Yeah, you know, just … *pspspspspspsps* … that sound you make when you want to call a cat," I say, recalling information I read about communicating with felines. "The *"ps"* sound supposedly mimics the rustling sound of prey out in the wild, or something, anyway, um … guess you're heading to work?"

"I was thinking we could go for tea and donut holes before I do," he suggests.

"Good idea," I say. "I could go for orange and cinnamon tea right now."

"Orange and cinnamon. Interesting," says Officer Cuetee. "I was thinking blackberry, pear, and vanilla."

"I'll have to try that," I say, thinking of pairing the blackberry, pear, and vanilla tea with donut holes rolled in powdered sugar.

"Or maybe peach and ginger," says Officer Cuetee.

"Good choice," I say. "What about lemongrass and hibiscus?"

"I'll have to try that," says Officer Cuetee. "Give me a few minutes to get dressed and we'll head out."

Chapter 58

"So, be honest with me," I start, staring at Officer Cuetee. "Do you really think Detective Francois will believe my theory? I mean, he's still hung up on the fact that my prints are on the murder weapon, despite all the other evidence that points to El Zapata's henchman as Ruth's killer."

Officer Cuetee takes a sip of his tea, a fragrant jasmine and elderberry blend. "Just because your prints are on the murder weapon doesn't mean you did it. You already explained that you were trying to help Ruth."

The two of us are sitting outside on the patio of Tea 4 Too, a quaint tea café overlooking the white sands of Golden Beach, which is five miles from my apartment. It's a balmy morning. Officer Cuetee has a few hours before his shift starts, so we'll have time to enjoy the tea and donut holes.

"But François doesn't believe me," I say, glancing down at my running shoes.

"Well, I do, and I'll talk to him about it," says Officer Cuetee, his frustration evident in his tone.

Encouraged and heartened by his ardent support, I say, "Thank you. I appreciate that."

Officer Cuetee gives me an enticing smile, one that makes me feel breathless and intoxicated. For a moment or two, I can't help wondering what it might be like to kiss that lovely mouth. But, I know that right now, when my freedom—my very life as I know it—is on the line, I can't distract myself with romance.

Clearing my throat, I say, "So, anyway … I'm sure Hector Gomez will talk to Detective Francois, but I'm not so sure about Zeke Kelly. He was so afraid to go to the police."

"I meant to tell you something about that guy," says Officer Cuetee. "Zeke Kelly."

"What about him?"

"When you first mentioned him," says Officer Cuetee. "His name sounded familiar, so I did some research. Turns out, he was involved in a bar fight."

Shocked and curious, I ask, "A bar fight?"

"Well, he got beat up in a bar," amends Officer Cuetee. "We got a call to break up an altercation at a joint in Guavatown."

"I think you mentioned this to me," I say.

"I might have," he says. "Anyway, the guy we arrested gave us a ridiculous story about how he was baited into hitting the victim—Zeke Kelly."

"What was the ridiculous story?"

"Something about the victim followed him into the men's room and offered him money to start the fight and punch him in the face, but he turned him down because it seemed sketchy."

"What?" I'm confused. "Why would Zeke Kelly pay someone to punch him in the face?"

"He wouldn't have," says Officer Cuetee. "Didn't make sense and we didn't buy it. But, that's why I remembered the name, Zeke Kelly."

"Poor Zeke," I say. "He's having such an awful time in St. Mateo. First, his good friend is murdered. Then he's attacked. Then he gets into a bar fight, which must have happened before the henchman attacked him because he told me he was too afraid to leave his motel so I can't imagine him going out to a bar."

Officer Cuetee takes another sip of tea, then says, "So much for a relaxing, island vacation. I'm surprised the guy is still here."

Nodding, I say, "After Ruth was killed, I would have thought that he would leave, but … I don't know why he stayed. But I need him to talk to Detective Francois about El Zapata's henchman, so I'm glad he stuck around."

Chapter 59

"Ms. Carter, thank you for agreeing to see me," says Detective Francois, taking a seat in the chair across from me. "I promise to get right to the point and not waste too much of your time."

"Oh, you're not wasting my time," I say, eager to speak with the detective, even though we're back in the interrogation room, where my nightmare began, when he arrested me for Ruth's murder.

Three days have passed since I was attacked by El Zapata's henchman in my apartment. Since then, Office Cuetee told me that he spoke to Detective Francois, sharing my theory about the Brazilian drug lord's motive to kill Ruth and how he carried out the heinous plot. Officer Cuetee assured me that the detective listened attentively, and promised to follow up with Hector Gomez, Ruth's former boss, and Zeke Kelly, her friend who was also assaulted by the henchman.

"Did you find the man who attacked me?" I ask.

After clearing his throat, Detective Francois says, "Ms. Carter, about that …"

"I'm pretty sure I know who it was," I say. "Well, I don't know the person's name, but—"

"Ms. Carter, are you sure your were attacked in your apartment?"

Confused, and wary, I say, "Yes, I'm sure. That's why I called the police—"

"The crime scene techs weren't able to find any evidence of a break-in," says Detective Francois.

My heart starts to slam. "Well, that's probably because the guy was a professional."

"A professional?"

"I believe that he was a henchman sent by a ruthless drug lord called El Zapata—"

"I'm well aware of El Zapata," says the detective, his dismissive. "And your theory about the Brazilian drug lord targeting your coworker."

"But my theory is true," I insist. "And maybe I can't prove it, but if you open an investigation, you'll realize I'm right. Ruth was writing an expose on El Zapata with the help of his former bodyguard, who fled Sao Paulo and changed his name to Ricardo Miranda. But somehow, El Zapata found out and sent his henchman to kill Ruth and Ricardo. The henchman killed Marlo, as well, because she discovered his identity, which she was going to tell me, but ... he killed her before she could."

The detective glares at me. "Ms. Carter, I don't dispute that Ms. Rice wrote stories about El Zapata or that Mr. Miranda was helping her with an expose of the drug lord."

My hopes rising, I say, "So, you do believe me!"

"What I believe, Ms. Carter," says the detective. "Is that you used the fact that Ms. Rice was writing a story about a dangerous drug lord to your advantage."

"To my advantage?"

"As a cover for your crimes," says Detective Francois. "You want me to believe that a South American drug lord sent a hitman—"

"Henchman," I correct, biting my lip sheepishly when the detective glowers at me.

"Excuse me?"

"I think he's more of a henchman than a hitman," I squeak, feeling utterly and immediately foolish.

"And I think," says the detective, "that you made up this henchman, hitman, whatever ... to cover up your crimes."

"You still think I killed Ruth?" I ask, frustrated.

"Not just Ruth," he says. "But Ricardo and Marlo Miranda, as well."

My heart drops as I stare at him, momentarily unable to speak. "Wait ... what?"

"Ms. Carter, do you remember the gun that you claimed the alleged attacker pulled on you?"

"It wasn't a claim," I say, indignation rising within me. "And the attacker wasn't alleged. He broke into my apartment and—"

"There were fingerprints on the gun," the detective says. "Ballistics determined that your fingerprints were on the gun."

My pulse races. "Well, that's because I picked it up when the henchman dropped it and I used it to make him leave my apartment."

"So you say."

"It's the truth," I insist.

"You know what else is the truth, Ms. Carter," Detective Francois says. "It's also true that the gun is the same gun that was used to kill both Ricardo and Marlo Miranda."

"Of course, it was," I say. "It was the henchman's gun! And he killed Ricardo and Marlo."

"If the henchman killed them, then why aren't his prints on the gun?" demands the detective.

Shaking my head, I say, "I don't know. I think he was wearing gloves, but—"

"I don't want to hear it, Ms. Carter." The detective stands, towering over me. "I'm placing you under arrest."

Confusion rocks me. "For what?"

"The murders of Ricardo and Marlo Miranda," announces the detective. "You have the right to remain silent ..."

Chapter 60

"You ready to order miss?"

Startled, I glance up at the waitress. "Oh, not just yet. I'm still waiting on someone who's joining me."

"No problem," says the waitress, giving me a smile before she pivots and walks to the next table.

At the moment, I'm sitting at one of the wooden bistro tables at Tea 4 Too.

Three days ago, following my arrest (again) for a murder—no, two murders—that I absolutely, without a doubt did not and could never commit, I spent a night in jail, then went to a bail hearing the next morning. Appearing before the judge with my lawyer, I was able to get bail, which I made. My lawyer and I spoke at length about the new charges, and how she would defend me against them. I told her my theory about the henchman, which she thought was perfect.

"That's the better suspect," she said, and promised to begin working on proving that El Zapata sent a ruthless killer to St. Mateo to get rid of Ruth, Ricardo, and Marlo.

Since then, instead of seeking tea and sympathy, I've been pondering how the jump drive might be the key to finding out who killed Ruth. As

I've enjoyed my customary tea and donut holes, I came up with a plan. This morning, I texted Officer Cuetee that I might have a way to discover the killer. He agreed to meet me at the tea café we both like.

Officer Cuetee was supposed to meet me at two p.m. Unfortunately, two o'clock came and went twenty minutes ago, but I figure Officer Cuetee got held up for some reason, or—

"Sophie?"

I look up from the menu I was staring at but not focusing on. Officer Cuetee walks toward me, giving me a dazzling smile that shows off his adorable dimples. After we greet each other, he sits across from me. Somehow, he seems to have gotten cuter if that's even possible. Which, I suppose maybe it could possibly be possible for someone to become even more—

"Have you ordered yet?"

"Oh, um …" I clear my throat and pray I wasn't doing anything ridiculous, like drooling or staring at him starry-eyed. "No, I was waiting for you."

"Sorry I was late," he says, picking up the menu. "I had to finish some paperwork about a call I took this morning."

"Oh, it's okay," I assure him. "I figured you were somewhere protecting and serving."

Smiling, Officer Cuetee asks, "What are we having?"

A flush of heat warms my cheeks, making it impossible for me not to smile. Officer Cuetee's use of the word "we" gives me goosebumps and a sly hope that something more might develop between us other than the standard reporter/anonymous police source relationship. But I'm not holding my breath. Or counting on it. Or taking it to heart. Or—

"Sophie?"

Clearing my throat again, I focus and glance at the menu. "Ooh … this cinnamon, mango, and blackberry tea sounds interesting."

"Let's give it a try," says Officer Cuetee.

Flipping the menu over, I peruse the pastries and other baked goods. "And maybe donut holes with lemon glaze?"

Officer Cuetee says, "Hmmm ... how about we do an orange glaze instead?"

"Sounds good," I say, though I'm not sure about the pairing of cinnamon, mango, blackberry, and orange, but I'm not going to make a fuss. There will be other times to debate tea and glaze pairings. Right now, I need to focus on what's most important—making sure I don't go to prison.

After we give the waitress our order, I tell Officer Cuetee about my plan. "El Zapata's henchman broke into my apartment because he thought I had the jump drive which he didn't find because I don't have it. But ... what if I tell the henchman that I do have the jump drive."

"But you don't have it," says Officer Cuetee, staring at me.

"But I can make the henchman think that I have it," I say.

Officer Cuetee frowns. "Why would you want to do that?"

"I want to set a trap for him," I say. "You know, set up a sting operation to draw him out."

Officer Cuetee says, "I don't know—"

"Here you are ..." The waitress is suddenly at our table, holding a tray with our tea and donut holes. She gives us napkins, eating utensils, and an array of condiments—sugar, honey, butter, plum jam, which I find odd, and a small jar of blackstrap molasses.

We thank her and proceed to partake of our meal. The tea is excellent. The donut holes with orange glaze are just okay, but Officer Cuetee seems to love them. I still think a lemon glaze would have been better, but at this time I have to pick my battles.

"What don't you know?"

"Sting operations are dangerous," says Officer Cuetee. "They have to be meticulously planned and—"

"Then I will plan the sting operation meticulously," I promise.

Shaking his head, Officer Cuetee gives me a grim look. "I really don't think you should put yourself in the crosshairs of a ruthless killer."

"Neither do I," I admit, trying not to feel desperate. "But my freedom is at stake. I can't just sit back and do nothing. It's like Callie says, I have to be independent."

"Callie says you have to be independent?"

Sighing, I say, "Well, she said I needed to conduct my own independent investigation and she's right."

Officer Cuetee gives me a strange look. "Wait. Callie is the cat who saved your life, right?"

"Right," I nod. And then I realize my mistake. Again. Gosh, when am I going to remember not to tell people things that Callie has told me? Not that Callie has really told me anything. I mean, the cat wasn't really talking to me.

"And Callie said—"

"You know, you're right," I say, giving Officer Cuetee a quick smile. "Maybe I shouldn't do a sting operation."

"Look, it's not that I don't think a sting operation isn't a good idea, because I do," says Officer Cuetee.

"I'm sensing a but ..."

"But I don't want anything bad to happen to you," says Officer Cuetee, reaching to take my hand.

His touch gives me a jolt, in the best way possible. Feeling a bit bashful, I say, "I don't want anything bad to happen to me, either."

"Sophie, if El Zapata's henchman killed three people already," says Officer Cuetee, "then he won't hesitate to kill you. He's already tried to hurt you once. You don't want to give him another chance."

Chapter 61

Later that afternoon, I'm still ruminating about the henchman and the drug lord, and the jump drive.

At the moment, I'm relaxing on the chaise lounge on my back patio, enjoying a cup of ginger tea.

As I drove home from the tea café, I kept thinking about my plan to draw out the killer by pretending to have the jump drive in my possession. Yes, I know it's risky and dangerous. And I don't know the first thing about how to conduct a sting operation. I might not be able to pull it off. I might get myself killed. I might actually succeed in catching the dastardly killer. The possibilities are potentially endless, I suppose. Who knows?

All I really know is I have to clear my name. And if clearing my name means I have to put myself in danger, then—

"Hay stissssss …."

The strange, slurring purr gives me a jolt. Praying I'm not about to be attacked, I glance left, toward the patio doors. There's nothing except the reflection of the setting sun against the glass panes.

"Othverrrrr herrrrreee …"

Huh? I glance right, toward the wooden railing wrapped around the porch.

"Oh my God!"

Sitting on top of the railing is Callie, the sassy, sarcastic Calico. And she's got something in her mouth.

It looks like a lizard.

Leaping from the railing to the ground, Callie opens her mouth. The animal falls out. I was right. It's a lizard and it is immediately scurrying away. Naturally, I scream and jump up, hoping the lizard doesn't scurry up my leg, but Callie is quick. She slams her front paw on the lizard's tail, preventing its progress.

"Not so fast," says Callie to the squirming lizard. "We had a deal, remember? And you owe me."

"What does he owe you?"

"Nothing much," says Callie. "Just his slimy, cold-blooded life. I saved him from a pack of feral goats when I was in the jungle a few days ago."

"What were you doing in the jungle?"

Callie says, "Date with the tomcat."

"How are things going?"

"So far, so good," she says. "I'll fill you in later. Right now, as I said, this lizard has guts to spill."

Seconds later, I hear low-fi screeching and glance down. The lizard's mouth is open. It must be spilling its guts, I presume. Callie looks at me. "He's got information you need to help clear your name. He didn't want to spill his guts, but I told him that if he didn't I'd spill his guts for him if you know what I mean."

"Um ... actually, I'm not quite sure what you mean."

Callie stares at me. Then she says, "Tell me again why you humans think you're the superior species? Never mind. So, you know that jump drive the henchman is looking for?"

Nodding, I say, "I was just thinking about that jump drive."

"Well, this lizard knows where it is," says Callie.

"Wait. What?" I stare at Callie, and then the lizard, and then at Callie again. "That lizard knows where the jump drive is? Are you serious?"

The lizard produces another low-fi sound.

"He's serious," says Callie to the lizard.

"How does he know?"

"Apparently, he used to live in your coworker's backyard," says Callie. "She had a habit of leaving her patio door open to catch the sea breeze and the lizard would slip inside her house sometimes. He was especially fond of hanging out in your coworker's bathroom."

Confused, I frown. "Why the bathroom?"

"Who knows?" says the cat. "Lizards are weird."

"Where is the jump drive?" I ask.

Callie repeats my question to the lizard who responds with a low screech.

Callie tells me, "He says it's in one of the pill bottles in the medicine cabinet."

"Are you kidding?" I ask.

Callie says to the lizard, "Are you kidding?"

The lizard responds.

"He's not kidding," says Callie. "He saw your coworker put the jump drive into the pill bottle. Of course, he's not sure which pill bottle because he can't read the labels."

Shocked, I say, "I can't believe this. A pill bottle? Wait. How does the lizard know it was a pill bottle? How does he know it was a jump drive that Ruth put into the pill bottle?"

Tilting her head, the Calico says, "Animals may not know how to speak human, but we know what things are, okay?"

Hands raised, I say, "Okay. No problem. If the lizard says it was a jump drive, then … Oh my goodness."

"What?" asks Callie.

"I have to go," I say.

"Where?" demands Callie.

"Ruth's house," I say, heading toward the patio doors. "I need to get that jump drive. I'm going to use it to catch the henchman!"

"Wait a minute," commands Callie.

Sighing, I pirouette to face her. "I don't have time to wait."

"What did you mean when you said you're going to use the jump drive to catch the henchman?"

"Just what I said," I tell the cat. "The henchman wants the jump drive. I'm going to get the jump drive and use it in my sting operation."

"Girl, what do you know about doing a sting operation?"

"Well … " I hesitate. "You see …"

"Have you ever done a sting operation before?"

"Well …" I clear my throat. "Technically, not exactly, but—"

"Yeah, just what I thought," says Callie.

Frustrated, I ask, "And just what do you think?"

Callie says, "You're going to get yourself killed. Girl, you can't pull off a sting operation."

"You sound like Officer Cuetee."

"He's right," says Callie.

"But I don't have a choice," I say, my frustration escalating to irritation. "I don't understand why you wouldn't support my decision. You told me to be independent."

"I said independent," says Callie. "Not idiotic!"

"Look, despite what you think, I have a chance to finally clear my name," I say. "Don't you want me to do that?"

"Girl don't get it twisted, okay," warns Callie. "You know I want you to clear your name. I have spent most of my time trying to help you clear your name, finding clues and witnesses, which is not something I had to do, but you needed all the help you could get, so—"

"You know, I have had quite enough of you taking all the credit," I tell the cat. "I may not be the world's greatest investigative reporter— yet—but I have been investigating, I have been finding clues, I have been interviewing witnesses and I have been coming to conclusions without your help—"

"Girl, didn't I tell you not to get it twisted," says the cat. "I am well aware that you have been investigating, but you have to admit that if it wasn't for me—"

"If it wasn't for you," I say. "I wouldn't have ended up with an infected hand. If it wasn't for you, I wouldn't have ended up in a coma!"

Hissing, Callie turns from me, jumps up onto the top of the railing, and then leaps down to the manicured lawn.

Staring after the cat as she scampers away, I take a few deep breaths, trying to process what happened.

That crazy cat tried to talk me out of finding out who killed Ruth. And why? Because I've never conducted a sting operation? Because it's dangerous? Risky? So what? Sometimes you have to take huge risks to get huge rewards.

I let out another exhale, then head into my apartment. I grab my keys and purse, then stuff my bare feet into a pair of flip-flops I keep near the front door. Minutes later, I'm in my JEEP, shifting into drive, steering the vehicle through the parking lot, and turning onto the boulevard.

As I speed down the road, it occurs to me that the cat's attempt to stop me from recovering the jump drive from Ruth's house might have been my own subconscious insecurities trying to hold me back.

That is ... from the moment the cat first spoke to me, I've been questioning if she and I were actually communicating. One moment, I was convinced there was no way that the cat was talking to me. And the next, I believed that the feline was absolutely speaking standard English.

But I suppose there's always been part of me that sort of knew Callie couldn't talk. Maybe for a moment, I wanted her to. Maybe I thought a talking cat would be cool and fun. But, the talking cat was all in my head. As I'd suspected before, the fever and subsequent coma—combined with the possible PTSD from the cat's attack—caused my subconscious to manifest a feline who could speak to me.

All this time, I must have been talking to myself.

Chapter 62

Nearly an hour later, I'm standing on the porch of Ruth's former home.

The sun is about to set but no golden orange rays can penetrate the thick clusters of overgrown bushes, shrubs, and palm trees. The snarled and tangled vegetation, which was unkept and wild when I first visited Ruth, seems to have grown into a thick jungle. After I walked up the path and entered the waist-high chain link fence, I had to push back broad leaves as I weaved through the dense foliage.

As I stare at the door, which is still festooned with yellow crime scene tape, I hesitate.

Then I take several deep breaths, which I hope will fortify and galvanize me into action. But they don't. So I take a few more. The second set of deep breaths doesn't help either. They make me feel panicked, like I'm going to hyperventilate. Suddenly, I'm starting to wonder if maybe this was a mistake. Maybe the cat is right. Maybe recovering the jump drive from the pill bottle in Ruth's medicine cabinet is not the best idea.

I shake my head. No, the cat is not right. Because the cat is not even real. Well, no, the cat is real. Callie is a real cat but she's not a talking cat. The words I perceived to be coming from her mouth were not real. Those words, that warning, were just a figment of my fears.

I have to get that jump drive.

I need it to carry out the sting operation I'm planning to conduct to catch Ruth's killer.

Resolved with my decision, I force myself to take a step closer to the door.

I haven't been back to Ruth's house since the cat convinced me to snoop around the place for clues the cops might have overlooked. Turns out, the cat had a good idea. I found Marlo Miranda's gun and listened to the message from Ricardo Miranda, warning Ruth that they should be careful. At the time, I thought Ricardo was talking about his jealous wife. As it turned out, he was talking about El Zapata's henchman.

Staring at the door, my mind floods with images of Ruth, stumbling toward me with a knife protruding from her gut.

Honestly, the last thing I want to do is enter Ruth's house. But, I also don't want to be afraid. I want to be bold and tenacious. A fearless investigative reporter. When I think about the stories my mentor Vivian Thomas wrote when she was a foreign war correspondent in Africa, I realize that I need to have guts and a spine.

When I worked at the main *Palmchat Gazette* office in St. Killian, Vivian often spoke of the dangers and perils she faced while chronicling crime and corruption in South Sudan. She often risked her freedom and her life to make sure the world knew and understood the atrocities taking place in a part of the world that was often overlooked and forgotten.

If I want to be like Vivian, then I have to suck it up, get over my trepidation, and stop being so hesitant. After all, if I want to be a great investigative reporter then I'm going to have to actually investigate, right?

Bending down to walk under the yellow crime tape, I enter Ruth's house.

I was expecting dim gloom, but several lights are on, illuminating the living area, which is a complete mess. Not surprisingly, the place looks like dozens of cops, CSI techs, and paramedics trampled and trod all over it. The living room, which along with the kitchen, dining area, and study nook form a large open concept space, appears as though it was tossed by looters and robbers instead of law enforcement. The orange couch cushions are all over the floor. Shattered glass from the coffee table Ruth collapsed on top of litters the rug. Furniture is overturned. In the kitchen, drawers and cabinet doors are opened. Dishes, pots, pans, and other appliances are crowded on the island.

A clean-up crew hasn't been hired, I guess.

But the jump drive isn't in the living room. According to the lizard, the jump drive is in a pill bottle in the bathroom, so …

I stop, arrested by a realization.

A lizard told me where to find the jump drive.

Well, no, that's not right. A lizard didn't tell me. A lizard spilled his guts to a cat who translated the lizard's story to me. But, even that's not right because the cat wasn't speaking to me. Maybe she was meowing and purring and trilling but I wasn't understanding any of those cat noises and sounds. Maybe, at one time, my trauma and PTSD from the cat's vicious attack fooled me into thinking I could understand Callie, but I was wrong about that.

And yet …

I bite my lip, reluctant to ponder how I could have possibly come to the conclusion that the jump drive is hidden in a pill bottle in Ruth's bathroom. I mean, there is no other way I could have gotten that lead. So, if Callie, translating for the lizard, didn't tell me then …

Shaking my head again, I decide it doesn't matter.

All that matters is recovering the jump drive.

Moments later, I walk into what I'm guessing is a guest bedroom. The bed doesn't seem to have been disturbed, but the drawers in the dresser are pulled out, their contents—mostly lingerie and undergarments—spilling over the sides. Other unmentionables are on the floor. The wardrobe in the corner is open. Inside I see three silky nightgowns and a robe.

Moments later, in the bathroom, I check the medicine cabinet.

Disappointment floods me. But it makes sense, I tell myself. This is a guest bedroom. Why would Ruth hide the jump drive in a guest bathroom?

Leaving the guest room, I hurry into Ruth's bedroom. It's a mess, like the guest room, but the bathroom is tidy. Approaching the medicine cabinet, my heart slams and my mouth goes dry. Please let the lizard have been telling the truth, I plead. And, yes, I do feel hypocritical. After all, I've decided that the tip about the jump drive in the pill bottle didn't come from a talking cat.

With a deep breath, I open the medicine cabinet.

A gasp escapes my lips.

There are hundreds and hundreds of pill bottles in the medicine cabinet. Okay, okay, maybe not hundreds and hundreds, but definitely about fifty or sixty of varying sizes. Some seem to be from prescriptions while others are over-the-counter medication.

Geez, was Ruth operating her own pharmacy or something? With a resigned sigh, I reach for a bottle of generic aspirin. I hold my breath and open it.

Inside I find … small white aspirin tabs.

Okay, so I didn't think I would find the jump drive in the first bottle I opened. I hoped I would, but I figured the probability was low that I would hit the jackpot on the first try.

After putting the cap back on the aspirin, I open more bottles. B-12. Vitamin C, Vitamin D, Melatonin, St. John's Wort, Zinc, Biotin, Flax Seed Oil capsules, and Fish Oil tablets. And inside the bottles, I find nothing but pills. Tiny pills. Large pills. Oblong-shaped pills. And capsules. Some are solid. Others are filled with gel.

Fighting discouragement, I grab the next bottle in my immediate line of sight. A bottle of antidiarrheal medicine. Glancing at myself in the mirror above the sink, I make a face, which is a mix of curiosity and shock. Did Ruth have intestinal issues? Not surprising, I suppose, if she was being threatened by a relentless henchman.

I open the bottle of antidiarrheal pills.

Staring inside the bottle, several emotions race through me. Shock, relief, and … and, okay, I guess, technically, only two emotions are racing through me – shock and relief. But those are huge, sweeping emotions, and I'm not surprised that I'm feeling giddy and dizzy.

The jump drive is in the bottle.

My heart thumping, I turn the bottle upside down. The jump drive falls onto my palm. Staring at it in disbelief, all I can think is the lizard was right …

And if the lizard was right, then that means …

No, no, I don't want to think about what that means. Not now, anyway. Right now, I just want to be happy that I found the jump drive. I can orchestrate my sting operation. I can catch the real killer and clear my name.

I glance up at the mirror.

And scream.

Chapter 63

Behind me, reflected in the mirror, is Zeke Kelly.

Spinning around to face Ruth's friend, I gasp and take a step back, but there's nowhere to go except into the pedestal sink, so I sidestep away from him.

"Ohmigod!" I take a deep, shaky breath. "You scared me!"

"What are you doing here?" asks Zeke.

"Oh. Well, you see … " I clear my throat. "Wait. What are you doing here?"

"I'm going to clean Ruth's house," says Zeke. "It's no longer a crime scene now that the cops have found the person who killed her."

I take another step back, offended by his fetid breath. The pungent stench of nicotine wafting from his mouth isn't surprising, considering he smokes like a chimney.

"I was going to pack up the rest of her things and ship them to her family," says Zeke. "She has a sister who lives in New Zealand."

"That's thoughtful of you," I say, distracted.

"Why are you in Ruth's house?" Zeke frowns. "Why are you going through her medicine cabinet? What are you looking for?"

"Actually, thankfully, I found what I was looking for," I say, holding the jump drive between my thumb and index finger. "Ruth's jump drive. It's going to help me clear my name."

"That's Ruth's jump drive?" Zeke stares at it. "The jump drive the henchman accused me of having and beat me up when I didn't know where it was?"

Nodding, I say, "This is Ruth's jump drive."

"I don't understand," says Zeke. "How will her jump drive help you clear your name?"

"I'm going to use this jump drive to trap the henchman. I'm going to conduct a sting operation."

"A sting operation?" Zeke looks skeptical. "You're not a cop. What do you know about conducting a sting operation? You're going to get yourself killed."

Rolling my eyes, I say, "You sound like that psycho cat."

"Psycho cat?"

"Callie," I say, thinking of the fierce, independent Calico who never was speaking to me, although I wish she had been. "She said the same thing."

"Wait. Did you say I sound like a cat who said the same thing?"

Realizing my mistake, I clear my throat. "What I mean is … I know conducting a sting operation is a risky endeavor, but I have to do it. I have to prove that I didn't kill Ruth."

"Well, I need to avoid a bullet between the eyes," says Zeke. "So I need you to give me the jump drive."

Shaking my head, I say, "I can't do that. I have to clear my name."

"The henchman who killed Ruth is going to kill me if I don't give him that jump drive," says Zeke, stepping closer to me.

I step back, trying to get away from his rancid breath. He should brush more. And floss. And use mouthwash. And maybe lay off the cigarettes, or—

"The hen says he almost set her on fire. Apparently, he was smoking. The hen followed him into the house since he'd left the screen door open. She walked inside and flew up onto the table. He yelled at her to get away and then flicked his cigarette at her. The cigarette was still lit and it landed on her and her feathers almost caught fire."

Callie's voice stops me cold. When did she say that to me? The hens, right? When she and I went to talk to Marlo Miranda. One of the hens told Callie—

No, that's not right. A hen didn't tell Callie anything. Hens don't talk. They cluck. And cats don't talk, either, and yet—

"Look, you either give me that jump drive," says Zeke, "or I'm going to blow up your sting operation before you get the chance to carry it out!"

"You would seriously sabotage my sting operation?"

"You would seriously let me get killed?" asks Zeke.

"Listen, how about this," I say. "How about we do the sting together? It'll be a win-win situation. You'll stay alive. I'll clear my name. What do you say?"

Zeke tilts his head. "Well—"

My cell phone rings.

With a slight curse, I remove the phone from my crossbody purse and glance at the Caller-ID.

Officer Cuetee is calling.

"Hold on ..." I hold up a finger. "I need to take this."

Making my way to the corner of the bedroom, I face the wall and answer my phone.

"Hey, where are you?" asks Officer Cuetee. "I stopped by your apartment, but you weren't there."

"I'm, um ... " I hesitate. I can't tell Officer Cuetee where I am because then he'll know I went searching for the jump drive so I could use it to conduct my sting operation, which he warned me not to do, so—

"Sophie? Where are you?

"Oh, um ... " I clear my throat. "I'm just running an errand. What's up?"

"Good news," says Officer Cuetee. "Detective Francois spoke to some law enforcement colleagues in Brazil about El Zapata. They gave him the name of El Zapata's top henchman and Detective Francois learned that the man arrived in St. Mateo a few weeks ago."

"Oh my God!" My heart starts to slam. "Are you saying that you know the identity of the henchman?"

"You're not going to believe it, Sophie," Officer Cuetee says. "The henchman is Ruth's friend … Zeke Kelly …"

Chapter 64

My slamming heart stops and drops into my stomach.

"Wait ... did you say—"

"Zeke Kelly," repeats Officer Cuetee. "Ruth's friend. Only, he's not really her friend. He pretended to be. Ezekiel "Zeke" Kelly is really a henchman for El Zapata."

"Are you serious?" I squeak, panic and terror racing through me. I can hardly fathom or process or believe what Officer Cuetee just told me. Zeke Kelly, Ruth's friend with the horrible breath, is a hitman for a South American drug lord. He's been lying all this time. Pretending to be Ruth's friend so he could get the jump drive and deliver it to his boss.

And I had no idea.

I was so wrong. I thought Zeke Kelly was a victim, like me. I wanted us to do a sting operation together, for goodness sake!

"Turns out Zeke Kelly—"

"Hey, remember you said that you like to get more information with a cup of peppermint tea?" I ask, painfully aware that I need to get out of Ruth's house. Now. And I need to leave without alerting Zeke Kelly to the fact that I know exactly who he is—a stone-cold killer.

"Yeah," says Officer Cuetee.

"How about you tell me over peppermint tea?" I suggest.

"But I thought you said—"

"But I think it might be best," I say. "You know, considering what you have to tell me."

"Well, okay," says Officer Cuetee. "You want to meet at Tea 4 Too in about twenty minutes? I'm due for a break."

"Sounds great," I say, and then end the call.

Taking a deep breath, I turn.

A gasp escapes my lips.

Zeke Kelly is gone.

Chapter 65

Pulse racing, I glance around the room.

My eyes scan the area from the wardrobe to the dresser to the bed.

The bedroom is empty.

I'm not sure if I should be relieved, or not. On the one hand, I'm happy that I don't have to face Zeke Kelly, considering he's a cold-blooded murderer. He's the guy who attacked me. The fiend with the foul breath who fooled me. I wasn't sure what to say to him. Didn't know if I could get away from him and out of the house.

Still, I wonder …

Where did Zeke Kelly go? And when did he leave? And why?

Did Zeke Kelly hear me talking to Officer Cuetee? Did he realize that Officer Cuetee was telling me the truth about him? I'm not sure. But it doesn't matter. I need to leave. Officer Cuetee is waiting for me. Securing the jump drive in my cross-body, I hurry out of Ruth's bedroom.

I hustle down the hallway and into the living room.

Once I get to Tea 4 Too, I think as I stride quickly toward the front door, I can tell Officer Cuetee that—

"And just where do you think you're going?"

My hand freezes just as I'm about the grab the doorknob.

Swallowing, I turn slowly.

Ten feet away, Zeke Kelly scowls at me.

Terrified speechless by the knife he brandishes, I nevertheless manage to say, "Um … Tea 4 Too."

Shaking his head, Zeke Kelly says, "I'm afraid not."

"But I have to go," I say, taking a step back as he takes a step toward me. "Officer Cuetee is waiting for me. And if I don't show up, he's going to be worried, and he'll come looking for me."

"How will he know where to find you?" asks Zeke. "You didn't tell him where you were. Just said you were, what was it? Running errands."

Mentally kicking myself for being so vague with Officer Cuetee, I say, "He'll figure out where I am."

"Maybe," says Zeke, smirking. "But by then it'll be too late … for tea."

"It's never too late for tea," I say, my eyes darting around the foyer … and landing on a vase sitting on a narrow side table beneath a mirror. "As a matter of fact, tea can help with insomnia. Especially chamomile tea. And lavender tea. And—"

"I meant it would be too late for you," says Zeke, taking another step forward.

"Too late for me to have tea?" I ask, hopefully, eyeing the vase again.

Zeke frowns. "Are you being obtuse on purpose?"

"No, not on purpose," I say, wondering if I should pick up the vase and whack him across the face with it.

"What I meant was," says Zeke, sounding exasperated, "that it'll be too late for your boyfriend to save you because you'll be dead."

"Boyfriend?" I'm confused. "I don't have a boyfriend."

"Weren't you just talking to him?"

Shaking my head, I say, "I was talking to Officer Cuetee. He's not my boyfriend."

"But you're meeting at Tea 4 Too," says Zeke. "That's a romantic place, isn't it?"

"Yeah, I guess it can be, but …"

"But ...?" prompts Zeke.

Confused about his seeming interest in my love life, I say, "But ... you don't have to kill me."

"I'm afraid I do ..."

"Actually, you don't," I say. "I mean, I'll give you the jump drive."

"I don't need you to give it to me," says Zeke. "I'm going to kill you. And then I'll just take it."

"So, hear me out, okay," I say. "I'll tell you why you don't have to kill me."

"I'm not interested," says Zeke.

"Speaking of interest," I say, hoping to keep him talking until I can figure out my next move. Although, technically, I suppose it would be my first move. "I'm interested to know why you killed Ruth."

"You already know," says Zeke. "Ruth had evidence, on that jump drive, that incriminates my boss. She was planning to write another expose. But this one would have been different. The story Ruth was writing would have put El Zapata behind bars for the rest of his life."

"Which is where he belongs," I say. "After all, he is a ruthless drug lord who got rid of the witnesses who were going to testify against him."

"That's what Ruth Rice wanted to tell the world," says Zeke. "And she got that disloyal snitch to help her."

"You mean, Ricardo Miranda."

"His name is Luis Inez Eduardo," sneers Zeke. "He fled Brazil like a rat deserting a sinking ship, then changed his name. The coward actually thought he could hide from us. He thought we wouldn't find him. That rat got what he deserved—a bullet in the head."

"And then after you killed him," I say, trying not to shudder, "you dumped him behind a fruit stand in Guavatown and went on a walking tour?"

"I joined the tour because I knew they would be walking around Guavatown, where I'd dumped the body the night before, behind the fruit stand," he says. "And I wanted to be there when the body was found."

Frowning, I shrink back. "Why?"

"Because the killer usually returns to the scene of the crime," says Zeke, shrugging. "It was risky, but I like the thrill. And I did want to learn more about Guavatown."

"It's a nice area," I say.

"Quaint and charming," Zeke agrees. "I enjoyed the tour."

"I'm sure the tour company would appreciate a good review," I say.

Nodding, Zeke says, "I plan to give them five stars. Anyway, Ruth made a big mistake thinking she could write an article exposing El Zapata and use one of his former bodyguards to give her inside information."

"Speaking of his former bodyguard," I say. "I understand why you felt the need to get rid of him but what did his wife, Marlo, ever do to El Zapata?"

"Marlo Miranda made the mistake of marrying a rat," says Zeke. "Also, I thought she knew about the jump drive that contained the evidence against El Zapata. When Ruth didn't give it to me, even to save her life, and I wasn't able to find it when I searched her house, I thought maybe she'd given it to the rat's wife. It also occurred to me that the rat might have shared secrets with his wife about El Zapata."

Thinking of Marlo's last message to me, I say, "So, you went to Marlo's house looking for the jump drive and when she didn't have it—"

"I got rid of her," snarls Zeke. "Just like I'm going to get rid of you."

"Well, speaking of me," I say, "Why did you think I had the jump drive?"

"Your coworker Candace thought you might have it," says Zeke.

My heart sinks. "Are you serious?"

"She said you were in the office when she was cleaning out Ruth's cubicle," says Zeke. "I'd called Candace to ask about the jump drive when I didn't find it in the box of Ruth's crap that she'd packed for me. Candace said she left you alone with the box and maybe you'd taken it."

"Is that so?" I'm fuming, thinking of giving Candace a piece of my mind—that is, if I still have my mind, which I won't if Zeke Kelly blows my head off.

Shrugging, Zeke says, "You could have found the jump drive in Ruth's things. I had to cover all my bases."

"But why didn't you attack Candace?" I ask. "I mean, don't get me wrong, I didn't want you to, but— "

"She was next on my list," says Zeke. "But then, you showed up at Ruth's place, and you found the jump drive, so …"

"How did you know I was here?" I ask. "Did you follow me?"

"Actually, I was already here," says Zeke. "I was searching Ruth's house again. Looking for the jump drive."

"But you don't have to look anymore, because …" Without thinking too much about it, I grab the vase and hurl it at Zeke.

Cursing, he raises his arm and ducks but the vase clunks against his left ear.

Turning toward the door, I grab the knob, and—

Something that feels like a vise clamps around my arm, and the next thing I know, I'm spinning away from the door in a dizzying circle, catching a frightful glimpse of myself in the mirror as I trip, and tumble to the floor. Screaming, I scramble to my hands and knees and crawl toward the couch. Glancing over my shoulder, I see Zeke lunging toward me, the point of the butcher's knife leading the way. Lurching to my feet, I sprint to the arched opening of the hallway that leads to the bedrooms.

With Zeke on my tail, I cut to the left, toward Ruth's bedroom.

Gasping and panting, I race into the room and slam the door. As I'm trying to lock it, something loud and heavy crashes against the doorframe. Screaming, I jump back. The door blasts open, slamming back into the wall behind it.

Zeke enters, scowling and sneering, wielding the knife.

"Please …" I hold up my hands as I stumble backward. "Don't kill me … you can have the jump drive … I won't—"

"Drop your weapon!"

The command, fierce and unrelenting, shakes me to my core and floods me with relief.

Zeke Kelly spins away from me as the sound of angry, guttural barking reverberates through the air.

Seconds later, Zeke lets out a fearsome howl as he leaps onto the bed.

Backing against the wall, I watch in fascinated astonishment as Dutiful, Officer Cuetee's Belgian Malinois, vaults through the air and lands on top of Zeke. The large, powerful canine barks viciously as he pins the henchman in place. And then, again to my astonished amazement, Callie comes running into the bedroom as fast as her legs can carry her!

The psycho cat who never was talking to me jumps on the bed and scampers on top of Zeke's chest.

"You leave Sophie alone!" says the cat before she batters Zeke's face with both paws, ferociously boxing his cheeks and jaw as he yells in agony.

"Sophie are you okay?" asks Officer Cuetee as he walks into the bedroom, pointing his firearm at Ruth's killer.

"Oh, thank God!" I exclaim, as Callie jumps from Zeke's chest and trots toward me. Officer Cuetee cuffs Zeke and then yanks the murderer to his feet.

"You gonna be alright while I put him in my squad car?" asks Officer Cuetee. "I'm going to radio for backup and then get your statement."

Nodding, I say, "I'll be okay … now that you're here."

After giving me a heart-stopping smile, Officer Cuetee marches Zeke down the hallway, while the Belgian Malinois follows.

"And what about me …"

I glance down at Callie. "What about you?"

"You're okay because Officer Cuetee showed up?" Callie asks. "But I'm the reason why he's here."

Staring at the cat, I'm stunned. "What do you mean?"

"Girl, how do you think Officer Dreamboat knew where you were?" demands Callie. "I told him."

"You told him?" I ask, not bothering to remind myself that the cat probably isn't speaking to me because the sound of her sassy, sarcastic voice is sort of making my heart soar.

"Well, I told Dutiful," says Callie. "And then he told Officer Cuetee."

"Dutiful can talk to Officer Cuetee?" I ask, sinking into a crouch next to the Calico.

"Girl, they have some way of communicating," says Callie as she stretches out on the hardwood floor. "Anyway, I told Dutiful that you were heading for trouble, and I was right—"

"Because cats know these things," I say.

Licking her fur, Callie continues, "I told Dutiful to make Officer Cuetee understand that he needed to get over here! If I hadn't talked to Dutiful, then there's no telling what would have happened to you. And I can't let anything bad happen to you."

Frowning at the cat, I ask, "What do you mean?"

Jumping up on top of the bed, Callie says, "Girl, it's not like I have a choice. I have to help you."

"Why do you have to help me?"

"Well, you are my human," says Callie, stretching out on top of the duvet.

"Wait. What?" Flabbergasted, I stare at the cat. "Wait. I'm your … human? Really? I am?"

The cat gives me a look, then starts licking her fur again, paying particular attention to her right leg.

"Oh, Callie! And you're my cat," I say, sitting on the edge of the bed.

Again, the cat gives me a look. "Girl, whatever. Don't get it twisted."

"What do you mean?"

"Who said anything about me being your cat?" demands Callie. "Miss me with those possessive pronouns, okay?"

"But, I don't understand," I say. "How am I your human, but you're not my cat?"

"Trust me. It's better that way."

A little bummed, I ask, "But … why?"

The cat says, "Because, sis ... I don't really know where I came from, or ..."

"Or?" I prompt.

"Or if I already belong to someone."

Even more bummed, I say, "Oh ... I never thought that you might be someone's cat ... "

"Or maybe I am a stray," says Callie. "That's the thing. I just don't know."

"What do you mean?"

"Sis, you remember when I told you that I attacked you because I'd had too much catnip?" asks the cat.

Nodding, I say, "Yes. Oh my goodness, Callie. Are you a ..."

"A ... what?" demands Callie, staring at me.

Trying to be sensitive, I say, "A catnipaholic ... because if you are, it's nothing to be ashamed of. I am more than willing to help you overcome your addiction, but the first step is admitting you have a problem, so—"

"Girl, I got a problem, but it ain't catnip," says the cat.

"If it's not catnip, then—"

"I have ... selective catnesia."

Confused, I say, "Selective catnesia ..."

"You humans call it selective amnesia," says Callie.

Worried, I ask, "What is the last thing you remember?"

"The last thing I remember is waking up tangled in that Seagrape tree," the Calico says. "But I don't remember much before that. I don't remember if I have a human or not. I have vague memories, but they feel like a dream."

"Oh, Callie, that's so sad."

"Don't cry for me, sis," says Callie, licking her fur again. "I don't need your pity. I need you to help me find out more about my past. And how I got selective catnesia. What happened to me? And why did I attack you? I was acting absolutely feral. But why?"

"Too much catnip?"

The cat gives me a look, one that seems contemplative and

worried. "I don't know. That's for you to find out. After all, you're the investigative reporter."

Nodding, I say, "Yeah, that's true, but ..."

"But?"

I glance away. The last thing I want to tell Callie is that I don't want to help her find out more about her past. And it's not because I don't think I can find out more about her. It's because I do think I can discover how she ended up stuck in that Seagrape tree. But, I'm not keen about it because ... what if I find out that Callie belongs to another human? Someone who's been looking for her? Someone who misses her? Someone who will claim her as their cat and want her back?

For some reason, even though I haven't known Callie for very long, I can't imagine her not being in my life.

Sure, she's sassy and sarcastic and ... maybe just a bit psycho ... but that's what I like about her.

Still, Callie deserves to know why she has selective catnesia and I'm going to help her find out the truth.

"Hey, sis ..."

I glance at the cat. "Yeah ..."

"Listen, don't take this the wrong way, but ..." Callie rises to her feet and walks toward me. "I kind of like you."

Smiling, and thrilled, I say, "You do?"

"I mean, you're goofy and quirky but you're not the worst egg."

"Not the worst egg?" I repeat, not sure if that's a compliment or an insult, or both.

"Girl, I'm not the sentimental type, okay?" says Callie. "Could I tell you that you're sweet and endearing and all that? Sure. But, I won't."

"Why not?"

Callie walks a bit closer to me. "Girl, whatever. If you want somebody to wag their tail so you can feel better about yourself, get a dog. I have to keep it real with you. After all, you're trying to become an investigative reporter, right?"

Nodding, I say, "Absolutely!"

"Well, you don't need me sugar-coating and mollycoddling," says Callie. "You need tough love."

Laughing, I reach over and pick up the cat.

The Calico stares at me.

Stroking her back, I tell her, "You know, I forgot to tell you how glad I am that you rescued me."

"Well, you should be grateful," says the cat, snuggling next to me. "Because, after all, I had to make sure my human didn't get herself killed."

I cradle the Calico in my arms and scratch behind her ears. "And your human is very thankful that you did ..."

Epilogue

"I can't believe Zeke Kelly killed Ruth," says Clark, shaking his head as he takes a sip of coffee.

Popping a donut hole in my mouth, I give him a look. "You still can't believe it? I would have thought you would have wrapped your head around it by now."

"Me, too." Clark shrugs. "But ..."

Three days have passed since my ordeal at Ruth's house, when Zeke Kelly, the henchman who killed Ruth, Ricardo and Marlo Miranda, and almost killed me.

Since then, I was tasked with and completed, writing a series of stories that detailed the gripping, sordid saga of the journalist, the henchman, and the Brazilian drug lord, El Zapata. In addition to my articles—all of which trended, thank you very much—I did two online interactive stories. I was even on the local television news.

I was not, however, booked for Good Morning America or Good Morning Britain, but I wasn't too upset.

Because, best of all, I was officially cleared of all murder charges by the St. Mateo Police Department.

Detective François, who was so totally wrong about me, did not apologize for wrongfully arresting me, but I didn't expect him to own up to his mistake.

Officer Cuetee, who'd believed in my innocence from the beginning, was overjoyed by the news about the dropped charges. We celebrated with too many donut holes and too much tea. Then we took Dutiful, the Belgian Malinois, and Callie to the park. The dog chased and retrieved a small rubber ball that Officer Cuetee threw at him while the Calico lounged in the grass and threw shade at the dog for his blind obedience. Later that night, we went to dinner—without the cat or the dog—and enjoyed each other's company in a very romantic setting.

"Speaking of things I can't wrap my mind around," says Clark. "How did Officer Cuetee know that you were in trouble at Ruth's house?"

"Well …" I trail off, knowing I can't tell Clark the truth about Callie contacting Dutiful, but I can tell him what Officer Cuetee told me. "Officer Cuetee says he was at the dog park with Dutiful when a cat ran up to the dog and started hissing and meowing at him. Next thing Officer Cuetee knew, Dutiful had jumped the chain link fence and had taken off after the cat. The dog followed the cat all the way to Ruth's."

Clark rubs his chin. "So … the cat led the dog to Ruth's place. But how did the cat know you were there? And we're talking about the same cat who saved your life, right?"

I clear my throat. "Right. Um … I don't know how the cat knew I was there. I guess animals just sense things sometimes."

Eyes narrowed and sly, Clark says, "Interesting …"

"You two want to know what else is interesting?" Marty's voice bellows.

I stare at the Managing Editor, wary of his stern expression as he stomps toward the table.

"Got a new story I need you to cover," says Marty.

"A new story?" I ask, excited. "What's it about?"

Groaning, Marty sighs. "Before I send you out to cover it, I feel it bears repeating that, even though I'm sending you to cover a crime, you don't cover the crime beat, and if you blow this story, I will ship you out if you don't shape up."

"Sophie has shaped up," says Clark. "Her recent stories were great and they're still trending all over social media."

"One good story doesn't mean you're good enough to cover crime," growls Marty. "You need to suffer more."

"And I will," I promise, even though I'm not excited about suffering, but I'll do it if it convinces Marty to let me cover more crime stories.

With reluctance and skepticism, Marty gives me the story assignment, and then says, "I want a rough draft by the end of the workday."

"You'll have it!" I say, excited and intrigued by the story.

"One last piece of advice, Sophia ..." says Marty.

"What is it?" I ask, hoping he won't tell me not to count chickens before they hatch.

Marty says, "Be careful."

Fifteen minutes later, I hurry across the parking lot to my JEEP, where Callie sits on the hood.

Happy to see her, I wave.

The Calico and I had a watershed moment when she allowed me to cuddle her, but since then, I've had to back off. But I don't mind. I'm just glad she's sticking around, even though she's made it clear that she's not my cat. I am, however, her human.

And as for my internal debate about whether, or not, she's really talking to me, I've decided not to worry about it. Somehow, someway, we can communicate. We understand each other and that's all that matters.

"Where're you headed, girl?" asks Callie.

"I'm off to cover a new story," I say, opening the door.

Callie jumps into the JEEP and settles into the passenger seat. "What's it about?"

Starting the JEEP, I say, "It's very mysterious. A body was found on the beach this morning and there was a strange note in the dead man's hand."

The cat stares at me. "What did the note say?"

I start the JEEP and glance at the cat. "Pay up … or you will never see your dog again … "

Can't get enough of Sophie and Callie?

Check out their next mystery in A Cold and Calculating Tail.

A scattered scribe. A fatal knot. Can she prove her detecting skills are up to scratch?

A Cold and Calculating Tail is the endearing second book in The Sassy Sarcastic Cat Cozy Mysteries. If you like tenacious heroines, sandy settings, and laugh-out-loud shenanigans, then you'll love Rachel Woods' head-scratching whodunit.

Buy A Cold and Calculating Tail to pounce on the truth today!

Hey, y'all, hey!!!

Subscribe to my newsletter and you'll get inspiring rescue stories, hilarious cat memes, and thrilling serialized fiction. Plus, you can find out first about new books featuring my fabulous life as a feisty, fierce feline, and much more!

Sign me up!

Sassy Callie

https://subscribepage.io/SassyCallie

Also by Rachel Woods

SASSY SARCASTIC CAT COZY MYSTERIES

Sophie Carter, a struggling reporter for the *Palmchat Gazette,* teams up with a sassy talking Calico cat to solve crimes as she strives to become an influential investigative reporter

A SLY AND SINISTER TAIL

A COLD AND CUNNING TAIL

A FOUL AND FEARSOME TAIL

A DARK AND DEVIOUS TAIL

REPORTER ROLAND BEAN COZY MYSTERIES

Roland "Beanie" Bean, husband and loving father, finds himself the unwitting participant in solving crimes as he seeks to make a name for himself as a reporter for the *Palmchat Gazette.*

HAPPY BIRTHDAY MURDER

EASTER EGG HUNT MURDER

MERRY CHRISTMAS MURDER

TRICK OR TREAT MURDER

GOBBLE GOBBLE MURDER

HAPPY 4TH OF JULY MURDER

SUMMER VACATION MURDER

HAPPY NEW YEAR MURDER

PALMCHAT ISLANDS MYSTERIES

Married journalists, Vivian and Leo, manage the island newspaper while solving crimes as they chase leads for their next story.

UNTIL DEATH DO US PART

NO ONE WILL FIND YOU

YOU WILL DIE FOR THIS

DON'T MAKE ME HURT YOU

THE PALMCHAT ISLANDS MYSTERIES BOX SET: BOOKS 1 - 4

RUTHLESS REVENGE ROMANCE SERIES

Gripping romantic suspense series with steamy romance, unpredictable plot twists and devastating consequences of deceit.

HER DEADLY MISTAKE

HER DEADLY DECEPTION

HER DEADLY THREAT

HER DEADLY BETRAYAL

MURDER IN PARADISE SERIES

A series of stand-alone women sleuth mysteries with murder, mayhem and a dash of romance, set against the backdrop of turquoise waters and swaying palm trees of the fictional Palmchat Islands.

THE UNWORTHY WIFE

THE SILENT ENEMY

THE PERFECT LIAR

About the Author

Rachel Woods studied journalism and graduated from the University of Houston where she published articles in the Daily Cougar. She is a legal assistant by day and a freelance writer and blogger with a penchant for melodrama by night. Many of her stories take place on the islands, which she has visited around the world. Rachel resides in Houston, Texas with her three sock monkeys.

For more information:
www.therachelwoods.com
rachel@therachelwoods.com

About the Publisher

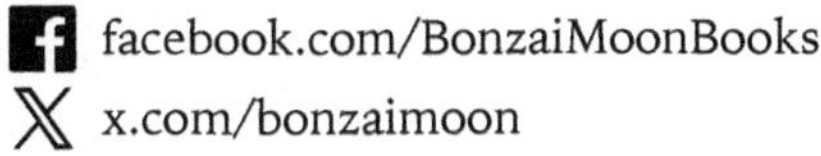

BonzaiMoon Books is a family-run, artisanal publishing company created in the summer of 2014. We publish works of fiction in various genres. Our passion and focus is working with authors who write the books you want to read, and giving those authors the opportunity to have more direct input in the publishing of their work.

For more information:
www.bonzaimoonbooks.com
info@bonzaimoonbooks.com

facebook.com/BonzaiMoonBooks
x.com/bonzaimoon

www.ingramcontent.com/pod-product-compliance
Lightning Source LLC
Chambersburg PA
CBHW070319190726
48291CB00014B/2282